Radiant

Abigail and David's story
as told by her handmaidens

Kirsty A. Wilmott

BEAR PRESS

ISBN
Softcover: 978-1-739-636777
eBook: 978-1-739-636784

A CIP record for this book is available
from the British Library

For Bear Press
Development: Bridget Scrannage
Editor: Ann Peacocke
Art Director: Sarah Joy

Cover Painting
Dawn Illumination 1
(detail) used by kind permission
©2021 Pip Sanday

The publishers would like to thank
Thomas and Helen Sanday for their assistance
in reproducing the painting for publication.

Set in 10/13pt PT Serif

1v05

For Mike, Becky and Jane

Prologue
Told by Hannah

She will not look at me, she will only stare down at her hands folded in her lap, speaking through gritted teeth and narrowed eyes. She forces me to shrink and fade, to become invisible. He asked her to be kind to me while he was away, and the bile chokes her. It doesn't matter that her body is tight with his child, it has squashed her heart, and there is no room for anyone else.

Abigail is calling, her voice growing stronger as she shouts away the drowsiness of waking. She is too small to climb down from her bed, so I am sent to get her. I breathe a little more deeply with each step away from my mistress.

Abigail's room is dim and smells warm, full with the dampness of restless stirring, for there is no breeze here near the middle of the house.

"Get up," she demands, raising her arms to me.

I am her way to freedom, yet I do not think she holds any great affection for me. Her little face is unsmiling, almost fierce. I lift her down and start to undress her until her quick little fingers push me away.

"No, I do myself."

Those dark eyes, framed by long lashes, frown with concentration. She is so very lovely. When she is done I hand her the pot and she squats over it, staring at something I cannot see, will never be able to see. She finishes and turns away, her nose wrinkling.

Abigail is an easy child and does not wriggle when I sponge her clean. She chooses a blue dress. It is her favourite colour and bodes well for an afternoon of good temper. I begin to brush her hair. When I snag a knot, she turns and wags a finger at me.

"Don't pull so, Hannah."

I want to pick her up and hold her close, for my sake as much as hers. I won't, for she doesn't like to be held.

When she is ready, I lead her back to her mother. She skips the last few steps, and I think, "Clever child, you know where the heart of this house lies."

In the corridor there is a small alcove, deep and empty. I'll wait there until the child is dismissed or I am called. The latter is unlikely. If he were home I would go and sit with them, sewing and listening. When he is absent, it is better for both of us, that I am invisible.

From within, I hear Abigail's small, clear voice. She is telling them the story I told her last night. She remembers it well for one so young, and even bleats when the shepherd boy calls his flock. She has a remarkable memory and mimics my own manner of speech in the telling. I squirm. It's as though the child has taken me back into the room to mock her mother, as if the tale were deliberately told. The shepherd, though of humble birth, is kind and brave and marries for love.

I hear steps, Abigail's sandals tripping across the floor. She stops and peers around. She is looking for me. At four years old she is delicate, arms and legs like a doll rather than a real child. I am ten years older, a young woman and yet she makes me feel ungainly and stupid.

"Mama says to go outside, I am figgy."

"Fidgety, sweet one, you are fidgety. You just need to play some hide and seek."

I am rewarded with a smile.

***

The garden is light and shade, colour and depth. It is why I could never go back to my father's tent. A garden is a hidden thing, a pleasure you cannot pack up and take with you on the back of a camel.

The child runs off to hide in her special place. I pretend to look for her although I know she is curled up under the bench in the middle. When I have walked past twice, it is time for me to go and sit above her, I have searched enough. Abigail giggles because I can never find her when she hides so well. I sigh.

"Oh where can Abigail have gone, where can she be?"

She stuffs her dress in her mouth. She is trembling with laughter.

"Perhaps she has been kidnapped by pirates. What will her father say? I must go to sea and search for her."

She lies very still. I look at her foot, so small between my own. I begin to speak from my own jealousy and pain; I cannot help myself.

"I wonder what the new baby will be like? If it's a boy, how happy everyone will be."

The words are gritty on my tongue, and I swallow them away. I hope she does not understand their portent.

"What is this?" I say, gently touching her ankle with my hand. She crawls out, brushing down her dress. She looks at me gravely and then climbs onto the bench, folding her hands in her lap, just like her mother. She sits quietly; her head tilted to one side. I tell her another story. I am careful to make this one about pirates and treasure and not about love and misunderstanding. I change the ending, just a little, so that it is the father who comes to find the lost heroine, instead of the prince. That pleases her and she smiles.

We go to the stables to see the camels and donkeys. Today, I am allowed to lift her up onto my shoulders so that she can see properly. A camel spits at one of the yard boys and she almost laughs, but not quite. I am ashamed, for I seem to have squashed her little soul. I have pressed her down, as I am pressed down.

Then Abigail points. Men begin to run and shout; there is a ripple of movement far off in the distance. We can almost see the air pushing ahead of them. The master is coming. We draw back into the shadows, out of the way, except that Abigail cannot contain herself. She wriggles and twists, until I have to put her down. I hold on tight but in the end she shakes herself free from my hand and runs to him. Perhaps I let her go, because at that moment I would not like to look too closely into my heart and what it desires. I pray that he will not be too weary or weighed down with business to greet her.

I need not have worried. He catches her up and swings her high. She laughs and tangles her hands in his hair. He lifts her onto his horse and calls her his princess, though he is turning all the while, peering this way and that, looking for me. I step into the sunlight, a small movement and my heart is filled with joy, for tonight I know he will come to find me.

"Father," she cries, as he lifts her down, "will you still care for me when the baby is born?"

I catch my breath. She will surely tell him that it was I who put this thought in her head and he will see me for what I am, twisted about with jealousy for what is not rightfully mine.

"Abigail, you will always be the love of my life, the princess of my heart," he cries. He sets her down and pats her on the head. "Go and play," he says, looking at me, "I have much to do."

***

There is wailing and darkness. The windows are shuttered and draped, for the little boy is dead. He breathed but a night and a day and never opened his eyes, nor suckled. The mistress screamed and turned her face to the wall. The master is distraught. He holds her close and weeps with her.

Abigail and I sit in the darkened rooms trying to stay out of the way. Last time she lost a baby, she dragged me into the centre of her anguish, raging against my presence. Last time she was younger and stronger and Abigail proof that she should hope. Last time she recovered quickly, fuelled by her passion to hurt me. This time she is weak and broken, ravaged with grief and it has made him doubt himself. He has become a man who sees only too well, so now I must become invisible.

Chapter One
Told by Hannah

Abigail has come to sit beside me. She leans against me while I sew so that if I pause, I can lay my hand on her head.

She is just turned eleven, is still small for her age and has a brother who is three years old. She often comes to hide amongst the mending when he is brought to his mother. I am glad, for she is my eyes and ears about the house and without her I would see very few people indeed.

Sometimes, Abigail brings me a pomegranate, my favourite, wrapped up in something torn or frayed, so that if anyone should ask her where she is going, she can say she is bringing me work.

He stopped coming a long time ago.

Today she is here to tell me a story. It is the one she tells most often, the one about a prince who can do no wrong, who grows up arrogant and spoiled. He is taught a lesson by the princess he hopes to marry, although she does not want to marry him. It's a sad story because at the beginning of the tale, the king dies and leaves the princess all alone.

Abigail has twirled a crimson thread around her finger. It is pulled tight, though she does not seem to have noticed. She tilts her face up to the light and says, "Hannah, I am to be betrothed." She speaks as if she were commenting on the colour of the sky or the sweetness of a peach.

"It is about time," I reply, carefully. "Who is he?" I ask, trying to not sound surprised or sad.

"A sheep farmer."

"Oh," I say smiling, "perhaps he'll be like our shepherd boy."

A shepherd who is really a prince because he falls in love with a princess.

"No, I don't think so. Mother is too pleased."

"Ah," I say, unpicking the last row of stitches. I have pulled the linen badly. "When is it to be?"

"After I am twelve."

One more year. That is a blessing. When Abigail leaves, my future here will be dark. She swivels around to look at me.

"Will you come with me?" she asks.

Even after all this time, her mother would never agree to anything that brought me happiness. I might hope, but it would soon become dust in my mouth.

Abigail puts her hand on mine, "I will beg Father. You can be my maidservant. It would mean they wouldn't have to send anyone else."

I wonder if she realises why her mother hates me so, why I have been banished to this small room, guarded by her mother's tantrums and wagging finger. She will come to understand it all, when she has her own husband and household. Perhaps then she will feel differently about me. Then I might find myself in another prison, this time one surrounded by sheep and stinking shepherds. She is still looking at me, her heart shaped face furrowed, her fingers tightly clasped together, and I realise she is waiting for a reply.

"Of course I will come with you, if I am able."

She flings her arms around me. I wish I had held her longer, for it is the last time she ever does so.

Chapter Two
Told by Jani

I forget to look at his dear face because I am watching his chest rise and fall. There is no rhythm, and I shrink and shrivel, listening for the next breath to come. My mother and sister drape me with shawls for I cannot stop shivering. They stand behind me, sometimes they bring me food which I cannot swallow and trim the lamp, but they do not try to make me come away or sleep. There is a buzzing in my ears and something terrible stands just out of sight. I begin to lose focus.

I doze, kneeling beside him. Waking is terrible. I watch for a breath, in fear that he has gone while I was sleeping. I was not such a good wife in life, in death I want to prove myself.

He said that God would help us, that God would give us a son when it was time. But the sands have run through the glass. I am barren, wrung dry and he is dying.

I fumble for the wine at my elbow. It was warmed some time ago. Now my teeth shudder as I gulp it down. It fills my empty stomach and is cold and hot together. A single tear runs down my cheek. It is not enough. I cannot even cry for him as I ought.

Mother whispers, "It's nearly time."

She gently turns my head towards his face. How does she know? I slip back to my knees and hold his damp hand to my cheek. Two, three heaves more and there is stillness. I stare. Fifteen years stopped, dammed, carved into stone. My sister starts to sway, she starts to cry, she starts to sing her grief and mine. Mother gently draws me away.

The priest comes and stands in the doorway. He does not enter, for I am unclean. He liked my husband, although he never cared for me, and I clearly see his soul fighting within to show some kindness. I am too forthright, too straightforward for his taste and he has already sent the news to my husband's cousin, now my nearest relative, despite the fact my mother and sister are standing in the room. He lives a long way south and I have never met him. The shop, my home, the goat, all belong to him now. I must wait for him. I hope to wait forever.

I wander through our rooms and touch all that my husband once touched. I sometimes feel for the pulse in my wrist, just to check that my heart is still beating.

***

I bring Nabal food and drink. He sits where my husband used to sit. When he takes my hand, I want to snatch it away. Each of his plump fingers carries a jewel and his cloak is shot through with gold. Such wealth so easily worn is disconcerting. He has decided to use my home as a place for his men to come and stay when they are meeting the ships down at the harbour. He talks of it as if it doesn't matter, tearing away my hopes like a fleece at shearing.

"Please let me stay," I plead, though I do not recognise the voice I use. He turns towards me, but not quite all the way. He looks over my left shoulder. I want to move so that he can't help but see my face.

"No Aunt Jani, it's all settled."

He speaks as a man not used to being questioned but hesitates, as if trying to make allowances. He calls me Aunt, even though I am only related to him through my husband and at best, I am a very distant cousin.

"I want you to come back with me. I have plenty of room."

"I will of course do whatever you wish." I don't want to go. I want to stay near my sister and mother.

"I want you to be comfortable."

It's a strange thing to say to such a poor relative.

"I shouldn't want to be idle," I reply, and feel as if I ought to smile but the muscles in my face won't work. His lips twitch oddly. It is disquieting. I do not know what he wants of me.

"When do we leave?" I ask, because I do not know what else to say.

"As soon as you are ready. I have arranged everything."

***

My belongings followed us, there was not much of worth, a chair, a few pots and my clothes. When I came to look closely at the things I had used every day, I realised that most of them were battered and shabby. My contentment had blinded me; grief has given me clear sight.

My new home is large and full of things I dare not touch. There is nothing to do. I have a room to sleep in and another to sit in. If I am hungry, a girl brings me whatever I ask for. I have even started sewing again, which I haven't done since I was a child. I am not very good at it, neither was I back then. Mother seemed to tut and sniff each time she held my efforts in her hands. This time I made a new tunic. I did not think it looked so bad, but the girl took it away. A few days later, it came back finished and I could see that all my seams had been unpicked and re-done. I tried to laugh about it with her, but she only shrugged and began to tidy the room, although nothing seemed out of place to me. I am tidied all the time, and I cannot bear it. Her name is Sarah. The other servants call her Little Sarah, for she is tiny. She makes me feel ungainly and wide, as if she would like to fold me away, or sweep me into a corner, because I am too messy, grubby and large.

We are nowhere. There is a town a long way north of us but apart from that smudge of life, we are surrounded by a flat, wide plain. I hear the wind at night; it is a dry desert wind that sucks the moisture from the air. I long for the breath and smell of the sea, the warm summery light that mottled the stones along the harbour.

Nabal comes to see me nearly every day.

"Aunt Jani, have you settled in? Do you like your new rooms?"

He always asks me this, as if my answers the day before did not satisfy him. I have become practised in my replies. I am beginning to understand what he needs.

"They are more than enough for me."

Today, he looks tired. There are fine lines and a pale moon of skin under his eyes.

"May I sit, Aunt Jani? May I sit with you?"

I nod, what else can I do? I call for peaches, almonds and some honey cakes.

"I am weary. There are many decisions to make," he says, as he stretches out. "Nobody realises how much of this," he waves an arm indolently around the room, "is dependent on me."

I wonder if he thinks I am not grateful enough. I murmur nothing of consequence.

"The shepherds up north have been having trouble with a lion. They have lost a lot of lambs; I have had to send more men to walk the pens."

I nod.

"That means I'm short handed down here and I don't want to employ anyone else just now."

"Why not?" The words spill out, before I can stop them. I forget myself.

He looks up and smiles.

"Oh, just that I'd rather wait and see what the summer brings."

Nabal has a secret. I should ask him what it is, only I do not want to pander to this spoiled child. After he has gone, my little Sarah appears. I wonder if she has been listening at the door. I would if I were her. I must ask her what she thinks about her master.

"Mistress, is there anything you need?"

"No, Sarah, you keep everything so well, what is there to do?"

She does not smile as I hoped she would. A little nod of her head, that is all. She waits for me to speak further, only I can't think of anything to say. She bows and turns to leave. I call her back. "Sarah, I would like to walk but not along a dusty road, where can I go?"

"I will take you to the garden, Mistress."

I did not know there was a garden.

We make our way around the courtyard. It is filled with bales of wool and camels; men shouting, a whorl of colour and heat, the stench of business. I envy them that business. We skirt the edge of it; she is careful to keep me in the shade. On the far side there is a gate, stiff and unyielding but she is strong and with a great shove it swings inwards.

Inside are hard baked paths between which are diamonds of soil, weedy with thistles and thorns. The beds are dry but there are also pomegranate trees, a small grove of almonds, patches of coriander, rue and myrtle. My mother used to say that weeds are only flowers growing in the wrong place. At last, I am in the right place. A garden held tight by a tall solid wall.

"Is there a gardener?" I ask, although I can see there is not.

"Not since the master's mother died."

There is a water channel running down the middle, however it is empty and at the far end, a small stone shelter, containing nothing more than a broken rake. I look down at my clothes, they are too fine. Sarah is watching me, she is curious.

"Come," I say, "I want to change."

At the bottom of my trunk are the tunic and sandals that I used for cleaning the shop, before we bought new pots from the ships just arrived from Egypt or Persia. I never thought I would wear such things again or feel the grit of dirt beneath my fingernails. Sarah is looking worried.

"You wait here," I command. "If Nabal comes, run and fetch me."

She nods but I can see that she is not reassured.

That first day, I hardly turn over more than a few square feet. The brambles tear my hands and there is dust in my throat, yet for the time it takes the sun to move a little way along the wall, I am happy.

"Aunt Jani, what are you doing?" Nabal sounds amused, not angry. I wonder that Sarah did not warn me of his coming.

"Do you mind?" I ask, spreading my arms wide, and his eyes fill with tears. At last, I truly understand.

"It will not be the same," I say. "Nothing is ever quite the same. That is the way of things."

I think he is glad that I have guessed, that he did not have to explain it to me. He has decided to trust me with this precious thing that used to belong to his mother. I wonder if it is because I am poor or perhaps, I am all that he has.

"What do you need?" he asks.

"I would like to get the water channel working. And some tools, a spade, a rake, a hoe."

"I will send my steward. He'll know what to get you and who I can spare."

"You don't need to spare anyone; I want to do it."

He frowns and turns to face the far wall.

"No, I cannot have people thinking that I am making you useful."

"But surely…"

"No," he retorts, more sharply than is warranted.

I have made him angry. He starts to walk away, slow measured strides, back to the gate. There he stops. He stands with his back to me, and I wonder if he expects me to run after him. At last, he turns around, looking troubled.

"I'm sorry, Aunt Jani. I was hasty." He sounds as if the words are sticking to his tongue. It is not something he is used to doing. Perhaps it is too much, perhaps it reminds him of my true value because he then spits out the words I have become used to. "I do not want people to think I am using you."

I nod, although I want to scream and then I smile, because it's what's required of me. It's what his mother would have done, only I feel a little grubby, like I used to when I short-changed the priest.

The steward, Matthias, is kind and helpful and before long, the gate swings sweetly on oiled hinges. I have two young boys to lift and carry and dig. When Nabal's men go to Joppa or Dor or to Hebron and Carmel, they bring me back seeds and herbs. Slowly, I am filling the beds with colour and light.

At last, I sleep and dream, and wake without a weight upon my heart.

Nabal comes to my garden. I have made a shady arbour for him under the almond blossom. I listen to his plans and sometimes I try to steer him back to kindness and love. He is hard in his dealings with others, yet as long as I do not press him too firmly, I can have almost anything I want.

Chapter Three
Told by Big Sarah

I milk the goats for my master. The herd is almost pure white. They are small and pretty, their little hooves cream and black. I smell of goat most of the time. It doesn't matter, for my hands are soft, unhardened by the work the other servants have to do. It makes them jealous of me, and they wrinkle their noses when I join them for breakfast.

I have dark brown hair, streaked light by the sun and I often wear it loose. I am tall, too tall for most men and there has been no mother to temper my language, not as far as I remember. The other women say that it is not good to be so like a man, so tall, so roughly spoken, that a little gentleness would soften my hard edges. I do not care, for there is much to swear about, and it makes me feel better. I swear at my goats for not standing still, for trying to lean on me, for chewing my hair. I swear at them when they spill the milk or butt my knees. I swear at them simply because they are so silly, but I also love them, and they each have a name which only I know.

This morning, while I was milking, I thought of Simeon.

Yesterday, I noticed him across the yard, and he gave a little wave when the foreman wasn't looking. He is younger than me, I think, but I am strong, and I make him laugh. He helps take the fleeces to the coast. He is often gone for weeks at a time. The other women have started to tease me about him. He is also tall and dark, and his eyes are brown. He smells of sheep. We go well together.

Chapter Four
Told by Miriam

I am sitting on a stool at my sister's feet. Our mother is on a chair, tucked about with cushions, her eyes closing against the sun streaming into the room. Despite it not being far across the town, the walk from our house was a struggle. I had to encourage her along, like a small child.

"It is not so far, Mother, and Rebekah will surely allow us to use the cart to come home."

"I mustn't stay too long. I don't know why she can't come to us. I don't want to miss your father coming home, I want to be there to greet him myself."

Our servant looks back at me. She widens her eyes as if there is something I ought to do. My father has been dead for a while, fighting with the King, but I know it is pointless trying to argue with Mother. She is contrary as the wind. Sometimes, she grieves as if the news were new, other times she sits waiting for him to arrive. Even Rebekah has given up trying to reason with her. And as for Rebekah coming to our house, she wouldn't dream of leaving her large safe abode, where there are countless servants and men to guard her. Heled, her husband, is wealthy. It was a good match, which Rebekah likes to remind us of, constantly.

I am watching the shadows moving across the floor, wishing that they would move more quickly.

"Miriam, you should get your girl to plait your hair. If you would only take some trouble, you would look less like a child. And do you not have a clean tunic?"

I do not always listen to what she says. It is always the same. That I do not take enough care over my dress or my hair, or our mother. She has even complained about the goat, my beloved Jani. She doesn't think that it is fitting for me to milk her, when we have servants of our own. Sometimes, I think she is a little ashamed of us.

I stifle a yawn. It is so warm in here and there is nothing to do. At last, there is a commotion outside, for which I am profoundly grateful. I want to run and see what is going on, but Rebekah puts a hand on my shoulder. It's not long before one of her many servants hurry in. Heled is back. He has come, with his men, to make sure that all is well at home. Rebekah stands and smooths her dress, she tucks non-existent strands of hair under her shawl, begins to press her lips together and constantly glances past us towards the door. Once seated again I notice that she is taking short shallow breaths. I wonder if it is because she loves him, or that it is because we are here, which might irritate him.

He strides in, unwashed and cloaked. When he sees us, he stops.

"What a tableau to come home to," he says, although he does not sound pleased. "Mother, are you well?"

"Do you bring news of my husband? I have heard nothing for such a long time."

"Hush, Mother, Heled will not have any news," Rebekah says, her hand squeezing Mother's arm so hard that she tries to pull away.

Why do they not yell from the roof tops that my father is dead? Instead, Mother should ask if there is any news of my brother. Rebekah's hand is also like a weight upon my shoulder so I would not dare speak to Heled, without some encouragement.

"And is this little Miriam?" So scrawny and awkward, I feel he would like to add. He looks with relief at Rebekah, he did indeed marry the right daughter.

"Are you staying long?" Rebekah asks quietly, as if we were not here at all.

"No, not even tonight. I must rejoin David, but we had heard there was trouble north of here and I came to make sure that you were safe. The King is undecided what to do, but if he thinks this town is for David, then he might well come to take his revenge."

I think Heled insensitive. We all know that King Saul is looking for the rebel David, and those men, like Heled, who follow him. Rebekah's hand clenches my shoulder even tighter. I glance up at her, her face has drained of colour.

Mother stands slowly; she has been sitting too long. She shrugs her shoulders and then turns to me.

"Come daughter, it is time for us to go. Let us leave these newlyweds to their precious time and perhaps we'll have a grandchild soon."

"Mother! There is no need to go," Rebekah says, her voice tight with shame. "You've hardly been here at all."

But Heled is already calling servants to bring the cart to the front door.

I drape mother's cloak around her shoulders taking care to fasten it tightly. Sometimes she tries to pull it off and drops it where she stands. I must take leave of my sister. She has risen from her seat and is calling for food and wine. She nods at me but quickly turns away to make sure that the men outside are also fed.

"Miriam, come here," Heled calls me, from the room. My heart beats a little faster, and I wonder what I have done wrong now. I'm not sure he has ever spoken to me before. I stare at my feet, because I know that Rebekah will be watching my every move. "I know your mother does not want to leave her home, but at the first sign of riot or fighting, you are to bring her here, to our house, where she can be protected. This is your responsibility, although I grow tired of her reluctance. It causes your sister much worry."

I can't imagine Rebekah worrying about us, but I nod and tie my cloak a little more securely. He at least thinks me capable of being more than an annoying appendage. When I wave to Rebekah, she looks at me with consternation. All she will have heard, is that Heled is cross with Mother because she wants to remain where she has lived, since the day she was married.

Chapter Five
Told by Hannah

Abigail is bleeding, her third or fourth time. She says she comes to me because she knows that my herbs can take the edge off her pain. She says, it's as if there is a deep wound inside her. The wound has nothing to do with the bleeding, she is simply learning what she has been born for. She is full of questions because we are awaiting the arrival of her betrothed. We know nothing of him, except that he is wealthy, and that negotiating the dowry took a long time.

I lay aside my sewing.

She asks me, "How will I know when he wants to be with me?"

"He will come to your room, or he will call for you."

"He won't just look at me in a funny way?"

"Well, yes, he might. Oh dear, I'm not sure I'm being very helpful. I don't know how to describe that look."

"What if he's ugly or fat?"

"Then you close your eyes and pretend he is someone else."

She shudders. She cannot help herself.

I shut my eyes and hope that he will be as her father was to me, at the start – gentle and kind. I kiss her on the top of her head, as noises from within the house herald the man's arrival. She gives me a look of desperation. I smile as best I can.

I sew on through the afternoon, but I have to unpick much of what I do. It is not that long by the shadow on the wall, but seems forever before she is back, dishevelled and in tears, her breath coming in deep shuddering gasps.

I have never seen her so affected, so uncontained. All hope is gone, as through her sobs she describes him, and it stills my hand. His face is round and flushed. He drank and ate noisily, he simpered over her mother and played too roughly with Samuel her brother, who ran from him, pointing accusingly at Abigail through his tears. She tried to find her father's face, but her mother frowned at her for raising her eyes beyond her lap. She was sent out and the deal was done; the day was set. Her father is still not able to look at her. Her mother, of course, beams with delight, it is a good match.

She dries her eyes on my skirt and says, "He waddles. He is not old and yet he waddles, and I swear I heard his mule mutter, 'oh no, not again'."

She is trying to make me laugh and I love her for it.

"You have been so quiet lately Hannah, are you alright?" she asks.

I am afraid that I will be left behind. The wretched hope she dropped into my heart, weeks ago, has flourished and grown wild. It is the start and end of each of my days. She kneels in front of me, her hands clasped in her lap, almost as if she is beseeching me to share my thoughts and yet I do not know how to ask her. Has she even dared speak to her father? She reads my thoughts, as always.

"Tonight, Mother is going to bed early. This new pregnancy is making her tired and her ankles are swollen. She doesn't want Father to see. Samuel, as usual, will fall asleep trying to stay awake. As soon as he does so, I'll talk to Father about you."

"Do you still want me to come?"

"Yes, of course. You will be all that makes it possible to live."

Suddenly, the window above my head looks pitifully small and I notice the plaster around it is flaking and cracked.

I am in bed when I next hear her calling me. She comes and perches on my cot so that we are sitting side by side. When I reach for the lamp she pulls my hand away. She is diminished and does not want me to see. She explains that she spoke to her father as promised, but she had to beg and cry before he would agree to let me go. She had hoped that she was still his little princess, that somewhere deep inside, he would remember. She is not. He is more concerned with angering her mother, for she has given him his beloved son, and he honours her above all else because of it. It is a bitter blow, and I think Abigail will carry it with her, forever.

I am sorry, very sorry that at last she sees how things are, but I am to go. I am to be free, and I tremble with joy.

"You must be cloaked and veiled, and you must stay at the back of the caravan, filled with the bride price. Mother may not notice you have left."

"Perhaps not," I reply. Inside I laugh, knowing she will notice soon enough – for who is going to sew and darn like me?

Chapter Six
Told by Jani

His secret is made known at last, although we had all guessed many weeks ago. His bride is here. He negotiated her price himself, so he is inordinately pleased with the wealth she is to bring. Yet, she is so tiny and delicate I am afraid that he will crush and break her. When we meet, she peers at me and then quickly looks away. I catch sight of dark eyes under long lashes. Her handmaid looks at me a little longer. She is trying to fix my place in the household. I wish her well with that, I am not sure where I belong. Still, it is clear Nabal is delighted with his Abigail and the noise and chaos of the celebration is wild and generous. There is feasting almost every night as he shows her off to his friends and neighbours. I wonder that he is still so rich, when he spends so much on eating and drinking.

He does not come to visit me as much now, because he has someone else to go to, someone who will nod and smile and laugh with him. I do not mind. I am happy to be left alone to tend my garden.

The weather is getting warmer by the day, new shoots are pushing through the dark red soil, and it is almost time for the shearing, my second in Nabal's house. Already, hanging in the air, is a strong smell of sheep dung and fleeces and I have to give up one of my boys, for everyone is needed. It doesn't matter, for the flower beds are trimmed and full.

I go to the garden every day. Little Sarah comes and walks beside me, like a dutiful maid, just in case I need anything. I think she likes it there too, although she has never said so. She doesn't talk much at all. I am beginning to think it is just her way. I've heard the others call her the butterfly, a fitting name for one who hardly seems to touch anyone or anything, as she flits about her duties.

I am as happy as I have any right to be, as a poor widow with nothing of her own.

***

Nabal has paid me a visit. He is striding up and down the paths, clearly angry, his fists clenched at his sides. The garden is hung with myrtle and each time he brushes past, a blossom is bruised or swept to the path. I do not yet know what is wrong; I hope he will tell me soon or there will be no flowers left.

"She is a witch," he hisses. I catch my breath. They have been married six months at most.

"Nabal, what is it?"

"Aunt Jani, she has shamed me in front of my friends."

I wonder at men's pride and the energy they spend on it.

"What did she do?" I ask, tentatively.

He storms away from me, as if he cannot bring himself to speak of it. I wonder if I should follow, only he is already turning back.

"I sent for her to come and wait on us as usual. She sent a message to say that she was not feeling well. I replied that she need not stay long, only she must come. I wished it. She sent another message, by that woman of hers, to say she really was too ill. It would not have mattered except that I went myself to see how she was. And what did I find? She and that woman laughing, laughing at me, for she was quite well, and I am labelled a fool."

He frowns at me, a small boy, a grown man, I'm not sure which. Then he strides away. A little further this time, before he turns.

"She was laughing at me, I know it," he says, and his voice quivers.

"What did you do?" I ask.

"I returned to my own rooms and sent Matthias to tell her how angry I was, only she bewitched him, too. He came back and said that I should go to her again, so that she could explain."

Nabal's pupils shrink within his eyes and become pinpoints of rage.

"How dare he take her side?" he almost chokes. "She must come when I call."

"Nabal," I say, "shall I go and see her? She will not bewitch me."

He nods, his cheeks purple and blotchy. I am worried. This little woman is playing with fire. I persuade him to walk, until he is a little calmer.

Abigail's rooms are large; they run down one whole side of the courtyard. I hope she is not getting too used to them, all to herself, for if he takes another wife she will have to share. I follow the sound of voices. She and her maidservant are sitting together. Hannah is sewing, Abigail is idle. There is no one around to announce my presence, so I enter with a bow. Abigail could, if she so wished, bewitch any man. She has a delicate beauty that seems to change, as if there is a curtain of light between us. Her dark curls fall around her face, unbraided.

The servant, Hannah, stands. Abigail does not move, neither does she smile in welcome. We have of course spoken, even eaten together, but I know my place. She might have sent for me before, if she had wished us to become friends, but she never has. It is only because I am here for Nabal, that I have dared come at all. I wait. At last, she says, "Fetch Aunt Jani a stool."

I am only just forty, yet she makes me feel like an old woman.

"Thank you," I say, keeping my eyes raised.

"You're here because he is angry with me," she says, returning my gaze. Her eyes are calm, and I am stunned at her candour.

"He is very upset."

"Did he send you?" she asks. She tilts her head very slightly to one side and I feel her scrutiny.

"Not exactly."

At this, she smiles at her servant. This is the moment I think she makes her mind up about me.

"I am bleeding. I am unclean. I could not serve him or any of his friends and I did not know how to tell him in so public a place as the meeting room."

I do not understand why something so simple has caused such a disagreement.

"You need to talk to him, to explain, to work out some sort of code for the future," I say, although I feel I am stating the obvious.

"Yes, of course but I can't go to him now unless he sends for me and he will not see Hannah, he is too angry."

"I am surprised that he has not guessed."

"That's my fault too. When we were last together I may have suggested I was pregnant."

I am disarmed by her.

"I have an idea. It is quite simple," I say.

Hannah serves figs and wine.

"Come to his garden."

"Can I go uninvited?"

"It was his mother's. He has let me tend it," I add, so that she understands a little better, *my* place.

"When should I come?"

"Tomorrow, just after the sun starts to drop. He may or may not visit but that is his usual time. It will be as if you have met there by accident and then you can explain your mistake."

"You will not see him before then?"

She is asking whether I go to him unbidden. I shake my head.

"We only ever meet in the garden."

She is satisfied by that. So I stand to leave. Abigail does not detain me, and I find I am a little saddened by that. Of course, Nabal will be displeased, it seems his tiny wife has bewitched me too.

***

I am up early. I pick pomegranate flowers for my room, just a few so that I will not spoil the crop. I get the boy to sweep the paths. He also opens the sluice gate to the channels, and the earth turns a deep red where the water spills over the soil. After breakfast, I idle in the shade of the almond trees, trying to mend a hole I tore in my shawl the day before. My sewing has not improved, and I am irritated by the large and ugly stitches. Abigail comes when I said to come and comes alone.

It is a precious moment when she beholds my garden for the first time. Her face lights up as if the sun has turned full upon it, she claps her hands, and I remember then that she is barely beyond childhood. She greets me and can hardly contain her joy.

"It is beautiful. No wonder he loves you so well. Why was I not invited to come before?"

I allow the rebuke to flutter past me. It was never my place to invite her here. I am just the gardener. After that, we walk and she asks me the names of the flowers, but I am afraid that he will see her with me, that he will leave before she has a chance to explain herself, so I take her to the bench just by the door. It is shaded by a vine, the grapes still hard lime clusters and the leaves a deep reddish-brown. I go back to sit in the arbour, where he will expect me to be.

The shadows begin to settle under the western wall, and I think that perhaps today he will not come at all. That she will have waited for nothing. I jump when the gate is flung back. Nabal, as angry as ever, strides over to me.

"Aunt, did you see her?"

"Yes. But please do not be angry with me or her, these things cannot be predicted or changed."

He does not understand, and too late my eyes have flickered over his shoulder. He turns. She is standing humble and penitent but clever, clever child, she has moved in front of the gate. I notice now that she is dressed in pale blue and her veil is the finest silk, edged with silver. Her hands are clasped in front of her, and she raises her face, just for a moment, as if she is searching his face for a small sign of love, her own filled with fear and remorse. I gasp at her beauty, at her skill, but I wonder if it will be enough, for Nabal has stretched tall. He is fierce and cold. I wait for him to sweep past her, yet, as surely as my Lord made the skies, Abigail is not defeated. She comes close and falls to her knees. She will not let him leave, until she has him once more cradled in her lap. I am impressed, that one so young, sees so clearly.

"Husband of my heart, I have hurt you and I cannot bear it."

He is lost and is already lifting her up.

After that, I am not sure how many weeks pass before I start going to my garden only if Abigail is not there or if she thinks something particular needs doing. I do not see Nabal at all, except when he passes me in the courtyard.

Now, everything is as it should be, except that I am blessed beyond measure, because Abigail often invites me to come to her, and when Hannah can, she seeks me out too. I've even taken to sewing, now that Hannah is on hand to show me how it's done properly. I am learning to be less impatient. Hannah is also a fine storyteller and I love to hear her tales of pirates and princes and faraway places. Abigail likes me to speak of my old home, the shop and the harbour, which I am glad to do. At last, there is joy in remembering, which I did not expect.

When we are alone, Hannah has even asked me about my beloved husband and although she is much younger than I, and has never been married, she seems to understand. I am sure she has known loss, as I am also sure, one day, she will tell me her story, because now she knows a little of mine.

Chapter Seven
Told by Hannah

It's been nearly a year since we came to this place of sheep and heat and the days have passed as in the blink of an eye. I am settled, beginning to feel free, to enjoy the sky above my head and to walk without glancing over my shoulder. At night, I love the dark mantle of blue, hung with stars and the pale washed dawn that races across this desert of shepherds. Abigail is less settled; there is still no child. Today, when she awoke, she could hardly bear to answer the simple questions that I must ask. She ate breakfast and hurried away to the garden, leaving me chastened and disconcerted. She needs to be alone, to walk in the shade, to think her thoughts, trying not to hope too much, that this month will be the month. I decide to sit and wait for her, watching the commotion of the central yard, the animals and men crowded around the bales of wool and feed. I see Nabal's steward Matthias. He comes over, dipping his head in greeting. He is a kind man.

"Let me get you something to drink. It's so hot today," he says.

"Thank you, Matthias."

He raises a hand, and it is done. He sits down beside me. The bench is long. He keeps a good distance between us. He is a man of propriety.

"And how is your mistress?"

He is probing for his master.

"She feels the heat. She cannot sleep, it is so still and hot."

"The shepherds say the weather will break soon. They always know," he says, looking up at the sky. Then he glances at me sidelong and says, "You seem tired."

"I am a little."

He stretches out and touches my hand with the tip of his index finger. He runs it under the palm and lifts it. I watch fascinated, as if my hand belongs to someone else. He is staring at it intently. She calls. I go to her and later I wonder whether he dropped my hand, or did I snatch it away?

Abigail is thirsty. I give her the drink that Matthias brought for me. She continues to walk slowly along the paths. I do not go back to the bench outside the gate but hide under the vines by the door. I watch the lizards running across the wall until it is time to go back to our quarters.

Chapter Eight
Told by Big Sarah

Milking my beloved goats has been forbidden. I weep, feeling as if everyone is looking at me, that I am outlined in light. I'm also trying not to think of Simeon. He is lost to me, for he would not dare touch me now. I am set apart. They have even given me my own room, which is small and bare, for I have nothing that is mine. It's a sad place, somewhere to hide. I have never slept before where I cannot hear others breathe and stir. I do not like it.

For two weeks, no one has spoken to me except the steward and the master. Sitting with the others in the kitchen, I used to laugh and gossip. They used to tease me. Now they whisper and stare. Sometimes, I manage to turn away before I weep.

The day it all changed, the goats were restless, they wriggled and squirmed. I knew I must make the tethers shorter. The next goat was old and was ready for me. She pulled away, turned and butted me hard, catching my knee with her bony head. She was always trouble. The pain made me cry out. I shouted at her until the throbbing subsided.

The men were laughing, my burst of cursing silenced them. Later, he said my eyes flashed. He said he had never seen me before. He said I was striking. God was laughing too, for that night there was lightning all around, no thunder, just flashes that splashed the mounds of cloud with brightness. The other girls were asleep, snoring gently.

"Sarah, Sarah come out. The master is calling for you."

Even then, I did not realise what was happening. As Matthias led me across the courtyard, the lightning flashed again and again, a scarifying white that left a blank darkness. Now, it is how I feel, even in the light of the brightest day.

He said he liked the smell of goats, yet after the first couple of nights he made the steward find me another job. Now I work washing clothes, although they won't let me do anything strenuous. They are worried that I will get over tired and that will make the master angry.

But it doesn't matter how light my duties are, falling asleep is the one thing that is not difficult to do. I have only to sit for a moment, and my eyes close and my limbs melt with heaviness. It means I don't get much done. My mind swings wildly from wishing my old life back, to wanting nothing. It was a good, old life and I miss it terribly, but I cannot imagine going back to it now. My misery is deep.

Hannah, Abigail's maidservant, came to the well today. The women stopped what they were doing. They are shy in front of her, respectful. I suppose she is only one step away from Abigail. She spoke to one of the women about some washing for her mistress. It was strange, for although she had her back to the light, I knew she was staring at me. Wondering at that, I began to fear. Abigail is clever and beautiful; I am rough and thick edged but could be pregnant with her husband's child.

Returning to my room to lie on the cot I notice there is a crack that winds across the ceiling from wall to wall. It is like a great river. I trace it from its source and imagine a tiny spring up in the mountains. Down on the plain it would become sluggish and wide and that is where I would wade across it or sit on a stone dangling my feet in the water. Last night he could barely touch me with kindness.

I look up at my river and wish I could truly walk beside it. Leave this place, wander into the desert, or up into the mountains. Of course I would not get far. I am always watched. To begin with I thought it was because he really cared for me. Now I know it's because they want to see if I am pregnant.

Abigail is still without a son, and they have been together for over a year. He is using me to see whether it's worth taking another wife. He's a careful man; he wouldn't want to marry another Abigail without good reason. It could be expensive trouble. He's not stupid. Neither am I.

He lies with me, he rolls off, I get up and leave. I wash, and wash, and then I curl into a ball and sleep. No one dares wake me and sometimes I do not get to the well before the sun is high. Hannah comes more often than she used to, to talk of this or that stain, the best way of washing this fine silk or the beaded linen. Abigail is watching. Everyone is watching.

***

It has been three months since Nabal started to lie with me, most nights. It is my third bleeding since then. I have told the steward, Matthias, I don't feel well, that I have a fever. I have stuffed the soiled rags under the bed, until they can be washed or buried out of sight. My stomach hurts, low and nagging, and so does my head. I have a pain that runs up my neck and across my forehead. Perhaps God has truly given me a fever because I lied to Matthias. Although I only did so, to give myself more time. Surely God will understand, for what happens next will not be good. I wonder what they will do with me.

I whisper to God, "I am little more than a whore, for he only ever sends for me at night, when none can see. And now, no man will ever touch me in love or take me to be his wife. Why have you set me on this path, why did you allow this to happen?"

I expect nothing, yet am surrounded with a strange, dark silence, even though the sun is high. I feel pinned to the bed and the pain in my head begins to wane. I do not want to move because for a moment I am at peace, and I will not willingly spoil it. There is a soft knock at the door. The darkness stays with me, in my head, behind my eyes. There is another knock. Who would extend me the courtesy of waiting?

"I'm not well," I call, sitting up. I can only move slowly, every muscle stretching and pulling with the effort of simply standing.

"I know. I have brought you something for the fever."

It is Hannah. I am frightened but I have no choice. Pulling the door ajar she slips inside, as if she does not want to be seen with me either. I am getting used to that. She looks around my room, then peers into my face.

"Do you have water?"

I nod.

She goes over to the jug and hands me a beaker. "This will help your pain," she says, holding out a bag of herbs.

I start to weep. Standing in front of this woman, I cannot stop the tears. She waits, standing with me.

When I have cried away the lump that was in my chest I say, "Please do not talk of pain."

She nods and says, "The mistress wants to see you."

I shake my head. I cannot go to her.

"She is not angry with you. You are just the first of many, until her own womb is opened."

I sit down on the bed, ashamed that the sheets are tangled. I had not thought there would be others. Of course, there will be as many as he wants.

"You are falling from favour," she continues.

Is she saying it, to make me feel better? No, it is to reassure me that nothing happens that these women do not see. I wonder if the herbs are poisoned.

"Come to Abigail."

I cannot refuse, and yet neither can I gather strength enough to get up. Hannah moves closer.

"You are exhausted."

She pushes me back until I am sitting down. She mixes the herbs in my water, and I drink. Lying back, she pulls the sheet over me;

she tucks it under my feet, she smooths the hair from my face. I look into her eyes, but she is not looking at me, her gaze is turned inward. When she is gone I want to cry again, only the herbs are taking effect, I haven't noticed the cramps for a while. It's the middle of the day, and yet I fall into blessed sleep.

When I awake the room is dark and I know that many hours have passed. There is a candle, although I cannot see it properly. I rub my eyes which are thick with stickiness. A cramp gripes from deep within my belly.

"How are you feeling?" Hannah asks. Abigail is sitting on a chair. Hannah must have brought it in for her. She herself is perched on my old milking stool. I sit up quickly, my heart beating so fast that my ears roar. I swing my legs onto the floor. My tunic is stained but I must stand. Abigail looks up at me. She neither frowns nor smiles.

"Sit down, Sarah," she commands, "Hannah will help you."

Hannah has a clean tunic. She pulls the soiled one over my head. I turn my back. Naked she helps me wash my face, my breasts, my belly. She hands me a wad of clean rags, and I push the others under the bed. Hannah straightens my sheets and comes to stand beside me. She begins to comb my hair. Enough is enough. I shake my head and take the comb from her. The strands are tangled, thick and long. Hannah goes back to her stool, I go to the window and push open the shutter. The night air is cool and the breeze like a blanket. I am ashamed, for my room stinks. How can they be here amongst my filth?

"Sit, Sarah," Abigail orders.

I drop onto the bed.

"How is the pain?" Hannah asks.

I shrug.

"I will leave you more herbs."

"Thank you," I whisper, "it won't be long, only one more day and night."

"Sarah, you will come to me," Abigail says.

I nod and wonder what that means.

They leave. I take the herbs quickly though they are bitter, for I long for the darkness.

Waking late there is no pain, so I rise and dress, taking the stained sheets from my bed and the rags from under it. I must go to the well, and walk with my eyes to the ground until the courtyard. There I yearn to scuttle around the edge, only when I remember the dark peace of the day before and Hannah's kindness, I straighten my back and step into the sunlight. My eyes are open but blind. The women look up and away again. After all, it is only me, spoiled Sarah.

I work hard washing my own sheets and rags. I also wash the floor clothes and the aprons from the slaughterhouse, beating and scraping them until the skin on my hands is white and flaking. I lay them on the rocks to dry in full view of anyone who wants to see. The other women are scared; the steward will be furious. I am unclean now, by my own hands. Let them suffer, only then one of them brings me water to drink. It is another small kindness, and I remember the laughter we shared in the past, but I do not try to thank her.

When the shadows spill across the yard I stretch, my back is aching. Yet I don't mind, because something has changed. I decide to go and stand with my beloved goats. The girl who milks them now will be long gone and I will be alone. I want to breathe in my old life and not worry about what is going to happen next.

The steward Matthias comes. He will know what I have done. Yet he comes in full view of the household. I look around. The boy is turning the spit and the old man tethering the camels. They pretend not to watch but their bodies are stiff with listening.

"The mistress wants you to help Hannah."

There is relief in his voice, and I realise he had not known what to do with me. Abigail has saved us both.

"Do you know what my duties will be?"

"You must ask Hannah."

I will be a servant to a servant. It is fitting. He turns to leave.

"Where do I go? When?"

He turns back.

"To Abigail, now."

I wonder if she will take in all of Nabal's discarded women. Perhaps, as long as he does not take any for a wife.

***

I help Hannah. She is kind and clever. I even have some new clothes. Abigail is generous and Hannah good with a needle. I sit at their feet. I am responsible for keeping Abigail's clothes clean and perfumed. It is not an onerous job and today I laughed, I could not help myself. Abigail raised an eyebrow, Hannah and Jani smiled.

When we went to the town, on the last feast day, I sacrificed two doves, one for my sin and one for my rescue.

Chapter Nine
Told by Miriam

"Sister, let me in. Please let me in."

"Who's there?"

"It's me, Miriam."

Rebekah's steward grasps my arm and pulls me into the house. I overbalance and he has to steady me. My legs are splashed with dust and muck; my tunic and cloak pulled to one side. I don't know why I am suddenly aware of such things.

"I'm so sorry Little One. Are you hurt?"

"No, I'm not. But it wasn't a very ladylike entrance." I laugh; the sound is high pitched and thin. He does not respond. I suppose, because he is worried too.

"It's just that the mistress said that no one was to be admitted, so I thought the least amount of time the door was open, the better."

I nod. I'm not really a good enough excuse for him to have gone against her wishes. We should have come yesterday, when I first heard the commotion in the marketplace, but I was too frightened to venture out with Mother.

"Where is she?" I ask.

"In her room."

I turn to go. He clears his throat. "Shouldn't you tidy up a little?" he says, quietly.

He's right. I smile at him, desperate for a little reassurance. He is usually so kind. Today he remains grave, so I shrug, and he calls for one of the servants. She comes and starts to undo my cloak. She gives me a cloth. I rub my face and hands. She rinses it in a bowl and hands it back, then straightens my dress and reties my belt, tighter than I like. She points to a dark smudge across my chest. I rub it away, leaving a pink mark where I rub too hard. She wipes my legs and feet. Another woman appears and inclines her head.

Rebekah wants me to hurry.

"Where's Mother?" Rebekah asks, before I have even caught my breath.

"At home."

"You've left her alone?" She is incredulous and it is worse than she thinks, for our servants have gone, too.

"She would not come. She cried and wept and when the mob ran past she would not talk to me at all."

"Why didn't you send one of the girls to alert us?"

"They left early yesterday and did not come back."

"You should have stayed with Mother."

She is disappointed in me. She is always disappointed in me.

"There is no food in the house and only a little wine," I say, and I force anger into the words so that they cross the distance between us too quickly. "We have not eaten since yesterday."

Rebekah is startled that I have dared speak to her so. She shakes her head and angrily calls her steward. I cross my arms over my chest. She calls for the cart to go and fetch Mother, immediately.

"You had best go back with him," she says. "You should not have left her. I will speak to Heled when he returns. He is on his way. They were close, when he heard about the mob, so David said he could come to us."

We are to return home immediately. I am so hungry. Did she not hear me, when I said we had not eaten since yesterday? I bow, but it is more of a stiff leaning towards her. I will not remind her of what I said, for in truth, Mother is alone, and we do need to get back to her. A servant is waiting. She smiles at me. I am so grateful. So pitifully grateful.

"The steward is getting the cart," she says. "He will not be long. He hopes you won't mind sitting here for a moment, to wait."

I sink down onto the bench. I do not understand why my sister's servants are so kind to me. The woman turns to go and then as if she has just remembered, she turns back and points to a beaker of wine and a plate of bread and cheese. My eyes fill with tears. Perhaps it is not kindness but pity, because there is no family left to love me as I would like to be loved.

When we get home, the door to our house stands open. I am afraid, for I am sure that I pulled it tight when I left. The steward has to hold me back. He pokes his head inside. Mother is not there. I run past him into the yard where she is sitting on her weeding stool with Jani, our goat. Jani bleats. Mother does not stir, she simply stares at the ground. I think she is humming.

The steward begins to supervise the loading of the cart. One of the boys stands guard outside the door. The streets are still mostly empty, silent, except for one or two hurried figures, so he soon changes his mind and calls the lad in to lift and carry. I want to help them, only mother won't let go of my hand. Jani pushes her nose into my lap and tries to eat my skirt. I scratch behind her ears. She looks like she could do with milking.

"Mother, as the girls aren't here, shall I see to Jani?"

"No child. One of them will do it. They always do."

The steward comes out to us and beckons me in. He looks stern and my stomach drops to my knees. I pull roughly away from Mother as she still won't let me go. It could not be worse, Heled has come. He looks hot and the smell of leather and sweat in our small kitchen is overpowering.

"There you are. Where is your mother?"

"With Jani."

"Who's Jani? I thought the servants had run away." He frowns, opening and closing his fists, flexing his blunt fingers as if he needs something to do with them.

"The goat," I mumble. I catch the edge of a smile from the steward. He is safely to one side, so that Heled won't see. It is a good job, for Heled is getting angry. I take a very small step backwards.

"Enough. I'm not sure why I am here except that your sister was upset and frightened for you." He gives a small shake of his head. "You and your mother will come now. I cannot have people think I neglect her, and it is far too dangerous for you to go on living here alone."

I can see his men outside, those he took to war. They have blocked the street, their horses squeezed shoulder to shoulder, their legs pale with dust. They are slumped in their saddles, not at all interested in what is going on inside our small house. Heled turns to leave. One of the boys, is so nervous in the presence of his master, that he drops a pot. It shatters. Heled turns back, but it is me he looks at. I'm angry and scared at the way his eyes run over me, from head to foot and I wish with all my heart that it was Joel, my brother, standing there, deciding my future. He *should* have come home to see that we were safe.

"It is time," he says, but it is a thought voiced, nothing that demands a response from anyone else.

Heled mounts, hesitating a moment before heaving himself into the saddle and rides away.

"Mother will not want to go," I say. I am worried about the fuss she might make.

"I have something that will calm her down. Do you mind?" the steward asks.

"No. I think a few moments of forgetfulness will be a blessing." Although, I'm not sure we should tell Rebekah. She will feel ashamed that Mother was so difficult, and I would surely get the blame.

Jani begins to bleat.

"Do you think she'll ever be herself again?" I say, peering out into the yard. I can just see Mother, sitting with her back against the wall. I should not have given voice to my thought, but I have known this man since Rebekah became Heled's wife. He is kind and wise.

"Your brother ran off to ride with David, the rebel, whom your father was fighting against. She knew, that one day, they might have to fight one another. Her grief is heavy and difficult," he says.

"But Father was killed by the Philistines, not by David's men. And Heled also rides with David against the King," I said, feeling the unfairness of it.

"Heled is not her son. That is for your sister to worry about."

I take a cloak out to Mother. The sun has not crept into the yard, for the walls are high and it feels chilly. I am careful to stay out of her grasp. I pull Jani to her stall and milk her.

A scream tears through the streets, a woman howling. It is a cry of great loss. We cannot stay. I tug Mother to her feet and lead her to the cart. It is only when I have settled her, that I realise I am trembling.

***

I am clean. My hair is braided, and I wear one of Rebekah's dresses.

It is too big, and a servant has tied the belt too tightly again. She has pulled the excess wool to the back where it is bunched up and uncomfortable. I have nothing to do but feel uncomfortable. Rebekah has of course spent the morning scolding me, she does not waste a single opportunity to point out my faults. Some of them are true, others she has made up. When I tried to speak, to argue my case, she slapped my face, which shocked me into a spluttered silence. She says I must keep my head down, literally; I am not to look up or speak or move. Heled would not like me to be so bold.

He comes into the room. He brings shadows and stirred air.

"I cannot stay long, wife, but I will leave more of the men at home this time. You will be safe, but you also need to be ready to move quickly, if I send for you."

Rebekah is pregnant and the riots have frightened them. We are all scared.

"The town is trying to prove its loyalty to the King. It will fool no one," Heled continues. "Too many of the men have gone over to David and that promises vengeance on those that are left."

When we crossed the market square in the cart, there was a patch of trampled rags, and I thought nothing of it until I saw a scrawny hand stretching from under the fabric. I wish with all my heart we had gone a different way. I cannot get that picture out of my head.

I wonder that he can leave Rebekah so. He is a wealthy man and could easily come to the attention of the King. His family would be a good example to make.

Heled paces up and down the room, filling it with his presence.

"Is she ready to marry?" he asks.

My sister nods.

"She is fourteen. Older than I was, when I came to be your wife." Once again, she is disappointed in me.

"I've a mind to take her myself. She would be a great help to you and a comfort to your mother."

I know he is looking at me. I wish he would look at Rebekah. I can only see her out of the corner of my eye, but her lips are thin, pressed together and her cheeks flushed. He continues, "But I have a better idea." He turns away to summon the steward, which is a relief because he might have been greatly irritated by the relief on both our faces.

He says, "David will want to move again soon, so send one of the men to find where I can meet him." Turning back to Rebekah, he continues, "Prepare your sister for a journey. Only pack her best things. Can you ride?" he asks.

"No," says Rebekah, "of course she can't."

"I can," I say and wish that I had kept quiet, for her look promises me at least one more slap. Heled is surprised. His head tips to one side and he raises an eyebrow. It makes him look younger.

"My brother, Joel, taught me," I say, quickly before Rebekah has a chance to silence me. She frowns and looks away.

That had been a good time. Father had been away fighting for King Saul. Joel and I sneaked out to the stables whenever Mother wasn't looking, me to wonder and him to boast. He'd help me up onto one of the horses, would lead me around and around, talking and talking. Even then he loved an audience, and I loved him, so there was nothing better for either of us. And he only had to make faces behind Mother's back while she lectured me on my latest shortcomings, to bind my love. I would have ridden to the gates of Sheol if he had asked me to. I miss him, it is like a lump inside me.

Heled sits down beside Rebekah. He puts his hand over her stomach. It is a large hand and Rebekah shrinks underneath it. A servant is standing to one side of the door. She gestures to me to come out to her. I am too scared to move. A moment later, the steward himself comes and beckons me away. They must need me for something urgent with Mother. I rise to take my leave. The steward gives a small shake of his head, and I come away without turning to my sister or her husband. I wait for Rebekah to angrily summon me back, but she does not. I am led to the kitchen, and I spend some time with the servants stoning peaches. The steward comes and goes. He is always listening for his master's voice. When next he looks in on us, I catch his eye and ask, "Have you heard what happened to our servants?"

I do not understand the expression on his face.

He says, "They won't be coming back. Heled was very angry that they left you alone."

"It's a shame, for Mother was used to them. Where is she?"

"Resting."

"Will I be able to see her before I go?"

"Of course," he says, turning to leave. At the door, he adds, "You had better go to your room and wait for your sister to call you. Try not to worry about your mother; we will be kind to her."

One of the women throws me a peach. I will try very hard not to drop its juice down Rebekah's dress.

Chapter Ten
Told by Big Sarah

Nabal has taken another girl. Little Sarah, Jani's servant. My heart darkens for her. She is no more than a child. Jani is angry, spitting dust and rage. When Nabal came to see us she could barely speak to him. He sent her another servant. Jani sent her back. Then he returned Little Sarah to her, not because she was angry but because the child had cried and trembled. She did not understand the honour he was bestowing on her! He tore her, then discarded her.

Jani keeps her close now, out of sight, lets her sleep alongside her so that when she wakes, Jani can soothe her. Hannah is making her new things to wear, for none we have are small enough.

Little Sarah does not speak and jumps at the sound of voices. She squeezes into corners and drops her head if anyone but Jani, Hannah or I come into the room. She is a tiny woman, enveloped in fear.

Abigail watches. Sometimes there is nothing she can do.

Chapter Eleven
Told by Little Sarah

Jani stands in front of me. Her back is broad. I do not like it when she moves away, for then the air grows heavy, and I cannot suck enough of it in to breathe.

When I was brought back to her, she was so angry she could barely look at me. I was afraid that she would send me away. Yet, even from that first day, after he said he couldn't bear my crying, Jani allowed me to stay near her. I must do as I am told, I must stay out of sight. She has said I can trust her.

I have new clothes that Hannah, Abigail's handmaid, has made for me. They are fine and one has a small silk trim that I sometimes rub when I begin to feel scared. It is smooth and helps me listen. When Jani goes to work in the garden, I bring her things I think she might need. Drinks and a shawl, cheese or fruit. She calls me Little One. The others call me Little Sarah.

Abigail does not seem to see me, for which I am grateful. She is so beautiful, so clever. I would not know how to answer any of her questions.

He will never call for me again, because he did not like my weeping.

Chapter Twelve
Told by Miriam

I ache from head to toe. Even my fingers are stretched and sore. We have ridden all day and when Heled lifts me down, my legs collapse under me. The men laugh. They have erected a small tent for me, although I have difficulty walking to it. The food his servant brings is more than I can manage, even though I am hungry and yet when he comes to gather my far from empty plate, he smiles.

"That's better. You won't be skinny for long."

He turns away quickly, as Heled, his master, is coming towards us.

"Sleep," Heled says. "We'll be setting off at first light and if you think you are sore now, then tomorrow will be agony."

I curl up in my tent and sleep until Heled shakes me awake. He looks happier, younger. He even smiles at me. It is hard to smile back, for my legs hurt so badly. Everything feels tight as if I am suddenly grown old. My horse is saddled, but I know that today my muscles are too stiff to clamber up by myself. Heled takes me around the waist and lifts me as if I were a child. I try to pull my tunic down over my legs. His servant comes and gives me bread and cold mutton. I don't taste it. I am trying to find a comfortable way to sit and when we begin to move, I cannot help the tears that fall. The servant hands me his cloak. I don't know what he wants me to do with it, so he bundles it up and points to my saddle. The men are howling with laughter. He does not laugh with them, for which I am grateful. It brings gentle relief, until the new muscles begin to ache, too.

The men stopped laughing and talking a while back. They have spread out, two riding in the far distance ahead of us. We must be a long way from any of the towns and nowadays no one is safe outside their walls.

We are heading for Ziph in the pasturelands of Carmel. I know nothing of it, never having been beyond the boundary of Netofa. When we camp, I need somewhere to relieve myself. I squat, but I can't help wrinkling my nose in disgust. I smell and I long to wash. My stomach has begun to clench, and I am frightened that my bleeding is coming. How much further do we have to go? I rub sand and grit into my hands, adjust my clothes very carefully and begin the slow walk back to camp. I do not see the horses until I am quite close but there is no disguising the thin plume of smoke that drifts high and feathery into the growing darkness.

I sleep until they bring me food. I ask God to protect me and my mother and the little one inside Rebekah. I ask him to keep my brother Joel alive too, although on this he is strangely silent. Perhaps I will never see my brother again. My eyes prickle with tiredness and the dust thrown in our faces by the wind and the horses. Through my tears I see Heled lying near the fire, in the centre of his men. The flames shadow his face, but I realise I am no longer afraid of him. He lies long and relaxed; out here he seems always to be laughing. It smooths away the lines around his mouth and I wish he had been like this at home, so that I could have felt as if I belonged there, once my father and brother had left us.

The next morning Heled rides beside me. His short beard still looks neatly trimmed only there is stubble on his cheek, and I can see the scars across the muscles of his arms and legs. I have never dared peer at him so closely. Before he was simply my sister's husband, now he is all that stands between me and the next part of my life.

Today, I do not ache so badly. Today, I have remembered to look at the land around me, to watch the men and how they live, to try to remember everything that I see, for it might be the most exciting part of my life and I do not want to miss a thing.

"Tonight, you will meet a man who will take you as his wife," Heled says, at last, talking quietly, without turning his head.

We ride a little further. I can see a town in the distance, no more than a smudge across the horizon.

He continues, "He is very rich, and I've known him a long time."

I do not know what to say to either of those things. I have no dowry, apart from what Heled gives me and I wonder what Joel my brother will think of this, for it is really his responsibility. I wonder whether he has even been consulted and what Heled brings as my bride price?

"Will I ever come home again?" I ask.

"I don't know, although you might see Joel. You'd like that wouldn't you? Rebekah said you were fond of him."

I am surprised and suspicious. Rebekah always stood apart from us, took her position as the elder sister very seriously. It felt as though she despised us both. Now it feels as if Heled is offering me something in return for what happens next, that he seems pleased to do so.

He continues, "Sometimes we pass near here and David has a high regard for kin. He will surely let Joel visit."

I have not seen my brother for nearly two years. Heled has no idea how my heart lifts at the thought of such a meeting. Perhaps God had been silent in the desert, when I prayed for my brother, because he knew that this gift was just around the corner.

"Will you take him a message, Heled?" I ask boldly.

"Of course," he says, although he has stiffened as if afraid of what I might say.

"Tell him, he was a good teacher, and that I did not forget how to ride."

Heled laughs. He laughs until his eyes water.

It is late afternoon when we reach the town, but it is not where we are going. We pass by on the southern side, and I start to see sheep, hundreds of them. So many, that I cannot imagine their number. Sometimes we see the shepherds. They stand together and watch us. We cannot see their faces, for they are wrapped up against the sun and wind. I do not blame them, everything that I wear is gritty with sand. Heled always acknowledges them yet never rides close enough to speak. I am beginning to think that I shall fall asleep on this horse.

There are lights up ahead, fires and twinkling lamps, a range of buildings that spill out to meet us. A man runs forward, and catches hold of Heled's bridle. Heled will not like that. Another man is waiting for us, further on. He calls loudly, so that all can hear.

"My master wants to be sure that you come in peace, Heled."

"Tell him I come in peace. I come, bringing the gift I promised."

We stop just short of the buildings. We remain mounted although I long to slide to the ground. Servants bring skins of water for us to drink and many come crowding around. We wait. I droop over the pommel of the saddle because it is too hard to sit upright anymore. I dare not take a drink, I do not know what is expected of me.

At last, the people part and a man comes towards us, surrounded by other men, though there is an arms width of space about him. He is massive, I have never seen a man so tall and wide. Even Heled is dwarfed beside him. His cloak is rich-red and glistens in the torch light, for there is a fine gold thread running through it. He has a full beard, and his cheeks and nose are pink, the skin stretched tight over jowls, that vibrate with every step. He is magnificent and gross. I keep my eyes down and pray and pray that it is his son to whom I am betrothed.

There is a lot of laughter, as if someone has just said something funny. Our men remain silent and Heled sits upright and stiff, his horse's ears flicking back and forth, however I think the beast would be too tired to run.

"Welcome Heled, welcome to my humble abode." His voice is loud and deep.

Heled climbs down.

"A welcome it is, Nabal, and I have never seen an abode less humble."

Nabal laughs, and then a hair's breadth later his men join in.

Nabal and Heled embrace. As they do, I see Nabal peer over my brother-in-law's shoulder. He is noticing how many there are of us. Is he counting the shekels to keep us, or the knives and swords we carry? I think both. Heled waves his hand and his men begin to dismount. They are still uneasy. Heled's servant comes to help me down and then stands in front of me. I want to bury my face in his back, so that I am hidden. He inches a little closer, as if he understands.

I suddenly wonder what this servant is really like, this man who seems to know me so well. He gave me his cloak as a cushion, didn't laugh at me with the others and is now helping me stay invisible. I am fourteen years old, a grown woman, only suddenly I wish that our journey had not ended quite so soon.

"So show me what you have brought me, Heled."

The servant still does not move from in front of me. He is looking to Heled, who is hesitating. Then there is a different feel to the crowd of men. My servant shield drops his shoulders and at last moves, just a little, so that I can see past him. Nabal stares at me for a long moment, and then turns to the woman who has appeared beside him.

"Abigail, my wife, my jewel. You have heard that we have guests. Look, our old friend, Heled."

"You are welcome." The voice is mellow, gentle. "You bring your sister-in-law to see us. Heled, she must be exhausted. Husband, allow me to tend to her, let me take her to my quarters and then tomorrow, when she is rested…"

"See how thoughtful she is." Nabal speaks a touch loudly, and I detect the tension stretched taut between them. "Tomorrow, Abigail, rested and refreshed." His voice is firm. He continues, "Come, Heled, let us eat. I've hardly tasted meat all day and I am hungry."

I wonder what I should do. The men are beginning to move away; I wait until at last the servant stands aside and bows low. There is a shimmer of gold cloth, feet that flash coloured gems, and jewelled hands that rest at her side. I look up and then I cannot look away.

"I am Abigail. I am Nabal's wife."

"I am Miriam, sister-in-law to Heled," I whisper, "daughter of Baanah, though he is dead."

"That we know of and are sorry."

She turns and I follow. I try to stay back from her. I must smell awful and I'm sure that my bleeding will start any moment. I long to lie down and sleep, yet I want to see everything.

We walk through what feels like a palace. There are three or four rooms filled with braziers, red and purple hangings twinkling with mirrored glass and soft rugs that my feet sink into. I am very sorry that my sandals are so dusty, that I am filthy from the journey.

She is slender, delicate and dressed as a royal princess. I trail behind her as the lowliest of women. Her eyes are dark brown, almost black and she looked at me with such intensity that I felt she already knows who I am, knows my true worth.

I am led to a small room. Abigail leaves me there with three women. They help me undress until I stand awkwardly before them. I am offered perfumed water to wash in, and my dirty clothes are pushed into a linen sack. I steal glances at these women, when I think they are too busy to notice. They are easy with each other, gentle and careful with me. They speak quietly and I strain to hear all that they say but it is only ordinary speech, spoken lightly at the end of a long day. The youngest woman unpacks my bag. She brings my festival dress. It is the best I have and yet it is so plain. I feel the poverty of it, of all my things. They start to brush my hair. They braid it with silver thread, winding it through my pale locks. Abigail has thick dark hair, mine is light and fine. All that I am is thin and scrawny.

When I am ready, her servant comes to fetch us. Her name is Hannah. I am not afraid of her; she reminds me of the kind servant from Rebekah's household. She leads us into a much larger room. It is warmed by a brazier of acacia wood and there are lamps all around, so that many shadows splay out around me, like dark stars on the floor. There are five of us and Abigail. They are all looking at me.

"Eat," says Hannah, and hands me a plate of lamb. The plate is silver, and I run my fingers around the edge. It is smooth and thick and heavy.

"You are very pretty," Abigail says. "There is something about you." She speaks quietly and I stop chewing in case I miss what she says next, although I'm not entirely certain she was talking to me at all. I know I am not pretty, so I shake my head, swallowing the food in a lump.

"Speak," she commands.

I dare not speak, for I would not contradict her, that would not be the right thing to do.

"I will save you from him," she says. "I know it is not what Heled came for, that his debt will remain outstanding and yet I wonder if this isn't what he had in mind all along." She speaks thoughtfully, as if she is alone and we are not crowding around her. At last, she looks up and smiles. "I think that you would do better to serve me than my husband, at least for now."

I wonder what Heled's debt might be. The tall woman with the dark hair begins to chuckle. Perhaps she knows. One of them called her Sarah and although her laugh is infectious no one joins in. The others look at Abigail, who leans back on her cushions. Hannah hands me more of the lamb. The herbs are fragrant, the meat tender, and as always I am still hungry.

"I used to tend goats until I came to serve here," Sarah says. The others turn once more to their mistress. Abigail nods and then looks down at her hands. Sarah may continue. "And this is Sarah, too." She turns to the youngest of the women. "We call her Little Sarah."

She is thirteen or fourteen at most. I am glad, for I think I may be older, perhaps only by a few months. She does not quite look at me and does not smile. The oldest woman pats her hand.

Next to Abigail is Hannah, who came to fetch us. She sits closest to Abigail and was the one who reminded me of the servant from home. I think she is in her mid-twenties, much older than Abigail, I am certain.

"I am Hannah," she says.

"I am Jani," says the older woman, "I am a distant cousin, through marriage, to Nabal."

I bow, for she is a relative. I thought she was a servant. I am also trying not to laugh. Jani looks at me through narrowed eyes.

"Speak child," she says.

I dare not.

Sarah laughs again, her deep throaty laugh.

"Jani is such a good name for a goat, or a donkey perhaps, is it not?" she says.

I am astonished, truly astonished. What kind of women are these that can see my thoughts, with such ease? Jani is shaking her head, and I hope that she is not too angry with me. "She was a very good goat, was she not?" Sarah continues.

"The best," I whisper. Inexplicably, my eyes fill with tears.

Abigail rises from her cushions and turns to look at us.

"Now I have five women to advise me. Truly, as the Lord lives, I am blessed."

I think she has chosen her words carefully so as not to offend Jani, any more than I have already.

Abigail and Hannah leave us. Little Sarah at Jani's prompting takes me to another room at the end of a long passageway. When I take off my robe we see that there is blood. It has come at last. I stand very still; I will make her unclean. She regards me with her strange, quiet eyes and nods.

"The Lord is truly good and smiles on our mistress," she says, so quietly I can barely hear her.

Little Sarah finds me clothes to sleep in, she even brings me herbs for the pain that has begun to nag across my back, as usual. She flits about my room arranging my sparse belongings, but it is a struggle to keep my eyes open. I do not want her to think me rude, but I cannot help myself. There is dimness and warmth, and I do not wake until bright morning light is streaming through a tiny window above my head. Now there are men shouting, the bleating of sheep and the bellow of camels.

Chapter Thirteen
Told By Jani

Heled stays two days after it is all settled. When he leaves, Abigail gives him a jewelled bracelet for Miriam's sister, Rebekah, and a tiny gold cup for the new baby, yet to be born. She says many kind things, things that, perhaps, Miriam should have said. Heled is not reassured, he still seems nervous at leaving his sister-in-law here. I suppose, because now, she is not to be married. He must wonder if he is doing the right thing, what her status will be. Of course, I doubt that it is Abigail he mistrusts, but Nabal. Abigail, as always, sees his unease. She says, "She will be like a sister to me."

I am glad Miriam is here, for she and I will stand together, in that we are neither truly servant nor equal to the mistress.

Abigail had spent the evening with her husband and his friends, with Heled and his men. She did not come back to us until very late. She was tired but she had done what she'd set out to do. Miriam is to stay, to be her companion, her maidservant, we are not sure which. It doesn't seem to matter to Miriam, she was just scared they would send her home.

Tonight, there will be another feast. Nabal does not seem to need much of an excuse. Miriam will not go, she is still unclean, which is fortuitous, as in Nabal's case, out of sight is out of mind. But she is avidly watching Abigail dress. She and I sit together, and I enjoy the wonder on her face, for Abigail wears the finest silk and linen.

"I would hardly dare touch such fabrics," she whispers to me. "They run through Little Sarah's fingers like water, so soft." Little Sarah also dresses Abigail's hair. She braids pearls on gold thread and uses ivory combs and silk ribbons. Hannah paints Abigail's eyes and lips.

"You'll get used to it," I say. I like this young woman. There is an honesty about her, an openness that is easy to sit with. I'm going to stay with her tonight, which I don't mind at all, although Miriam cannot understand why I would want to miss the excitement of a banquet.

There is so much that she does not understand, that she has yet to learn.

***

There is a butterfly hovering among the juniper bushes. It is grey-veined and when it rests above my head I can see the sun through its wings. I rock back onto my heels and become aware of the ache in my back, just around the middle. Spilling the loose soil from my lap, I realise I have done more than enough today. It's an effort to stand slowly, to walk up and down the path until my muscles loosen. Miriam is at the far end of the garden with Little Sarah. They are sewing in the shade of an almond tree.

Miriam has settled well and does not seem homesick at all. She is, as I thought, easy to be with, and quick like Abigail. Her previous life was quite sheltered, so she knows very little of the world and I do not think it would ever have been enough for her. I don't doubt she would have gotten into trouble, sooner or later. So I am glad that she has come. She questions us relentlessly on all that she sees. It's all so new to her. Her eyes sparkle with curiosity and Abigail is right, when she fills out a little, she will be quite lovely.

She sees me walking stiffly among the myrtle bushes and calls out, "Jani, come sit with us, here in the shade. You've been working all day."

It's a joy to stretch out on the rug. Little Sarah jumps up and is gone in a moment.

"She will have gone to get you water for your hands," Miriam says, holding her fingers out in front of her, her sewing discarded across her lap.

"They are dusty more than anything," I reply, brushing them against my skirt. They are not pretty hands and are ingrained with the dirt of my morning's work. The fingers are strong and blunt, but the nails have grown since I came here. They are polished and neat, but I still can't soften the hard skin on my palms. I was brought up to work, so these leathery patches are old friends. I pick at them whenever I am anxious and rub them smooth when my mind wanders. Miriam's hands are soft and delicate, little white fingers that are good at pulling out the tiniest splinters or using the finest thread.

"Poor Little Sarah, she does so hate the dirt and dust, and I suppose she thinks we do too," Miriam murmurs, leaning back against the tree.

We laugh because neither of us are worried about such things.

"What happens if Abigail cannot have a son?" Miriam asks. Her sudden question makes me open an eye. She is staring at me, unblinking.

"He'll have to take another wife. He needs a son," I reply.

"Will she come and live with us?"

"Yes, where else would she go?"

"I mean, actually in Abigail's rooms."

"Mmm," I reply, again closing my eyes against the harsh light. I am beginning to feel sleepy.

She squints down at me as the sun hardens the air around us.

"Another wife," she whispers, and I realise that she is worried that it might still be her, that Nabal would not treat her as he has the two Sarahs, that she would have to marry him.

"Don't worry," I say, "I'm sure Nabal doesn't think of you anymore and anyway, you belong to Abigail now."

Miriam is right though. Two wives would mean jealousy and power struggles; our easy lives would be over in a moment.

"I could never serve another," Miriam says, "I am Abigail's..." and she hesitates for a moment before saying, "companion."

I can see her mind open before me. The word sister would have implied equality, and she sees quite clearly that that is not the case.

She is staring at her embroidery. She is learning to scallop an edge of silk, her young eyes able to see the tiny stitches. Hannah has high hopes for her sewing, although I am not so sure. I think, once the novelty has worn off, she will grow impatient with it. I know I did. I like doing the simple things, and I'm sure I sew the straightest hem of all of us, except Hannah of course.

Little Sarah comes slowly through the gate. She brings a bowl of warm water and a fresh linen towel. Big Sarah comes behind with a tray of fruit and a flagon of watered wine. I can't remember exactly when we started calling her Big Sarah, but it was definitely after Miriam came. Now it seems right, natural. Big Sarah, and my dear Little Sarah.

"That's more like it," I whisper to Miriam, who jumps up to take the tray from Big Sarah. Miriam never allows anything to bother her for long. She is good at putting things to the back of her mind. It will help her as she grows, she will not carry any unnecessary burdens. She kneels, holding out the cups for Big Sarah, their hair blowing together dark and fair as they lean in close, so as not to spill a drop.

Big Sarah looks over at me, and nods. Her eyes are ringed with dark shadows and her hand trembles. Now, she is a woman who does not put things away lightly. She is a woman of depth and height. Easy laughter but heavy thoughts, that pull on her face. I would like to reassure her that I have noticed her pain, except she would only tell me to mind my own problems. She is strong and I will respect that.

We stay seated together, laughing and talking, trying to answer Miriam's many questions until I doze. As I sink into delicious sleep, listening to their voices, I hold this moment as a precious jewel.

Chapter Fourteen
Told by Hannah

Abigail is weary because she was sitting late with Nabal. This time, there was no feast and few friends. It is much harder for her when there are not so many to entertain him; she always comes back exhausted and stretched. Last night, on her return, she was irritable and walked her rooms a long time, before she would settle. I could find nothing that would soothe her, so it was nearly dawn before she lay down and her breathing deepened. Sadly, a particularly large caravan left early this morning, and she woke with the noise of it. Camels and donkeys laden with skins, and dressed carcasses, braying and bellowing interminably. Since then, she has spent the hours yawning and lethargic. I hate it when she is like this, she will not be roused by anything and her indolence spreads through our quarters, until everyone is affected. Nothing will be done properly all day. I have tried to persuade her to go back to her couch to sleep, now that things are quieter, but she will not.

I watch her staring into space, willing her to close her eyes. It would be best to concentrate on my sewing, but I am disconcerted too. The morning stretches. We are both silent. She picks at her food, gathering crumbs with her fingertips and then she stands, so swiftly that I jump, dropping my needle. Abigail disappears into her room, the door closing with a bang behind her. With relief, I call one of the girls to come and sit outside. She will find me if Abigail needs me again.

I pick up my sewing basket and walk across the courtyard to the garden. I see Matthias, Nabal's steward, talking to one of the men from the fields. He nods to me, and I reply with a sombre tilt of my head. He deserves our respect. He has always treated us with the utmost dignity, except for that one moment, just before Miriam came, when he touched my hand with the tip of his finger. It seems a long time ago now. Before I have gone more than a few paces, he returns to his work for already there are more men waiting to speak to him.

Pushing open the gate, I can see at the far end of the garden, Big Sarah is lying back against the trunk of the almond tree, her eyes closed and a smile playing around her lips. Jani sits against her and Little Sarah lies curled in a ball between them, her head in Jani's lap. Jani strokes her hair and Little Sarah fiddles with the fringe of her scarf. Miriam is opposite them, her sewing lying idly beside her. When I get closer I can hear that she is plying Jani with questions about her life in Dor and what the sea was really like. She is leaning forward, her fair hair falling from the clips, her arms clasped tightly around her knees. Just for a moment, I do not go any closer, content to watch them.

"When the ships unfurl their sails, why do they not blow over and turn upside down?" she asks.

Jani replies, "Child, I have only watched them, I do not know how they work, but sailors are the roughest, strongest men I have ever seen."

"Trust you to notice how strong they are," Big Sarah says. She keeps her head bowed over her lap, as if she doesn't want the rest of us to hear, but I can see that her eyes are crinkling with silent laughter. Jani frowns at her, although I see her mouth twitching too, as she swallows a chuckle.

Little Sarah says, "They cannot be as scary as shepherds."

"Oh much worse, Little Sarah. You would not dare go near one," Jani replies.

"And you would have to block your ears. Their language is rough, from what I've heard," Big Sarah mumbles, suppressing a yawn. Her voice is almost slurred, as she fights off sleep, her lashes long across her dark olive skin.

"Yours is not always the most ladylike, from what I've heard," Jani retorts. Before Big Sarah can speak again, I move closer so that they notice me.

"Hannah," Miriam calls, with delight, making space for me beside her, "Big Sarah is too weary to tell us one of her tales, so could we hear one of yours? Please Hannah, just a little one."

I reach for a fig. They are past their best, but I love them like this, juicy and soft.

"Please tell us the one about the shepherd boy," Little Sarah asks, sitting up. She is pale but her eyes are bright, and she would be lovely if she would only smile a little more, but then perhaps she is wise to stay so grave. I find it hard to refuse her, she so rarely requests anything.

"Is it really about David, the rebel?" Miriam wonders.

"No, I've known this story since I was a girl. Well before David killed the lion, and a long time before we first heard of him."

Little Sarah is disappointed, for the rebel David has become a great favourite among us. I pretend to yawn. Big Sarah flicks open her eyes and then closes them again. She knows I am teasing them. I can keep nothing from her.

"Miriam, show me what you have done this morning," I say, keeping my face still, trying hard not to smile, as if I have made up my mind. Her mouth droops, as she reaches for the fabric on the ground and hands it to me, first smoothing it across her knees. Her shoulders have slumped, just a little, and her eyes are shadowed. Enough teasing, I cannot do it, I am no Big Sarah, so pushing Miriam's sewing away, I lean back to begin the tale of the shepherd boy and the princess.

Little Sarah and Miriam listen to every word, but I am sure that not long into my story Big Sarah and Jani fall sound asleep. I don't blame them. The sun is sinking low, its light mellow and gentle, and although we can hear the shouts of men, the bleating of sheep and goats, even the throaty belch of the camels, here in Jani's garden, there is peace.

Chapter Fifteen
Told by Miriam

I hardly ever think of my life before this, of Mother, Rebekah, Heled or the baby. Once Joel left us, nothing back home seemed to matter. Here, everything seems to matter. Nabal's land stretches far, there are strangers coming and going all the time and sometimes when Nabal calls for Abigail, she allows me to go with her. Nabal does not seem to recognise me when I am veiled, and I am able to sit at her feet watching and listening to my heart's content. I have seen men from Egypt, Persia and Lebanon and have touched cloth from across the sea. My head is full of the world, yet I remain safe and happy under Abigail's care.

This week, Nabal left us to go and survey the shepherds and his flocks. Abigail says it is an excuse to feast without restraint. I do not know how that could be true, for when he is here, there is no one who would dare counter his wishes, and his eating and drinking are already fabulous. Still, I would not have him shirk his duties, because in his absence, it has been the best four days of my life.

We tied our hair into scarves; we put on our old clothes—for me a dress of Rebekah's—and we went into Nabal's quarters, where we cleaned and scrubbed and shook things until the air was thick with dust and our buckets scummy with dirt.

Today we are beating carpets and sweating with the effort. Little

Sarah comes and laughs at me. She does not often laugh. My face is streaked grey, and she says I look like a foreigner from the north. I easily forgive her, for when she returns she carries a glass of sweetened lemon juice.

We hear singing from the banqueting room. A line of women are cleaning the floor. Behind them small boys replenish their buckets with fresh water. They fill the room with their sloshing and the stones shine honey hued where they have scrubbed them. We are also washing the hangings and the cushions, although a huge pile have been discarded. Nabal's wealth is legendary and yet his quarters foul and this is the only time everything can be sorted and made new. I wonder if he ever notices or cares about the trouble everyone goes to.

Abigail wanders from room to room, dressed in a plain blue gown; her hair pulled back from her face in a simple braid. Nabal's steward, Matthias, walks beside her, turning her wishes into orders. There is singing everywhere, a sense that this is a holiday, a celebration.

Little Sarah and I return to our carpets. The servant girls watch us out of the corner of their eyes. They are not used to seeing us working so hard, I am not used to working so hard. I am already exhausted. Little Sarah now also has a fine shadow of grime across her forehead and her eyes are red-rimmed, still she has found a rhythm, and I don't know if she will ever stop beating the dust into the air.

Abigail and Matthias come to laugh, and I stop because my arms are so heavy. They are discussing how much they could sell us for. Of course, Little Sarah is worth double of me because she is still going. I shake my head until Abigail says to him, "Mmm, but Miriam is very clever and is learning more all the time. She reads almost as well as Jani now."

"In which case, let's sell her as a scribe," he replies.

My price comes up and equals Little Sarah's. It's such a silly thing, they are only teasing us and yet it makes me stand tall, for Abigail has honoured me.

The young women around us suddenly stiffen and then begin to peer about. We feel the moment before we notice its cause. Everything stops, as we wonder what is happening. Apparently, a servant sent to watch the northern road is riding back. For a moment, Abigail actually counts on her fingers, shaking her head. It is too early for Nabal to return, unless something is wrong. The steward speaks low so that I can only just hear him.

"Perhaps it is not him, Mistress."

Abigail moves towards the gate. Little Sarah and I fall in behind her. She is walking out to the watch tower. Jani is also hurrying towards us, from our rooms. She won't want to miss anything out of the ordinary.

The watchman calls down, "It's Josiah, riding like there is a demon on his tail."

Josiah was the man sent to watch the northern road.

"And behind him? Can you see anyone coming behind him?" Matthias calls up.

"Yes," he hesitates, "though not many of them."

Abigail clasps her hands and waits. At last, he calls down, "There are two behind Josiah and they are not riding fast."

She turns to the steward.

"Tell me when you know who it is. I will wait in my rooms."

Matthias is already preparing a servant to go back to where Josiah was watching. If this is not his master, he will still need to keep an eye out for him. Our work was going well, but Matthias will be anxious to get everything back in place before Nabal does come back. The women return, reluctantly, to their beating.

At last, Josiah slithers to a halt, his donkey's head drooping, its sides heaving. There is lather across its neck.

"Who comes?" Matthias asks.

"Two men from David. One is Joel, son of Baanah."

My brother. It has been a long time. I stare at the animal, feeling sorry for its beating, but its state is a measure of David's standing, not mine.

"There is also a servant of Heled, who brings a message and gifts from his master."

Jani and Little Sarah turn to me. It is wonderful news.

"Your brother," Jani cries, with delight.

I don't know how to express my joy; no words seem sufficient. Jani raises an eyebrow at that; it is not often I am speechless. Little Sarah begins to pull me towards the house. The line of rugs has disappeared, the singing has stopped, and just before I am dragged into the dimness I see the new watchman riding off to the north.

Little Sarah is fussing. She has loosened my hair and is brushing away the dust.

"What's he like, your brother?" she asks.

"He rides well and is a good teacher. He used to make me laugh." It's how I think of him.

"I don't think I ever had a brother," she says. I must ask her one day, what she remembers of her childhood. She sounds so sad.

She is choosing my dress and has laid out for me her own red shawl, a gift from Jani, her most precious possession.

"My brother was scrawny. And if I remember rightly, his grin was lopsided, as one of his teeth is missing," I continue, remembering the boy who led me around on one of our father's horses.

"A front one," she says, ignoring my protestations about the shawl.

"No, but he can whistle in a most peculiar way."

"But when you last saw him, he was still a boy."

It is the most she has ever said to me. I wonder if she has begun to trust me at last.

"He broke Mother's heart when he ran away," I say, remembering the tears and red blotchy face. "She scratched her arms with her own fingers, until they bled."

Little Sarah watches me intently, she thinks I'm going to cry. I will not, I have practised the telling of this many times and I am ready for the wave of sadness that comes with such a memory.

My mother waited many days before she sent word to our father that his son, his only son had gone. She had hoped he had simply run away to join the King's army, that he had gone to join his father and that before long they would send a message to say that it was so. No message came. Then she received news that my father had been killed fighting the Philistines and that her son had gone instead to join the rebel David. She was beside herself with grief and none of us knew how to console her. Her only hope was that my father had died ignorant of his son's rebellion, that there hadn't been enough time for her own message to have got through to him. When the servant she had sent, did not come back either, she agonised over my father's last hours and what he might have known.

Mother must have gotten well used to losing those she cared for. People didn't ever seem to come back to her. I am suddenly sorry that I have thought so little about her over the last few months. I begin to pray that my mother's heart would stop waiting, that she would start living again, as I have.

"I don't remember my mother," Little Sarah says. I am so deep in thought, I jump when she speaks, even though her voice is soft. I notice that she is now dressed in pale green, and I see that she is beautiful.

"Little Sarah, from now on I am going to call you Beautiful Sarah."

She blushes.

"You must not," she says.

"Why?"

"Because that would mean that Big Sarah is not beautiful."

"I see," I reply, but I do not think Big Sarah would mind at all.

We return to Abigail's room. We take our place beside our mistress. She is veiled. It does not help; her beauty cannot be hidden. I stare at her fingers resting in her lap. They are slender, the nails shaped and polished.

At last, there is a clatter of noise, feet stamping and a clearing of throats, the men enter. I cannot see the boy I knew but undoubtedly, it is my brother. He is tall, broad and dark. He has washed from his ride, but I see that his sandals are worn, and his clothes stained. He bows low. At least he has learnt some manners.

"Mistress Abigail, I have brought a message from our kinsman, Heled."

It is him. I hear the laughter in his voice, and I do not know how I can bear to sit still. I cannot, I jump up and run to him.

Heled's servant stands behind. It is so good to see him, too. I bundle the edge of my brother's cloak into a ball. The man's laughter is deep. Abigail must think I have gone too far. She clears her throat, and says, "Joel, please come and tell us the news."

He sits before us, relaxed, squashing pillows until they are just right. He does not seem cowed by Abigail. Heled's servant and Matthias wait by the door. I pour wine for my brother, hardly daring to believe that he is really here. He looks at us all, though it is Little

Sarah on whom his eyes rest longest. Big Sarah notices and grins at me, but mercifully, she stays silent.

He eats, he is hungry and when he is satisfied he speaks his message.

"From Heled. Greetings, to the woman who gave his sister-in-law a home, who treats her with the due courtesy of her rank."

He speaks as if he has learned it by rote, it is a careful message and Heled would not have wanted him to get it wrong. I remember him reciting Scripture to us as a boy. That was always word perfect, but with no feeling or passion to it. He only warms to his task when he tells us that Rebekah has produced a little girl. To begin with Heled was disappointed; he had so wanted a son, only then David sent him home to see them and when he returned he was a changed man. She is apparently the most beautiful child that ever existed and has truly won her father's heart.

Abigail smiles.

"You have a niece," she says to me. "There is time enough for a nephew, and a daughter will always be the apple of her father's eye." She speaks with sadness however, and I wonder at her words.

Joel looks away, he must surely remember that Rebekah, our sister, had indeed been the joy of our father's heart. She was spoiled, she could do no wrong, and Joel, on whom all our hopes rested, had been unable to do a single thing of worth. He remains quiet, so I ask the question I need to ask.

"How is Mother?"

"Heled says she is frail but well. She dotes on her granddaughter."

"Does she send a message?"

"Only that she remembers us fondly."

I don't know why, but I am sure that Heled lies. There was no message. No recollection.

Later, we walk in the garden together. There are almonds and pomegranates, and I can see that Joel is impressed.

"When Heled said you had become a handmaiden, I imagined you little less than a servant. I was very angry with him. It was like he had sold you as a slave for his own profit, to pay some outstanding debt. I am your nearest kin, it was not his decision to make, it was mine. It's why David has let me come to you. David is wise, he always knows what's best to do."

"Then he is like Abigail. She too always knows what's right for us and sometimes it's as if she can see inside our heads."

Joel nods. He walks between Little Sarah and me. She keeps trying to drop back, only Joel slows his own steps to match hers until, in the end, we almost stop. I persuade her to sit on the bench in the middle of the garden so that we can walk and talk and she will still be in sight. Joel is then able to concentrate on me. Little Sarah is confused, and I think frightened, but she is always frightened, so it's hard to tell what she is really feeling.

We talk of home. There is more in my head than I realise. My childhood was larger than the stables and Jani, the goat.

"I cannot think of Rebekah kindly," I say.

Joel stands still for a moment and then replies, "She was younger than you when she married Heled and the night before she left our house, she wept in terror. I could not sleep for all her crying."

"He is not such a bad man."

"But you did not always feel so, did you?"

"No. It was only on the journey here that I began to see him, past my fear."

"Well, she had no journey on which to get used to him. She was a child going to be a wife and there was darkness and then morning and she was married."

"I never saw. I never thought," I replied, feeling selfish and mean.

"No, and yet if we'd asked her if she were scared, she would have denied it, would have found a way of twisting it around, of accusing us of being cruel or some such nonsense."

"She seemed to really hate me."

"Of course, sister, although only while she thought you were going to be a wife of greater standing. Let's face it, you are prettier and better company; you would have fetched a much larger bride price if only Father had lived." He then pauses and adds carefully, "And then later, perhaps, she was scared that you would become wife number two!"

I hit him hard on his arm, but he doesn't flinch. My brother doesn't know how close he has come to the truth, even though in jest. He looks down at me, raises an eyebrow and brushes his arm as if I were an annoying fly.

"I have ridden too long and fought too hard to feel a little bump like that."

Although I am exasperated by him, I suddenly see him wielding a sword and I see the strength in him, that only comes from fighting.

"Oh Joel, has it been difficult? Have you shed much blood?"

"I will not speak of such things to you, Little One."

I remember the body in the marketplace, on my way to Rebekah's house and I thank the Lord for such a careful brother.

"Let's go back and sit with Little Sarah. We've left her alone too long," I say.

I know it's what he wants, and I wish to please him, though I am sure that Little Sarah would rather be back with Jani.

I am learning there are many different types of love, and mine for him is an easy sort. It comes like breathing. Perhaps when he leaves, I will cry for home and Mother and my new little niece Chloe, whom I may never see.

Chapter Sixteen
Told by Little Sarah

Joel, Miriam's brother, is different from other men. I saw him look inwards and find only pain. It twisted my stomach into a knot. He touched my hand to say goodbye and I felt so wobbly I had to concentrate on standing. I did not look at him. Perhaps next time I will have more courage.

Chapter Seventeen
Told by Big Sarah

There are two of me. The loud woman who says what is in her head, who makes them laugh and the frightened woman who thinks she can see into the future.

I am now sure that I will never be held or loved except by one of these four women. That should be enough for me, more than I might ever have had, but the wound from the past is deep and raw and seeps around the edge of my good fortune.

Little Sarah fell in love today, even though she didn't realise it and I was jealous. I watched her cheeks flush with the first sparkle of womanhood, then she remembered, and her feelings turned to fear. I watched her trying to swallow it down, to regain control but there is already too much squashed inside her tiny frame. There doesn't seem room for anything else, certainly not for love. She hides behind Jani's wide back. I wish there was room for me. But I am too tall, too long limbed. I have the manners of a common goat girl and a tongue that is coarse and unlettered. Abigail saved me but she did not know what she was saving.

Before the lightning, I knew how to laugh, I knew how to tease the women in the kitchen, I knew how to swear at the goats and untangle my hair from their horns, I even knew how to smile at a man. But I do not know how to deal with the hard questions that God seems to be asking of me.

When I am with my dear sisters I sparkle and shine. I know how to do that. When I am alone, I fight a heaviness which I am afraid is too strong for me. I am afraid that it will swamp the light and the kindness of these beautiful women. I curse Nabal and how he has covered me in grief, left me hiding. It is not who I am meant to be, yet I do not know how to get out from underneath this rock, that sits so heavily upon my chest.

Perhaps I have too much time to think, my duties are so light. I carry our clothes to the well, I sometimes help with the laundry, but I am not that Sarah anymore, I am Abigail's pity, Abigail's compassion, Abigail's kindness.

Jani is calling me. She does not like it when I lie late. She will also see that I have not slept again. It will worry her. So, for her sake, I will get up, smile and make comments that Miriam will not understand and that Jani will refuse to explain. I will make Hannah sit back, close to Abigail, listening and watching. She thinks that she understands everything. Everything, except that which is under her nose.

There are two women inside me, two women who rise and leave their bed, but I would like one of them to stay hiding under the covers. I would have her leave me alone.

Chapter Eighteen
Told by Hannah

Abigail has called me so that she may lay her head in my lap. I stroke her hair. The sun is warm, the light heavy around us and there are dust motes dancing in the air. Nabal is out with his men, so the inner yard is quiet, even though it is nearly time for the shearing. I feel uncertainty and anticipation all around.

"Hannah, call for Matthias. These next few weeks will be…" Her voice fades and her hand falls heavily across her waist.

"Why don't you walk in the garden?" I suggest. She shakes her head. There is such a dullness about her. Of late, she has struggled to shine, although I think I am the only one who has noticed. There is still no child, and I fear that God has more sorrow for her.

I send the message to Matthias. He will of course come, when he can, but Nabal has him running ragged and it is a while before he finds the time. The shearing lasts for nearly ten days and the population of our household triples. He has much to do. Abigail understands that, but it still irritates her.

***

The ranunculus has started to flower, and deep patches of colour are spreading across the plain. There will be perfume in the air, at least until the stench of sheep overpowers it. Dawn is the best time. I often go to the garden in darkness. I lean against the wall, feeling the warmth from the previous day's sun at my back. I wait until I can see a pink glimmer across the high coping stones, then it is time for me to return to Abigail, so that I can be in place when she wakes.

Today, as I come back across the yard, everything seems to be moving slowly, a weary yawning, as night keeps its hold as long as it can. The boys are winding water up from the well. There is a stiff squealing of rope on wood, tight and rhythmic in its turning. In a few moments, the sound will be lost amongst the babble of morning. The men will gather; the yard boys will drag fodder to the animals, and the herdsman will snatch breakfast before going out to the sheep.

Matthias crosses the yard. We are both in a hurry, so we only greet each other with a smile. Of late, the lines around his eyes have deepened and I have caught him sitting with his head in his hands. With despair or weariness, I do not know. I have tried to show him that I notice what he does, that we are grateful for his good management but there is never enough time, and there is always a line of men waiting to speak to him.

Our quarters are in darkness. Little Sarah is setting the room straight and laying out the clothes she thinks her mistress will want. She is invariably right, although how she sees in this light I do not know. I envy her skill of putting things together just so, always mixing the colours and fabrics to their best advantage. Abigail rarely questions her choices unless she is feeling particularly irritable. Who would trample over so fragile a flower, as our Little Sarah? She has always been hard to fathom but recently I have noticed a tightening about her mouth that never quite goes away. She seldom speaks. Still, as she leaves Abigail's chamber we touch as we pass, fingertip to fingertip. This is how we comfort each other, for when Abigail is out of sorts, then so are we.

"Hannah, are you there?"

"Yes, Abigail."

"Pull back the curtain, I want to see."

The pale thin light of morning fixes the room with its ordinariness, and I begin to feel a little better. Jani appears yawning. She is stiff first thing and we try as much to ease her waking as we do for Abigail.

"I'm cold, Hannah," Abigail says.

Little Sarah returns from the dressing room with a light silk shawl, and a slightly heavier one for Jani. She always seems to know what they need.

"You are all so good to me," Jani says, her hands wrapped around the hot cinnamon tea I have had made for her. The steam lights up her eyes, which begin to twinkle, as she sloughs off the night, although she is having difficulty getting comfortable. We hear Miriam calling from outside for us to come and see. We smile, it will just be more sheep and shepherds, or another string of camels from Dor.

So begins another day, and yet I feel that with this shearing, change is coming. Not just because of Abigail but the rumours of David and the King. No good can come from a country divided. Big

Sarah has felt it too, although when we tried to speak of it, we could not find the words. We can only hope that such things will pass us by. We will have to wait and see what the summer brings.

Chapter Nineteen
Told by Big Sarah

I open my eyes with a sense of foreboding, but am relieved that it is at last morning, a bright glow of yellow light across the wall and the smell of sheep. At night I sleep quickly and deeply, yet past the first or second watch, I wake. Then I lie in darkness until dawn. Hannah and Jani have noticed, and they are working on a stronger sleeping draught. The usual one of rue does not help at all. I feel such a heaviness about my limbs that I wonder if I am on the edge of a sickness. Neither Jani nor Hannah thinks so, but I feel a weight on my ankles like shackles, and simply rising can sometimes leave me breathless. There is not enough air in my room, and I am afraid that it is the wings of death that cover the door and window. I try to look forward to the days to come but there are swirls of darkness, of which I am afraid.

"Please Father, show me what I must do," I beg.

Again, there is no answer, so I get up, easing my way to standing. Testing muscles and balance, before I dare rely on them. Little Sarah knocks. How I love the child. What sorrow she has, she buries deep so that she can live. I will follow her lead and do as she does.

"Hannah sent me to see if you need anything."

"Nothing, dear one. Tell her, I'll be along to help with breakfast in the shake of a goat's tail."

She smiles.

"Shall I lay out your clothes for you?"

"No, I am not your mistress, and I am still just about capable of dressing myself."

I chase her from the room and wear what I wore the day before. My tunic is only a little stained from the figs we peeled. I know that it will displease Little Sarah, but I honestly do not have the energy to choose something new. Tomorrow, I'll let her help me.

Hannah is already over at the kitchen. I see one of my old friends, finishing her breakfast before leaving for the laundry. She smells of soap and lavender, although her apron is stiff with muck.

She wants to stop and talk but I'm in a hurry. I really do want to help Hannah, so I promise to come and find her when I am free. A gossip will make me feel better and before Nabal, she was a very good friend.

Hannah has the trays ready; still her face lights up when she notices that I am here. She could have asked anyone to help her. I am secretly pleased that she has waited for me.

"Your night was just as bad as ever," she says, looking at me through narrowed eyes.

"Can't we just double the dose of rue?" I ask.

"It's not quite as easy as that. Too much and you could fall asleep forever."

"That doesn't sound too bad," I reply, only Hannah looks so alarmed I am ashamed. "Don't worry," I add, "I am only tired and grumpy."

She tries to see past my eyes. Luckily, she is no Abigail so I will not have to taint her with my sense of dread. She turns back to the food. I realise with surprise that she trusts me, that we are friends. I am grateful and lay my hand over hers.

"You help me sleep and all will be well, I promise."

She nods.

***

We are all together. Breakfast is done and the noises of morning have settled to a grumbling murmur beyond the walls.

"We will go to the shearing," Abigail announces. "It is the first day, the best day."

"It's a fine sight," I add.

Little Sarah looks troubled.

"Will it be crowded?" she asks.

"Yes, Little One," Jani says, and then adds, "I will stand one side of you and Miriam the other."

Miriam laughs.

"It will be fun," she says.

"We must go veiled," Abigail reminds us, "the men must not be distracted."

Jani shakes her head.

"Jani," I say, trying to look serious without laughing, "despite all that you say, you are still a handsome woman, and I have seen how

Kenan's eyes follow you."

Kenan looks after the shepherds. He has been overseeing them for as long as I have been here. He is grizzled and ageing, but still strong and to my delight, Jani colours pink. We laugh, even Abigail.

Jani has been a widow a long time, but we all envy her, for she has known love.

Matthias stands in the door. He has been there a while. I feel it. He is drinking us in like a man who has been in the desert too long. When Abigail notices she stiffens, as if she resents sharing the moment with him, sharing us.

"Matthias, what can we do for you?" she asks.

He looks at each of us in turn, all of us but Hannah.

"Mistress, the master has asked that you would come. There are things he would like to discuss concerning the shearing."

Abigail rises.

She is gone a long time. Hannah leaves us to wait nearby in case she is needed. We go to the garden to help Jani gather flowers. We will not visit the shepherds today.

Chapter Twenty
Told by Little Sarah

It is the third day of shearing. It is not a good day to go and watch. I am a little frightened. The stench of men and animals hangs in the air, so that it is hard to breathe. The sheep bleat and scream. The men handle them roughly. We dare not get too close for fear we will be in the way. Miriam has my hand tucked over her arm. She feels my trembling. She has offered to take me back, only it is too long a walk for me without the protection of Jani and Big Sarah.

Miriam is excited. She has heard that David is near, and she longs to see Joel again. Now even Jani has stepped away from me to get a better view. Big Sarah is teasing her. She says, "Oh Jani, I think I can see him over there. He is shearing a sheep just for you. He is showing you that he is still strong."

I don't think Abigail can hear what she is saying over the noise. Jani can, quite clearly, although she pretends she cannot.

The gap between Jani and me is too big and I can't help myself; I grasp her cloak to fill the space. Miriam sees and nudges me over until the gap has gone. She squeezes my hand. She does not understand my fear, but she acknowledges it. I stay close to her and resist the temptation to run.

Chapter Twenty-One
Told by Jani

I do look at him, just a glimpse. I will not stare. I should know better and feel slightly ashamed, as if I am some young woman, with no self-control. Big Sarah laughs again, of course, for she does not know the ache inside. I'm sure that she would be less hard on me if I were more honest with her, of how I still long to be touched with tenderness, how I long to be drawn down onto a bed and for his hand to search out my breast. I shiver at the thought and flush with embarrassment. Surely this will pass, it cannot go on. I have lived and been loved more than most, what more do I want?

I want to be young again. I want to stop aching.

He is coming over to pay his respects. His eyes flicker over each of us. We are all heavily veiled. I am glad, for my face would betray me. He is everything that my dear husband was not, with grey, close-cropped hair, broad shoulders and thick arms ending in stubby fingers. The nails are black with grease and his accent is heavy. The desert is probably all he has ever known.

Abigail is leading us away. He did not say anything, but she feels we are a distraction. There is at least another week's work, and he must keep the men going. I feel the determination all around me. I am not paying attention, and I stumble. Little Sarah grips my arm, and he stretches out a hand to steady me. I deliberately reach for him. I cannot help myself. His eyes widen in surprise, as I hurry away. Only Miriam or Little Sarah might have seen, and I know they will not say a word.

"I'm sorry, Abigail," I say, "I'm feeling a little dizzy. If you do not need me, I would like to lie down."

"Can I bring you anything?" Big Sarah asks. I shake my head but not long after, Miriam brings me a tray of food.

"How are you now?" she says, carefully laying out the plates on my little table.

"Much better," I reply. "It was probably all the noise and the heat of the sun."

"Jani," she says, wringing her hands together, "do please rest. I could not bear it, if anything were to happen to you." Her eyes fill with tears.

She sees me as an old woman, a little of the mother she has lost. Inside, I am still young and lovely, my skin pale and tight. Why can no one else see it? I roll over to face the wall and try to remember.

I was younger than Miriam when he first came to see my father. I was only just her age when he tugged me down that first time and pulled the blanket over us. His smooth skin and his shining eyes looked at me as if I were the most precious thing he had ever seen.

I shiver now, only because I am cold and I cannot remember clearly what my husband looked like, the man I had grown comfortable with. Today, when I touched the rough skin of that shepherd, there was only surprise in his eyes. What would I have done if there had been something else?

Chapter Twenty-Two
Told by Miriam

Abigail cannot sleep. She has sent the others to bed. Big Sarah could hardly keep her eyes open and kept yawning. I think it annoyed our mistress. We play backgammon and when I have beaten her twice, she pushes the board away. She looks pale in the lamp light and there is darkness around her eyes.

"There is something going on tonight," she says. She stands up, peers around the room as if looking for something, walks to the door as if listening.

I've heard nothing unusual. The feasting has been loud, the men raucous and stumbling, but it is always so at shearing time. We simply stay in her quarters until the morning.

"What have you heard that has worried you so?" I ask, putting the counters away. They are made from cedar, inlaid with gold and silver. They feel heavy in my hand and smell of forests and soft light. I am reluctant to close the lid.

"Men came earlier, five or six of them. They didn't stay."

Men come all the time. Big Sarah and I were fetching food from the kitchen, so I saw this group. They were a little unusual, as they were mounted on horses and had brought a string of empty donkeys. I did not know they had left again. Abigail must have eyes and ears everywhere.

"I think it is beginning to quieten down for the night," I say, although I can still hear some awful singing from the sheep pens. "Lord save me from the clutches of a drunken man."

"What's that?" Abigail says.

I had not realised I had spoken aloud. She stares at me, trying to fathom my words and yet she does not ask me to repeat them. The lamp flickers and I rise to trim it. She returns to her chair and lays her head down on her arms. I think perhaps she is beginning to fall asleep. I tidy the cushions, pushing them into piles and smoothing their rumpled fabric.

"Miriam, I would never send you into danger unless it was truly important, but I am sure there is something wrong."

I wait, wondering what she would have me do.

"Will you go and find Matthias? He will be sober and he will know what is happening."

I breathe a sigh of relief. That is not such a hard task. I can keep to the shadows and if I move swiftly, no one will see me.

I find my cloak, for though the summer is just beginning, the warmth of the day is already lost to the stars. I pull my hood over my hair and step out into the dimness. A wind from the north shivers around my legs. I wrinkle my nose. I would much rather look at the bright, clean sky than at the foul mess around me, but I must look down, if I am to find a clear path.

A fire burns in the centre of the yard. The men sleep beside it, some completely still, others moving and murmuring to the beat of their own dreams. The hall doors are open and light pools across the hard packed ground. It seems to me it must be like the aftermath of a battle, the dead and dying uncaring as to how they lie. Matthias will be near his master, which means that I must cross to the banqueting room. There is too much light.

I pick my way through the shining pools of vomit, not yet covered with sand. My stomach heaves of its own accord and I swallow hard to control it. Why do men do this? What can be gained? What is it that they find at the bottom of the skins?

I approach the door from the east. That way is darkest. I peer into the room. It must be late, for there are only four or five men upright. I see Matthias. He is laying a blanket over his master. I watch fascinated as he lifts the great head and places it on a pillow, arranging the mighty bulk, almost with tenderness. It is a private moment, one that I should not have seen. Matthias looks up and catches my eye. He nods. He will come. It's almost as if he were looking out for one of us.

As I cross to the safety of our rooms, I hesitate, I cannot see my way clearly, the moon has dipped behind a cloud, and I am concerned at what I might walk through. A white hand shoots out and grasps my ankle. His grip is like iron, and I know that I cannot struggle free. It is Kenan, the chief shepherd, the one that we tease Jani about. His eyes are unfocussed; he is not looking at me at all. He runs his other hand over my calf. I wonder at kicking out at him only there is a reluctance in me to hurt this man. He truly does not seem to know what he is doing.

I hiss, "Kenan, let me go. I must get back to our mistress."

I bend down to try and prise his fingers off my leg. He catches my hands in his own. I am frightened now, and I try to twist away. The moon slips out from behind the cloud, and I see him. His eyes are narrowed, he smiles, and I feel like a lamb confronted by a lion. I will never forget how he looks at me. I kick; I do not care now if I hurt him. I twist and wrench with all my might, yet he pulls me down to my knees. His breath is sour, and there is spit at the corner of his mouth. It is strange, because I never think to scream or shout. A shadow cuts across the light, Matthias has come. Kenan drops my hands as if I have burned him. He rolls over and curls into a ball. Matthias hauls me to my feet.

"Are you hurt?" he asks.

I rub my wrist, which is painful, but shake my head. I find I cannot speak. My breath is ragged and shallow. I straighten my clothing as I follow him back to our rooms, blinking away tears. I feel foolish and ashamed.

Just inside, Matthias asks, "How much does she know?" He puts a hand on my shoulder. I flinch at his touch, but only a little and I hope he doesn't notice.

"She has said nothing to me but that she is uneasy."

He nods.

"Good."

I lead him to Abigail.

To begin with she looks as if she is sleeping, however, as I reach out to touch her arm, she rises, uncurling smoothly. Matthias bows low and Abigail motions for him to come close. I stand awkwardly to one side, burning with curiosity. I stay very still in the hope that she will forget that I am here, otherwise, she might dismiss me, and I do not think I would have the courage to eavesdrop.

"When David's men came tonight, they did not stay. Why not?" Abigail asks.

"Nabal was not himself," he replies.

Abigail drops her head.

"When do you last remember him, truly himself?" she whispers. "Was he discourteous?"

"Yes, very."

"What exactly did they want?"

"They asked for food."

"Nothing more?"

"No," Matthias's voice cracks, grows husky. I should offer him a beaker of wine, but I really don't want to draw attention to myself. He continues, "they've been camped on the northern border for weeks and up until now, they haven't asked for anything. In fact, the shepherds say they've been helpful."

"How so?" Abigail asks.

"They've kept the thieves at bay and have even hunted the lions and wild dogs. We've never had such a good yield at shearing time."

"And Nabal sent them away empty-handed?"

"It's even worse than that. He asked who David thought he was, that he, Nabal, should support him?"

Abigail shivers.

"Was Joel with them?" I ask.

They turn to look at me, although I have shrunk back into the shadows, wishing I had kept my mouth closed.

"No, he was not."

Abigail's face pales and her eyes shine with fear.

"I've heard he has over six hundred fighting men and if he is angry, he would be quite capable of killing us all." Her voice trembles. I have never seen her frightened.

"How can he fail to be angry at such inhospitality?" Matthias replies.

Over the months we have heard rumours about David, the King's son-in-law, the rebel. When Joel was with us we never tired of asking questions about him and Joel never seemed to tire of answering them. We found much to our liking. David is young, and as handsome as we could want, wise and Joel says, burning with injustice. He has been unfairly treated by the King and longs for some resolution. Joel and the others with him, long and burn too.

I have seen what men are like at the festivals, as now during the shearing, when they feast and drink to oblivion. In the dark hours before they fall insensible, reason and honour die. If David thinks he has been mistreated by Nabal, there will be trouble.

"Matthias, I have to do something to turn this away!" Abigail declares.

"Mistress," I say, "send me to him, with food. I am Joel's kin, he will not harm me, and it may soothe his anger."

She looks up.

"You would do that? Ride out into the night to meet six hundred rebels?"

"One of them is my brother. What harm can come to me?"

She and Matthias exchange a glance, one that I now understand. She rises.

"Matthias," she says, "only I dare defy Nabal and live. I have done it before, I will do it again, for all our sakes."

"Mistress," he replies, "I must counsel strongly against this." His voice is loud and a little fierce.

She smiles at him. He continues to shake his head.

"How long will it take me to reach his camp?" she asks.

"Four or five hours by donkey."

"Then we must leave immediately."

Matthias is also frightened. I have never seen him so either and it is disconcerting. I suppose, for him, it is an absolute step, he is going against Nabal's own drunken wishes and angry Nabal will not listen to reason. He is used to being obeyed, totally, even when his wits have left him.

"I will need an hour to put together the food and wake the servants, those I can trust," Matthias says, even now planning what needs to be done. I marvel at his courage, for I think he could have washed his hands of this and walked away. He is Nabal's servant first and foremost.

"Miriam, go and get Sarah, I want her with me," Abigail commands.

"May I come, too?"

She looks at me, a look that peels away my skin and leaves me transparent to my bones.

"Yes. You have a brave heart and a sharp mind. I may have need of both tonight."

Chapter Twenty-Three
Told by Big Sarah

I lie in darkness, warm in a deep, honeyed sleep. It is a place of peace. There are shadows, only I am not afraid.

Miriam shakes me, she wants me to wake up. I try to roll over, to turn my back on her. She whispers, urgently, things I do not understand. She almost pulls me from my bed. She is pale and shivering.

"Abigail? Is it Abigail? Does she need me?"

She begins to talk of a journey. I am still drowsy and wonder if she is sleepwalking, and that I am part of her dream. She tells of a meeting with Matthias and Abigail. The foreboding that I usually carry with me, moves into my throat like vomit. Our lives are at a sheep gate. It feels as if we are about to step into the wilderness, without a shepherd.

"Remember, Miriam, how cold the night can be. You'll need a warmer cloak," I say, grasping at the ordinary. She is grateful. We both have to be stronger than this.

Abigail has dressed herself. She wears her finest tunic but it is covered with a woollen dress and a dark cloak. There is a single pearl at her throat, and she wears a ring, the garnet engraved with Nabal's seal. She is however thinking clearly and pulls her scarf so that the pearl is covered. We could be robbed for much less and perhaps a great deal more.

Matthias has hand-picked five men to come with us, to guard us from harm. They are fighting drink and tiredness. They are unsure, as to who is giving the orders. They know if they cross the master, they will have to run and continue to run, until there is a world of space between them. It would have to be a good way; Nabal will have a long reach. Matthias looks at me as if he has read my thoughts. He is not sure that he trusts me. To him, I am the woman who milked the goats.

A shepherd boy, a young lad of no more than eleven is with him. Matthias has his hand on his shoulder, and I can see the grip is tight. He is to be our guide, and Matthias does not want him to alert anyone of our departure, except that we are a circle of commotion, among the restlessness of drunken sleep.

The shearing is the best it has ever been, and Nabal could not help himself; the celebrations have been wild and lavish. It serves us well, as we prepare to leave, for no one has the wits to notice or to care.

Chapter Twenty-Four
Told by Miriam

I begin to see a pink rim to the world. I am glad, for until now I have been barely able to see the donkey in front of me, and each footfall rings out into the darkness, calling down on us all manner of evil. We have been riding half the night.

We stop, for a moment, to stretch our aching limbs. I study Abigail's face. It is still and quiet, set with resolution and I marvel at her bravery. I only hope that Joel is with David. He holds kin in high regard, and a brother is the closest kin I can think of. Heled, too, would surely speak for us. Yet still there is fear mingled with my excitement. Will David be like Nabal when he is angry? Will his mind be unbending? Will we simply be swept aside, as they ride down to kill those we love?

We head on towards the hills. They have grown large in the dimness, rearing up from the plain with steep suddenness. Big Sarah rides behind Abigail. I see a dagger in her belt. Her head twitches back and forth, listening, staring. As the light grows the path narrows. We begin to move past the pack animals, the servants are beginning to doubt. Only the boy, awkwardly sitting astride his donkey, is ahead of us. He stops and points to a crack in the rocks, hardly visible at all. The path disappears, twisting out of view. The oldest servant beats his beast hard to catch up with us, grabbing Abigail's bridle. She glares at him, but he is too frightened to see.

"Mistress, this is dangerous. We cannot see far enough ahead."

She does not deign to answer, only narrowing her eyes slightly.

His voice falters.

"What if they are waiting for us? How can we fight in such a place?"

"If we have to fight we are dead. You may go back to the food. Sarah, Miriam and I will go ahead of you. Hopefully, they will be less inclined to kill women."

He is ashamed. He does not raise his eyes from the ground, as he waits for us to go on.

We pick our way forward, the young shepherd riding just behind me. He is more afraid of mountain lions than of rebels and his knife is in his hand, his sharp ears straining to hear the slipping of stones or the scrabble of claws.

He catches his breath. I turn. Dawn is almost here, and I can see his features clearly. He is pointing and shaking his head.

"Big Sarah," I call, my voice low.

"Abigail," she calls ahead.

We stop. Our breath hangs in the air, and I would like to snatch it back, proof that I am alive, for I cannot get enough of it into my throat. I can hear harnesses, horses, the slither of stones under hooves. They are coming down to us, many of them. Our donkeys prick their ears. Abigail smiles, her beautiful, reassuring smile, the one she has used on each of us in the past, to say that all will be well. I realise now that it has little value. She steps forward into the future with as little certainty as any of us and I wonder if I will ever truly trust her again.

Big Sarah pushes up close behind her and I kick my donkey forward to join them. The boy is still behind me. He is a good lad, and I suppose, until now, he has only ever been treated with kindness by these men of David and would wonder at our fear.

The ravine is narrow, the sides steep, the sky a strip of pink and grey above us. They come three abreast, filling the space, moving forward to overwhelm us. They are all mounted and on such magnificent beasts. Where can a man, a simple rebel get this sort of wealth, unless he is, as they say, blessed by God? There surely cannot be space in our land for both these men, David and the anointed King, still living and ruling. The times ahead of us will be troubled and dangerous.

The men stop; they are relaxed and ordered except that they

stare in wonder. Their eyes see, yet their heads do not understand. I look for Joel or Heled, but I cannot find them. We wait. Big Sarah and I edge closer to Abigail. She stares forward, careful not to catch the eye of anyone in particular. My heart is beating hard, and I feel my hands trembling.

The front row parts and a horse rides through. It is black, from Arabia, its head fine and delicate. Abigail slips from her donkey. Big Sarah and I climb down too. I am stiff and I walk heavily, hardly in control of my legs. Abigail drops to her knees. It all happens so quickly. No one can be thinking beyond this moment. Big Sarah and I kneel behind her, except now, Abigail is prostrate. We stay upright to protect her. Big Sarah has her hand on the dagger's hilt.

He has dismounted. He is coming forward. I dare not look up although I long to. I am frustrated, that I am so close yet can see so little. The ground holds no interest for me.

"What have we here?" His voice is light; there is a tenor quality that makes me want to hear him speak again.

"My Lord, please hear what I have to say." She sounds so dignified, despite the fact her head is in the dust.

"Who calls to me from the ground?"

"I am Abigail, wife of Nabal of Carmel."

She rises to kneeling, but her head remains bowed. The men behind him begin to mutter.

"Please my Lord, let me speak. He has not sent me, although I come to plead for him and all that is his."

The man folds his arms. I am unashamedly watching him now, though I don't remember lifting my head. His brow is wide above piercing blue eyes. I cannot say why he makes my heart falter as it does, but I will have no difficulty describing him to Jani and Hannah, if we live. Abigail remains upon her knees. He says nothing. He continues to frown, his eyes are narrowed and his lips pressed tightly together.

"At least hear me, before you kill me," she whispers.

"I will not kill you," he says, but he sounds angry, perhaps because he does not know what to do.

I see movement behind him and at last I see Joel and Heled. They have also dismounted and are standing with the other men. They nod but do not come any closer.

"Get up," David commands.

We move to help her. She does not need us and rises easily without our aid. She looks up into his face for a moment, and then drops her eyes quickly to the ground, again.

"Why are you here?" he asks.

"You were treated badly."

I can barely hear her words, and I see him lean in. She lifts her head just a little and her voice becomes stronger.

"Nabal's house was inhospitable. It is not our usual way. I did not even know your men had come."

"You have ridden through the night?" He is wary, looking for a trick.

"I have come with a gift, many gifts, to thank you, for your great kindness to our shepherds."

David shakes his head. He is still looking for a trap. Heled tentatively steps forward, Joel too, a little behind him, a little more hesitant. Joel mouths my name, and I hold his gaze. He will surely not let anything bad happen to her.

The sun flashes the first dawn rays into the ravine. David is caught in the light. He is striking, broad and tall, so sure of himself, standing at the head of those that would die for him. But Abigail, too, is bathed in the glow of morning, her eyes bright and her skin radiant. Big Sarah and I, as always, are in her shadow.

"I have heard of your beauty," he says, his hand still hovering over his sword.

"And I of yours," she replies, and although her head is bowed, we see the hint of a smile. There is a ripple of laughter from those behind him. David narrows his eyes, again. I can see that he does not know what to make of her. "And that you are blessed of God," she continues.

"So all that I see, is all that there is?"

"Yes, my Lord, except for the many laden donkeys stretching down behind us."

There is a tiny change in his stance. I breathe.

"You would not want to displease God with an action born of anger," she says, lifting her head a little more, so that he can see the long, dark lashes on the edge of her cheek.

He shakes his head again.

"We will camp and eat," he calls behind him.

"We have brought figs, raisins and bread, dressed sheep and some corn. Will that be sufficient?" she says, her voice reaching now, beyond the first lines of men.

He laughs and she dares to lift her head a little more. He stops and stares and I hear Big Sarah sigh, with such sadness. I do not understand why, for surely we are now safe.

We move to the bottom of the ravine. He posts men above and below. They light a fire for him. He and Abigail sit either side of it.

We are allowed to move away to a smaller fire, tended by Heled's servant. Joel and I hold one another very tightly. We do not let go of each other's hands even as we sit to share our news.

"Your mistress is bold," he says. There is a muttering from those sat with us, I hear the word brazen.

"She is clever and only does what has to be done, to save our household." I do not understand why they cannot see her wisdom. I suppose, they do not know her as we do. Perhaps she should not be laughing quite so much or allowing her eyes to meet David's quite so often, for her veil has slipped from her face.

"If I were her husband, I would be disquieted by such..."

I let go of his hand.

Big Sarah is silent. She watches David and our mistress, barely taking her eyes off them. We cannot hear what they are saying, and Abigail is animated in a way I have never seen before.

When at last it is time to leave, David says that Joel and Heled may accompany us, at least until we get to the edge of Nabal's land. I am pleased to spend a little more time with them, although Joel and I are now struggling to find things to say. Big Sarah's face is troubled. I suppose she is worried about what awaits us at home. It casts a shadow over my own heart too, but I will not think about that yet.

When we finally part, my brother and I, I look back over my shoulder as long as I can see him, only turning to face the desert when I am sure he is no longer in sight. Then weariness sweeps over me and my eyes sting and water with the need to sleep. I push my knuckles against them. For a moment I can see clearly but all too quickly everything blurs again, as I yawn and wipe away the tears.

Chapter Twenty-Five
Told by Big Sarah

When they parted David touched her hand and before she fixed her veil she looked full into his eyes. It *was* brazen. He openly returned her gaze, as if there were some understanding. I am disappointed— he is but a man. They talked, until the morning stretched beyond what was safe for us. She has nonplussed him, and he is caught.

Nabal will be sobering up and he will want to know where his wife is. Who will tell him?

Oh, Abigail. You have met your rebel king and conquered him. We are safe, although I wonder if Nabal is. Who would raise a hand to stop David, if he came to claim her; would Abigail herself plead for her husband?

I am unwell, my head feels as if it is being squeezed either side of my temples, one thought sneaking in, then hundreds crowding behind it, the pressure building as if I might burst. My beloved Abigail has displeased me, my heart is angry, yet what right have I to feel such displeasure? She is my mistress. I am who I am because she wills it and she has been so kind to me, rescued me when my life was narrow and hard. Yet I think, if I were her husband, I would take another wife and be done with it.

This man David has had the King's daughter and there is already another woman at his camp, a foreign princess. I am surprised there are not more. I think he could have anyone for the asking and does our mistress have any idea what it would mean to be a second or third wife?

I am twisted by premonitions of darkness.

There is something else I have seen, that has astonished me. Miriam stood close to Heled, to take her leave, and his servant was standing, as a good servant should, just behind his master. He was the one who came with Joel, when last she saw him. It was such an odd little moment. When the servant caught her eye she smiled. The man could not take his eyes off her. I suppose she has changed since she has been with us, filled out, even grown a little taller. As I watched him, for a blessed moment I stood in the light of God, a golden light that warmed my stomach. Sadly, I could not stay there, God wants me back down in the darkness where I can hear him.

As we ride away, Abigail begins to talk. Miriam draws close to her, to listen, despite the fact that she is exhausted. She is a good girl and knows what is needed. Abigail did glance at me. Perhaps she saw that I should be left alone, or that all is well, for my dagger is back in my belt. Her eyes do not seem able to pierce my soul like they did before. I wear an extra skin, which she cannot peer through. We go home with the sun on our backs. It is the only warmth I can feel.

We cross the edge of Nabal's land and Joel and Heled ride away. Our hearts turn to what awaits us there. We fall silent. Even the donkeys seem to have slowed their pace, yet time starts to move in great lurches. Before it can be possible, I see Matthias coming out to meet us. I wonder that he comes so far from his master's side. He is quick to speak, to explain.

"Nabal woke late morning, then just after noon he and his friends began to drink again. He is once more nearly unconscious and does not yet know that you have been away."

"God is good," Abigail says to the sky. She continues, "All is well. David has turned from his anger." Matthias stares at her, and I wonder if he sees it too. There is something different about her. She is changed. She shrugs aside his glance and says, "We must go and rest. Poor dear Sarah is beyond tired."

She even turns to smile at me, and I know that as I have seen into her heart, so she has guessed what is in mine, that it is now hardened against her, like never before. It seems to bother her. I feel a surge of power at my own self-importance, and I am unbalanced by it.

Chapter Twenty-Six
Told by Jani

Hannah was awake before dawn and the hours have passed painfully for her. She is worrying away the time we wait for Abigail, her eyes shadowed and her lips thin and tight. She is bereft that she was left behind, that she was allowed to sleep through their leaving and she paces our rooms unable to settle anywhere. I want to help carry this burden, but she will not let anyone near. She is surprised by the intensity and jealousy of her love.

Nabal roared like a bull mid-morning. I thought he had

discovered Abigail's absence and when he sent for me, I went trembling, dawdling as much as I dared. All for nothing, by the time I got there, a glass of honeyed mead had done more for him than I ever could.

I did not like his colour, it was grey and blotchy, his speech slurred. I could not understand what he was trying to say. He mumbled and waved me closer, until someone rattled dice. I could not wait to leave but just as I was about to breathe the clean air of the courtyard, he called me back. He winked and pulled me close, to pat my arm. His breath was foul and hot. He has drunk far more than usual, and I am worried, for all of us.

He said, "Don't tell Mother."

Don't tell Mother what? That he has lost his wits to wine and the false regard of his friends. That he is allowing his business to be run by Matthias, his steward and that if it weren't for the fact that Matthias is an honourable man, much would be lost already.

When I return, Hannah is still pacing her mistress's room. I make her a drink and drop in some rue. She takes a sip and instantly tastes the faint bitterness. She puts it to one side.

Little Sarah has been sent to watch for their return. I will go and join her. She hates beyond measure being out under the sky and I wonder that Hannah has asked this of her. Hannah looks up as I take my cloak.

"Where are you going, Jani?"

"To be with Little Sarah." It sounds like a rebuke.

"Must you go?"

"Well, I can't stand here and watch your despair."

She drops her head in shame.

"I'm sorry, it's just that I don't know what I'd do if anything happened to her."

"I know that, but this fretfulness is not helping anyone. Least of all Abigail."

Matthias knocks and enters. He speaks as though he has been listening to what we have just said.

"Mistress," he says, bowing to me, and yet speaking to Hannah. "Please don't worry, Nabal is back in his cups. We have a few more hours before he will be himself again."

Hannah looks confused. She doesn't care about Nabal, she only cares that her beloved Abigail is in danger and on that, Matthias cannot reassure her. My heart is pierced by his anguish for her, for his eyes cannot veil the hurt she is inflicting. They both stand in shadow. I want to catch her by her arms and shout into her face, make her see what she might have. I leave them. It's no use. No one can help her but Abigail.

I look out across the road to the watchtower. Little Sarah is beyond the safety of the walls. To begin with, I cannot see her at all, and I wonder if she has gone to hide in the garden. Then there is a shimmer of movement, and I spot her—no more than a tiny, flat blemish against the stones. The sun is warm and yet she is hooded, covered, hiding.

I decide to walk out to her. I am surprised that she has gone so far, but it is good to stretch my back. Powerlessness tightens and we are all stretched taut. As I get close, she hears me and turns. She is pale and sweaty under her cloak, and I wonder at the folly of her waiting here. Hannah must have been very firm with her.

"Oh Jani, there is no sign of them."

"Sarah, pull your hood down and get some air."

"I cannot."

"You can, now that I am here. I will stand beside you."

She does pull it back, but only a little. She is almost as small as Abigail. I am nearly a hand span taller and twice as wide. Her willowy youthfulness makes me feel aged, not wise but strangely wasted.

"Jani, they've been gone forever. Do you think they are alright? What will happen to us, if anything happens to her?"

"Now, what have I said about worrying about things you cannot change?"

"I'm not worrying Jani, I'm just asking questions."

We look along the road. It is empty. All this stillness feels like an ending, rather than a beginning.

"What will become of us?" she persists.

"You'll stay and work for Nabal, you belong to him."

"What about you, Jani?"

"I am Nabal's to command." My legs are beginning to ache; I move from foot to foot. "Perhaps he'll have need of me again," I say.

"What for?" she asks with wide-eyed candour.

"To reassure him, that what he does, won't hurt his mother."

She frowns, she does not understand. His mother has been dead for years and I have never shared with them, the things that he has said to me, concerning her.

"I'm going to walk around the tower, I cannot stand so long," I add.

Little Sarah begins to panic.

"I'm not leaving you," I reassure her, and although I do not walk out of sight, she still presses herself against the stones and pulls her hood over her face.

At last, when my back feels as if there are rods of iron piercing it and that they are twisting this way and that, when there are shooting pains up and down my legs, she points to the horizon. She can see dust. The watchman is already sending for Matthias. I do not see anything, until he himself, sets out to meet them.

∗

They are back and all is strangeness. Abigail is fevered with excitement, impatient, because we do not seem to understand. We stand about her, unsure what to do, what she needs. Hannah's agony has been waved aside as if she were an irritating fly.

We are lost in the shadow of Abigail's meeting with David.

Chapter Twenty-Seven
Told by Hannah

I'm breathing again, but my hands still tremble. Big Sarah comes and stands beside me until Abigail has swept past. Abigail neither looks at, nor reaches out to me. Miriam comes next. She smiles an awkward, crooked smile. She is weary and her eyes are bright with tiredness.

"You are too good to her," Big Sarah hisses in my ear.

I do not understand what she is talking about. She has grasped the sleeve of my dress. I pull free to follow Abigail. She will need me. Clean clothes, something to drink, food to eat. I have it ready. I move into the room of welcome, where she is waiting for me.

"Hannah, there you are," she says, as if she has just come back from a turn in the garden.

It's as if nothing has happened, as if she did not leave me, in the night.

"What can I get you, Mistress?" My voice is thin and scratchy.

"I don't want anything."

Jani and Little Sarah come in. Little Sarah looks relieved and begins to sort through the clothes that I have laid out for Abigail. Jani is wary and stands back against the wall.

"Leave that, Little Sarah," Abigail commands.

She speaks sharply. Too sharply. Little Sarah drops the scarf she is holding and scurries to Jani's side. Abigail must be very tired and does not realise what we have suffered. Miriam is slumped onto the cushions. Her eyes are slightly crossed. I fetch her a beaker of wine.

"I don't want a drink," Abigail snaps.

I hesitate.

"It's for Miriam," I say.

She stares at me as if I am a stranger and then she lies back too, and for the first time, I notice the tiny lines around her eyes and mouth do not smooth away when she slips into sleep.

This is how Matthias finds us. Jani tries to turn him away. He will not go.

"I need to speak to her. I will not stay long, but I need to know what she wants to do."

I whisper her back to us. She dropped so quickly into sleep she is disorientated, though only for a moment.

"Matthias," she asks, "is he awake?"

"No, Mistress."

"As soon as he is sober, you must fetch me. We cannot allow him to drink again, until he knows what I have done in his name."

Matthias isn't sure.

"Does he need to know at all?" he asks cautiously.

"He will notice. He will hear gossip, and he will not hesitate to check your ledgers. We took a lot of food and wine."

"I'm sure I can adjust them accordingly."

"I do not want you to," she says. His head comes up as if she has hit him. His silence eloquent.

"He must be made to see that he made a mistake angering David. That David was coming to kill him and that I saved him."

Matthias is uneasy. He needs time to think. He is confused by the change in her. She has not confided in him, has not told him what happened, and he is sorely worried. I see it in the way his nostrils flare, by the tightening of his shoulders and by the way he dips his head.

"Leave us now," she commands.

He bows. I want to follow him out to reassure him, yet I dare not leave her.

"Hannah, I must sleep," she commands.

She rises unsteadily. In her bed chamber I help take off her outer garments, still dusty from the road. She lies down in her tunic, just as she is and turns her face to the wall. When I return to the others, there is silence but for Miriam's quiet snores. I drape a blanket over her; she will sleep where she sits just as well. Big Sarah has gone to her room. Jani and Little Sarah are standing by the door. They look at me. I shrug. We are none the wiser as to what is going on.

"Miriam is our best hope," Jani says. "When she wakes, she will tell us all she knows."

"I'm going to check on Big Sarah," Little Sarah mutters.

"Little Sarah is trying to make sure we are all safe," Jani says, crossing her arms over her body, leaning forward. Holding herself.

I yawn. I have not been up all night, yet I am exhausted. Jani is the only one of us able to see clearly and she is staring at me.

"Hannah, why don't you rest next to Miriam and I will wake you as soon as Abigail stirs," she says.

I want to, but I am afraid that Abigail will call me and that Jani will not hear her. I shake my head.

"Oh, Hannah," Jani retorts and walks away, out towards her garden. Now she is angry with me too. My world is tilting, it feels unbalanced. What have I done to make it so?

I step into the courtyard and sit on the steps leading up to our quarters, not too far away if Abigail needs me. Matthias is standing outside the banqueting room. I wave. He pretends that he has not seen me. Again, my world shifts a little. I rest my head in my hands.

There is noise and movement all around, yet I can only hear my own heart beating. I am numb, empty and I decide that it is Big Sarah I must seek out. She will help me sort through what is happening and why I feel so dislocated from all that I know.

Chapter Twenty-Eight
Told by Little Sarah

I am scared for Big Sarah; she is tired and angry. I am worried that Abigail will notice and will send her away. There, I have said it. Jani said I mustn't worry about the things I cannot help, yet I must say what buzzes in my head, otherwise the thoughts spin around and around until sometimes I cannot move for the noise of them. I wish Abigail had not gone off on her adventure. Everything has changed and now I feel sick with what might happen.

I will go to the garden. It is quiet there. It is where I hide when no one wants me and sitting at the far end, away from the gate, I cannot be seen unless someone knows where to look.

It's getting harder to walk across the courtyard alone, so when I do sit down under the almond trees, I pull my cloak over my head and stare into the darkness, not moving until the light patches stop dancing behind my eyelids. It is a long time, for when I next peep out, the sun has moved across the sky and dropped behind the wall. I must go back, or I will have to cross the yard at dusk, when there are more shadows than people.

Jani is calling my name. She knew where I would be and is soon beside me. She looks closely at me.

"I thought you might be here, but you don't normally stay this late, Little One."

"Does Abigail want me?"

"No, she is still asleep."

I grasp her hand and hold it to my cheek. It's soft and hard. Patches of her old life grafted on to the softness of the new.

"Jani, what is going to happen?"

"I don't know, Little Sarah, I honestly don't know."

We walk back together. Hannah is already lighting the lamps. She has been crying. Her eyes are swollen, and I think I see a red weal across her cheek. When she sees me looking at her, she covers it with her hand. Jani fetches a cool cloth, and Hannah takes it without a word.

I hear Big Sarah shouting. I think she is calling for someone called Simeon. Jani nods at me, so I go to her. I light the lamp in her room and find her clean clothes. When I turn around, she is awake, staring at me.

"Whatever happens, I will not leave you," she says.

I know that she has no power over such things.

"And I will stay with you, wherever you go," I reply.

She blinks away tears, and I leave to get water for her to wash with.

Chapter Twenty-Nine
Told by Miriam

I wake stiff, my eyes glued with sleep. I have lain on the cushions all night, in clothes I have worn for nearly two days. The sun is already high. Hannah and Little Sarah are with Abigail. Jani sits with me, as I yawn and stretch. She tells me Matthias has come to say that the master is also beginning to stir. He will fetch Abigail as soon as Nabal is ready to receive her. I clamber to my feet and then help Jani get up. She comes with me to help me dress, because I think she doesn't want to be left alone. When we return, Abigail is already there. She is thoughtful, as she waits for breakfast. I do not think she knows what she is going to tell her husband.

Yesterday, in my last moments of lucidity I tried to explain to Jani, Little Sarah and Hannah what had happened, only Abigail had spent too much time away from us. She and David had talked and talked but we could not hear their words.

Hannah is pale and worn, as I have never seen her before. I hope that Abigail notices and is kind to her. We have come to expect our mistress's love and if it is directed elsewhere, it will be hard for us. Hannah is fussing around Abigail. When Abigail waves her away, she comes to sit beside us. Jani takes Hannah's hands in her own, an unusually tender gesture from Jani. Something is going on that I do not understand. Big Sarah does, I can see it in her face.

"I'm hungry," Abigail announces.

I realise that so am I. Ravenous. Hannah has breakfast ready and once Abigail is served, we sit with her as usual. I take a large hunk of bread and goats' cheese to still the growling of my stomach. Hannah takes a small piece of crust. I pour her some watered wine, for the bread is dry and she is having difficulty swallowing. Big Sarah sits silently, chewing, focussed elsewhere.

Nothing is resolved. We are all on edge.

"When Matthias comes, I want Miriam and Jani to come with me," Abigail says.

We nod. Big Sarah looks at Hannah. Hannah looks down at the floor and I begin to see where the problem lies. Hannah would normally have gone with Abigail. This is the second time she has been left behind. I hope that she is not jealous of me. I would not have it so, but I am also glad to have been chosen, for now I will have an opportunity to see what comes next.

I will also find a moment to speak to Big Sarah and get her to explain what is happening to us, what I am missing.

Chapter Thirty
Told by Jani

I am shocked at how ill he looks, even since yesterday. His skin is still so grey and there is moisture across his forehead and upper lip. He has been shaved, and his clothes are clean, but the room is stuffy and dim, for he cannot stand the bright light of morning. My heart is wrung out for him, for I can still see the young man I first met, underneath the skin that folds about him.

Abigail should run to him, call him her beloved, for all our sakes. David might cause her to dream, yet surely she must put away the blasphemy that I see in her eyes, since she returned from the mountain.

"Wife, Aunt Jani." His voice is faint, and there is a catch at the back of his throat. He nods to Miriam, even though he has clearly forgotten who she is. He is weary and motions for us to sit down. Miriam stays back in the shadows.

"Husband, are you well?"

He is patently not and he cannot be bothered to answer her. He looks to his right where there is a window, shuttered and curtained and yet through which light still filters.

"There is something we must speak of," Abigail says. Her voice does not waver, and I marvel at her strength.

I am aware that I am now included. She is clever. She uses all that she has at her fingertips.

"Must it be today? Can it not wait?"

"I am sorry husband, but when you hear all that we have to tell you, you will understand."

His eyes begin to light, and I see there is a misunderstanding. It is always the same between these two. He thinks she is carrying his child at last. His cheeks flush and he begins to smile. I turn to her, frowning, willing her to see what is happening. He is nodding, eager now to hear what she has to say.

"The night before last some men came to see you."

What have they got to do with a son? He is stuck in his hope; I can see it plainly.

"Do you remember?" she continues, "They came from David. They asked for food."

He does not remember. He spits into his bowl and mutters, "He is a wanderer, a rebel, not worth a moment's thought."

"Nabal, by turning them away, do you not see what you have done?"

He stares at her. She has used a tone that he has not heard since he was a little boy. This is not going well and unless Abigail is less haughty, it will not go any better.

"He may be a rebel, but he has six hundred men, warriors, all mounted and armed and he is camped less than half a day's ride from here."

She is almost shouting at him, willing him to understand how important it is that he listens to her. Nabal is beginning to see that there might be something in what she says. He is not a stupid man, only weak, I think.

"We'll send him food."

"I have done so, already."

He stares at her. His eyes narrow, as he comprehends what she has just said, and he allows his anger to come. I see it, as it begins as a thin-lipped smile that turns into a snarl. She has overstepped her authority. She is only his wife, and she is barren. He is looking at her with new eyes, far beyond her beauty.

"How much have you sent? Does Matthias know?" Nabal is hauling himself to his feet, his cheeks slashed with purple, his eyes tiny pinpoints of red and yellow.

Of course he knows. How could she do anything without Matthias's knowledge? And so Nabal screams for him. He spits out his name. Matthias comes quickly, his face like stone.

"Husband, you cannot blame Matthias for this. He had no choice but to do as I ordered."

Nabal stares at her. No one, no one interrupts his anger, no one. I draw back to stand beside Miriam.

"You will be silent. I will deal with this."

He speaks through gritted teeth, but his eyes are wide, all seeing, his voice like a serpent, his barrel chest heaving. He is having difficulty breathing; he needs too much air to fuel this kind of anger.

"Master," says Matthias, his voice steady and calm, although I see his hands are clenched, "I would do nothing to harm you."

"You are bewitched by her. Enough is enough. I will not have any child in my house, birthed by a whore."

Nabal is muddled and for a moment Abigail and Matthias exchange a look of surprise.

"But, husband, I did only what I had to do, to save you."

He waves her away. She moves to stand in front of Matthias. She is also flushed pink and her hands flutter at her sides. She speaks quickly.

"I took food to David. I could not be sure that it would be accepted, unless I went myself, to explain our mistake. David was gracious and turned back from his anger."

Nabal has turned to stone, his eyes wide in surprise, and I can see the purple blotches spreading down his neck.

"You have been with him? You have explained our *mistake*?" He hurls out the words, unable to believe them. And then he begins to topple backwards; there is a gurgling in his throat. I do not realise what is happening until his arms thrash, as he gasps for air. After a long drawn-out moment he falls limp. He does not move again, except his eyes, which roll wide with fear.

Matthias rushes to him, calling over his shoulder for the men who stand at the door. I cradle his head in my lap; it is heavy and stiff. He stares up into my face, beseeching me. He is unable to wipe away the tears that run down his cheeks, settling in drops upon his beard.

Abigail watches.

I send Miriam to fetch Hannah. He has some strange paralysis, and we need to loosen the rigidity. Abigail comes a little nearer. She stares down at him for a long time, before she turns and leaves.

Chapter Thirty-One
Told by Big Sarah

We are mourning, even though Nabal is not dead. The house is shuttered and dim. We sit around waiting. Jani prays for his recovery, and so perhaps does Matthias. I think they are the only ones. Abigail says nothing. When I asked her if she thought she was to blame, she stared at me for a long time, before there was the tiniest shake of her head. She believes that what she did was ordained by God. How dare I even ask such a question?

Jani and Matthias take it in turns to sit with the master. They drip water into his throat. Sometimes, he manages to swallow and sometimes he does not. He cannot eat, not even the thinnest juice or gruel. Such things simply bubble out of his mouth; they are afraid that he will choke. Matthias has called for two or three apothecaries. None know what to do. Jani is the only person who does any good. She and Hannah have filled his pillow with lavender, and they rub him with oil. They bend his limbs and talk to him.

I come often to his room, so Jani can rest. I sit with him while she sleeps. It is all that I can do. I'm not afraid of him like this, anyway I come for her, my friend.

Today, his breathing is jagged and sharp. I watch his nostrils flare; it is the only movement he seems able to make. When Hannah and Jani rub oil into his limbs, his skin ripples and their hands disappear into the flesh, as it rolls ahead of their kneading fingers. It is hard to watch them. I marvel at Jani's strange love for this man.

At last Jani's snores stutter and stop, she catches her breath and opens her eyes. As she stretches I notice there is a stiffness in her back, a little pain. I stand behind her and rub the tired muscles.

"What will you tell her today?" she asks me.

I shrug. "The same as usual I suppose."

Jani moves next to him, and I leave as she lifts his great head once more into her lap. She looks so small beside him, but her mouth is set in a determined line.

The courtyard is empty, the business of the day having been moved to the pens, so as not to disturb the master. Finally, a place to breathe. A place where neither of them are. A place where I am not stuck between them. Here, I walk slowly.

Abigail is waiting. She has sent Hannah to watch my door. We do not talk about this, Hannah and I. We do not need to. I turn and follow her. Abigail will not speak to Jani or Nabal, she will only speak to me. I am the bridge between them; a bridge with a span too wide to support its own weight.

"Is there any change today?" Abigail asks.

"No, Mistress, no change."

"How is Jani?"

"She is tired."

"Does she need anything?"

"I don't think so, except perhaps an end to it."

Abigail shakes her head.

"If that happens, then all our comfortable lives will be over."

I look at her, her hardness, her longing and the words spill out, even though I promised myself many times, that I would always keep them bound and gagged within me.

"Will he not come for you?"

She turns away, to face the bare wall.

"I do not know what you are talking about."

I laugh.

"Sarah, you are growing insolent," she says, turning to stare at me, now that I have made her angry.

I breathe and bow. I should have been more careful.

"I'm sorry, Mistress," I say, although she knows I am not.

"Why are you, of all people, so hard on me?" she asks.

She has spoken so quietly I wonder if Hannah and Miriam have heard her at all. Miriam is betrayed, her hand has stopped in her lap, her needle poised above the linen. With Hannah it is more difficult to tell, she can easily sew and listen even if her head is lowered so that her eyes are hidden.

I cannot explain to Abigail that I am disappointed, that when she met David there was no parting of the heavens, that these golden people were just like us, a man and a woman who looked and wanted. I thought they would be above such things, that there would be a higher purpose to it all. I am disappointed, because what drives them is only love, ordinary love, that has its roots deep in the earth. My waking moments are thick with this dark seeing. I wish to

God that I were blind, for I cannot help but judge her ordinariness.

I look back to that laughing servant, that dark-haired goat herder. Where is she? I do not recognise myself and I wonder what more God wants from me.

When I look up, Abigail has turned away. I ask permission to return to my room. I do not trust myself to stay near her.

Miriam comes later with a tray of food.

"Abigail said I should bring you something, and that you might need some company."

Later, Abigail will ask Miriam what we talked of, and Miriam will tell her.

"What is happening, Big Sarah? Won't you explain? So at least I can try to understand what you are going through."

I will not load any of them down with this weight of knowing, so I say, "Miriam, I am not sure what is happening to me, or why my thoughts are so dark."

"And why do you voice them to Abigail, of all people? Is it because of what Nabal did to you?"

"You know of that?"

"Yes," she says. "Jani talked of it, just after Little Sarah had one of her turns. That time she had difficulty breathing and could not leave her room. Jani hoped that if Little Sarah knew it had happened to you too, it would enable her to hold on."

"Jani is wise."

"Yet she cannot help you?"

I think about this and then I say, "She has been loved and finds it easier to love others. She sees the faults of those she walks with, but it does not stop her walking with them." I feel my eyes well up. "I envy her," I continue, "but no, she cannot help me."

"Abigail does not know what to make of you and your boldness, she is used to us simply loving her."

I know that, but I am surprised Miriam has seen it too.

"I hope that she will bear with me, so that I may stay with you." I sound a little desperate. Miriam flings her arms around my neck. It makes me jump. She is so afraid for her goatherd. As she clings on, I whisper into her hair, "I hope that you find happiness, Miriam."

"I thought I had," she replies.

Chapter Thirty-Two
Told by Hannah

Since Nabal's seizure, I have spent a lot of time helping Jani. Abigail does not need me as she did before, and I seem to irritate her. She still has Big Sarah, Miriam, and of course, Little Sarah. They comfort each other, so that I can come and comfort Jani.

It has created a small gap in my heart. When she stopped seeing me, I began to lift my eyes. I began to see for myself. Big Sarah helped too, when she slapped my face. At that moment, my world slipped back into place.

It was the morning they returned from meeting David. I needed to know what had happened, so I went to Big Sarah, to her room. She was not asleep, but staring at the ceiling, unmoving, unblinking.

"Sarah, why did she leave me behind?" I asked.

"Oh, Hannah. How can you not see? Is your blindness rooted so far down in your marrow." She got up and stood in front of me.

Suddenly, her anger uncoiled inside her, like a snake out of a basket.

She shouted, "You are worth so much more than this. What about Matthias?"

I knew what she was talking about, but I pretended I did not. She grasped my wrist. I tried to pull away. I was bewildered and perhaps a little scared, at what was happening between us.

"What has Matthias to do with anything?" I gasped. I lied.

She slapped me hard.

"You are a fool," she said.

We have not spoken since. I sit beside Jani and Big Sarah. I hand them what they need. I bring them food when they are hungry and shawls when they are cold. Jani is looking more worried as each day passes and the worry marks her face, indelibly. The lines do not smooth away, even when she smiles. She is ageing before our eyes.

"Hannah, will you go and find Matthias? We need to turn Nabal," Jani whispers, as if her words might disturb him. Big Sarah has gone to fetch water, and we are alone.

"Of course," I say, and laugh quietly to myself, for I too have whispered in reply.

Matthias is in the counting room, where he sleeps and works, where he keeps his scrolls and the money for paying the merchants. It is across the passage from Nabal's bed chamber, as mine is across from Abigail's. I knock softly, so as not to make him jump if he is concentrating, or even perhaps resting.

"Enter Hannah."

"How did you know it was me?" I ask.

"I know your tread," he replies, standing. He does not seem to know what else to say and I wonder that I so easily rob him of his voice.

"It's time to turn him."

"Please sit down," he says, clearing a stool. He pours me a beaker of wine. It is not what I am used to, and I cough. He laughs. "It's not the good stuff; it's what we servants drink."

"I am a servant, too."

He shakes his head. He's right. I have shared Abigail's food since we came here. I am used to the finest bread and the best cooked lamb, fruit, honey and nuts. I have long forgotten my days in the tower when I made do with dry crusts and cold mutton.

"You look tired," I say. He does. It must be so difficult for him.

"There is much to think about and if our master stays as he is, I'm not really sure what should be done."

"Abigail could easily run this place, with your help."

"Of course, but there is a lot of money at stake and there are relatives who might want to interfere." He is speaking what is in all our hearts.

"If he recovers, will he forgive her for what she did?" I ask, because it is a question that flares to life each morning.

"I don't know, Hannah, I honestly don't know." Matthias clasps his hands together. "Or me, would he ever trust me again?" he adds, quietly.

"Of course he would Matthias, why ever not? You have always been the most faithful of servants. You are honest, trustworthy, everything a man should be."

For me it is obvious, the truth. I see a glimmer of hope in his eyes, and his hands drop to his knees, he looks at me unblinking, his stare unwavering. I wonder if I should cast that hope aside, snuff it out forever or perhaps...

"You are a true friend, Hannah."

I reach out and touch his hands lying so still in his lap, I run my finger over each of his fingers. And I choose. In the end, it is not so difficult.

"We do need to go and turn him, Jani will worry," I say, rising. I dare not look at him now.

He follows me to the door. I feel strangely light, as if I have loosed something tight from inside my chest.

Chapter Thirty-Three
Told by Jani

Suddenly, he is gone. He does not even close his eyes. The life that was in him simply isn't there anymore. I remove his head from my lap and stand. The pain that shoots down my legs makes me stagger. Hannah steadies me, until I can walk without crying out, then she leads me away, to wash and mourn. I am surprised at the intensity of my feelings.

Matthias is also strangely touched by his master's death. He does not cry, but moves very slowly, as he begins to arrange all that must be arranged. He and I seem to be the only ones who can think of Nabal kindly, who regret his death, if only a little. They will bring in mourners to cry and wail, for Abigail is silent.

"Oh, poor Jani." Little Sarah cries, running to me. I hold her tightly and she weeps. Not for him but for me, and with a depth that is beyond all this. I look at her and wonder what is going on inside her head. At last, I manage to sit her down and to comfort me, she falls asleep in my lap. Strange little creature. At rest her face is smooth, so much closer to that of a child than a woman and I wonder if she will ever grow up. When Hannah comes to find us, she kneels and strokes Little Sarah's head with one hand, with the other she gently touches my hand, resting her fingertips on my skin. It is comforting. I am comforted.

"I'll bring you a drink," she says, rising.

"And a cushion for my back."

There is a dull ache and my legs are tingling. Hannah returns and rearranges me. She knows just how I should be, so that at last I am warm, and I can rest. We hear Abigail walking past the door.

"Can I do anything else for you, Jani?" Hannah asks.

I shake my head, and she rises to follow her mistress. Her movements slow and deliberate.

As if she were waiting for Hannah to leave, Big Sarah comes in to sit beside us. She does not look at me or speak. We sit shoulder to shoulder until Little Sarah stirs. Then Big Sarah pats my cheek and also clambers to her feet. Not long after, I hear the door to her room shutting. She hardly says a word these days. Perhaps if she begins to say the things that are on her heart, she may not be able to stop. She is like a pot bubbling under its lid. I am worried that Abigail will not put up with her behaviour much longer.

When I am done with mourning, I will take Big Sarah into the desert and force her to cry out. I will scrape away the surface of her soul, until she is able to shout and scream. But I will take her a long way away, before I dare open that well of pain.

"Jani, I'm so very sorry," Little Sarah mumbles, rubbing her eyes and yawning.

"It's alright, Little One, I think you needed to rest."

She stands up and starts to tidy the room.

"Did you cry too?" she asks. She doesn't wait for my answer before she says, "What happens next, Jani?"

His cousin will come and claim his inheritance. He is a man with three wives already and many children.

I say, "We wait. It won't be long before we know."

It won't be long; there is far too much wealth to be left lying in the hands of a wife. Little Sarah is rightly scared, Abigail has lost her power to shelter us, and we are all beginning to realise what that might mean.

"I'm hungry, Little Sarah. What about you?"

"What shall I fetch you, Jani?"

But this is not what I want. I don't want to let her out of my sight. Not just yet.

"No, Little One, let's go and find something together."

Chapter Thirty-Four
Told by Miriam

Nabal is buried, the house ordered and calm. We have been sprinkled with the ashes of a red heifer, all the rooms and our clothes. When the priest came, we also sacrificed two doves and a lamb. Yet people still fall silent as we pass, for rumours pile high around Abigail. She is linked with David, her adventure told and retold. I think she is a little proud, for he is considered a hero by many, but she has begun to worry, that some may think she has been unfaithful, behaved wantonly. Her reputation is thinly stretched and although she saved us from ruin and disaster, now we are fighting shame.

The nearest cousin, Nabal's heir, is married and has sons of his own. Abigail is beautiful. Even I can see there might be trouble. Nothing can be as it was.

I ask, "Mistress, may I send word to Heled? He knew Nabal, and I would not want the news to reach him as hearsay."

She shakes her head. "It is too soon."

How can it be too soon to inform my brother-in-law?

She continues, as if thinking out loud, "And yet he is a close relative. He would expect such news from you."

I nod. "My brother, too?"

She shrugs.

A great deal here is beyond my understanding. I have not learned nearly enough to know what is truly going on. I must watch and listen more closely.

Little Sarah is worrying me. She has become so withdrawn of late, hardly speaking at all unless to answer a direct question, and she cannot cross the yard without crouching under her cloak and clinging to the wall. It used to be difficult for her but with Nabal's death it has started to become impossible.

Big Sarah is hiding in her room. There is something of my mother about her. I worry when she is not with us but worry more when she is. She says such strange things to Abigail, sometimes interrupts her, challenges her orders. We are waiting for our mistress to get really angry. I do not think Abigail will take much more.

Jani is sad and in pain. She twists and turns this way and that, never getting comfortable.

Hannah is most strange of all, for she seems almost happier than before.

I hope that Joel, my dear brother, has not changed. I want someone to remain the same.

"Miriam!" Big Sarah calls from her room. I go to her. She looks so pale and tired. "Would you bring me some bread and wine?"

She missed lunch, for she was sleeping. When I return, I tap on the door.

"Silly girl, you don't have to knock." She sounds almost like her old self, except that her voice is dry and cracked and the room dark and musty. "Put it down over there," she says, pointing vaguely to a small table covered in mending. When I turn back to her, she is staring at the floor.

"Is there anything else you need?" I ask.

She shakes her head and then mumbles, "Would you stay and talk a little."

"Of course."

I'm not sure where I should sit.

After a while, she say, "Clear the stool."

That is also piled high with clothes. Most are Abigail's. I will take them with me when I leave. I do not want our mistress to know they have been left here to fester.

"What is it, Big Sarah?" I ask.

"I want to try to explain to you what is happening and why I need someone to stand in front of me, just for a while. Could you do that?"

Any of us would willingly do that for her, even Little Sarah. She has only to ask. I am flattered that she has chosen me and glad, for I do not think any of the others, though willing, would be able to help just now. I nod and wait. She sits back against the wall, drawing her knees up to her chest. She is trying to decide how to begin. At last, with a deep sigh, she starts to speak.

"I see how things are, as clearly as if God has shone a bright white light onto them. When he does that, it is hard to look away."

"What sort of things, Sarah?"

She lifts the wine and drinks, gulping it down. She wipes her lips with the back of her hand.

"Nabal, Abigail, David."

"Ah," I say as if I understand, although I do not.

She looks up at the window. The dark blue of night is a line of black at the curtains edge.

"Shall I let the moon in?" I ask.

"No, I'd rather you didn't. I don't want *him* to see me too closely."

I know she is talking of God.

"A curtain can't keep him out," I say, and smile as if I have made a joke.

"But it makes me feel better," she replies. There is an intake of breath. She is catching hold of her temper, before it starts to run.

"Why does this light of seeing make you so angry? Surely God doesn't want you to feel so."

"I like your God, Miriam. He is loving and kind," she says. She sounds so sad.

"He's your God too."

She smiles her angry smile and I'm afraid that she thinks I'm foolish.

"What do you think will happen, to us, to Abigail?" I ask, trying to turn the subject.

She stares at nothing for a long time. I think she has forgotten I am there. I wonder if I should leave, or whether I should ask her something else? I can't decide, so I am relieved when she begins to speak again. The room is now quite dark, but her voice is clear and strong.

"She will have a child, and I think the scales will fall from her eyes, only by then it will be too late."

She turns to me and smiles weakly or perhaps it's a grimace. It's hard to tell in this dimness.

"Please, may I light the lamp for you?" I ask. I can't hide the tremor in my voice; she has frightened me.

"Yes, of course. I didn't mean to scare you, Miriam."

I shrug my shoulders, as if it's alright but I daren't speak, for then she will catch me in my lie. She has always said that my voice tells everyone how I am feeling.

"Miriam, pray that the Lord will release me, that he will let me see again with my own eyes."

"I will, Sarah." I rise to leave. "Shall I come again tomorrow?"

"Would you?" she says, thankful, hopeful.

As I turn, she reaches out her hand and catches mine. She says, "Do you think of him often?"

"Who?" I ask, my eyes wide with astonishment, for I have told no one, that I do, sometimes, think of him. That the last time I saw him, I realised that his eyes were kind, his hands gentle, and that his laugh made me want to act the fool. Oh, how can she know what's in my heart? That I have looked at Gabriel, Heled's servant and thought him more than a good man.

"He is a good man," she says. "I can see that."

"He sees me as a child."

"Oh Miriam, he does not. He has loved you from the first moment he saw you."

"I was probably seven or eight," I say, laughing.

"Alright," she says, "the first time he really saw you."

And I know the exact moment. I've always known it. When in the desert, my pain became his pain.

I do not want to leave her here in the dark.

"Come and sit with us," I plead.

"Not yet, but soon," she says, trying to reassure me.

I am glad to be out in the hallway; I am glad to breathe the clear night air. I will pray for her, but I am now also worried, that she will say something of Gabriel to the others.

God must have a reason for the far sight that he has given Big Sarah, but it is putting her out of our reach and perhaps he is asking too much of her. Perhaps, he is asking too much of us all.

Chapter Thirty-Five
Told by Big Sarah

I am sewing a simple hem, to help Hannah, but I'm quite sure she will have to unpick it and do it all over again. My sewing has not improved, and I keep finding my needle lying idle on my lap. Maybe I ought not to wait for Hannah and should start to unpick it myself, for when I look closely, it is poorly done.

The others are running errands, except Jani. She is resting; she gets so very tired of late and takes herself off to her room at every opportunity. Perhaps I am not the only one who is finding Abigail difficult. It means that we are left alone, my mistress and I, sitting in awkward silence.

Abigail is looking at me from under her lashes, trying to gauge my mood. I pretend not to have noticed. It's as if we have swapped places and she is now worried about pleasing me. Of course, my momentary power is hardly more than a gossamer thread, for she can still send me away on a whim.

She has never had any difficulty reading me, I have never been able to keep my thoughts secret. I know she clearly saw the disappointment I felt, when I watched the easy regard which sprang up between her and David. That I feel disdain for the longing she feels, now that her husband is dead. She would not be human if it were not so and yet I am saddened that she is not greater than this. I felt that she should have been able to stand apart from this love, which seems to have tied itself around us, tripping us and choking us, at every opportunity.

The others are slow in returning. I do not know where they could have got to, and I know that they will be anxious. Miriam in particular loves me but does not trust me. She is reluctant to leave us alone, for fear of what I might say. She knows that when I sink into the darkness, I am unable to stay silent. That when God turns his bright eye of knowing onto those I love, I cannot control myself. I hope that Miriam is hurrying through her chores so that she can come back.

There is shouting in the yard. Abigail looks up, tilting her head to listen. Someone is arriving; surely it cannot be the cousin; he is not due for another week. We wait and I pretend to sew, although I long to jump to my feet and peer through the door. I listen intently but I cannot tell what is going on. The hem is a lost cause. At last, Miriam hurries in, bursting with news, her face pink with hope and love.

"Two men, Mistress, two men have come."

Abigail does not move a muscle, and it is me who wants to scream, "Are they from him?"

She has such control. I marvel at her strength as she waits for Miriam to speak again.

"They are from David. They want to see you. Matthias asks if you will receive them?"

A flash of irritation crosses Abigail's face. Of course she will see them, despite the fact that she is in mourning for her husband and should see no one.

"I will see them," she replies, her voice steady.

I hope that David is not testing her propriety, only her love. She turns and gives me such a fierce look, that I quail. She is daring me to show my disapproval. She has bared her teeth and in her fierceness, my true state is once more established.

They are indeed his men, well dressed, standing tall, his confidence radiating from them. They bow low.

"Lady, David sends his greetings. He is aware of your great loss and is sorry for it, but he would ask something of you."

She inclines her head.

We sit protectively around her, except that everything is different. Little Sarah stares at the floor because there are strangers in the room. Jani stares at the floor because she is angry at this breaking of tradition, this disrespect of Nabal. Has she forgotten what he did to Little Sarah and to me? Miriam and Hannah are watching intently, these men from David, Miriam probably hoping for a message from her brother. Hannah hoping, that despite everything, we will be able to stay.

"He knows there has not been an appropriate time for you to mourn but begs that you would join him and his people, as his wife."

His men seem so unconcerned, as if David has only asked for a little bread, yet can they not see that they have just dropped a huge, unyielding rock into our midst? That tall waves are rushing out from behind their words, to sweep us away.

He continues, "David must move. He cannot wait, the safety of all he holds dear is in his hands."

Jani has caught her breath. It is far too soon, scandalously, desperately, shamefully soon.

Abigail is veiled but all of us can see that she shines. The tremor in her hands, that I noticed when Miriam announced their arrival, has stopped and she is looking at me in triumph. My heart is squeezed tight, and my mouth is dry.

She sends the men away to await her decision. She bends her head to Matthias. Nabal's cousin is on his way, and he owns everything; she wants to know what she can take. It's as simple as that. Matthias thinks that Abigail must leave before the cousin arrives, or she will not be allowed to go. He is speaking with his head, but I can see that his heart is breaking because Hannah must go with her mistress. Hannah does not look up, but for once her sewing is stilled.

I notice that Jani is cradling Little Sarah in her lap, that the child is crying. I can see that Matthias wishes that he and Abigail were alone. I think he would like to speak frankly to his mistress but cannot do so in front of us.

Jani bows to Abigail and leaves. I go after her, I do not seek permission, and Abigail does not call me back.

Chapter Thirty-Six
Told by Jani

It is not that I loved him, it is just that he gave me so much more than I ever thought to wish for. He allowed me the garden, he gave me a little of his regard, he even asked my advice, although he never took it. His need of me, before Abigail, allowed me to breathe again, to leave my husband buried. My old life became a memory, no longer such a terrible ache. Of course, he was not the son I never had, he was too cruel for that. I would have been ashamed to have been his mother, yet... I do feel the loss of him. And despite what Big Sarah thinks, I have not forgotten what he did to her and my dear Little Sarah. I will never forget that. I suppose I am confused, for I am tired, very tired. My back aches and will not be eased. I have not slept well for a long time. I am worried, no... I am frightened. Now that David has made his offer to Abigail, she will accept and leave.

She will leave me. It is the adventure, the love, that she has longed for and if he is half the man that Miriam described to us, Abigail will not be able to resist.

Big Sarah, who I would have confided in, is disturbed, distant, troubled. She thinks she can see the future. I do not know what she sees, except that it is upsetting Abigail. If Big Sarah does not catch hold of herself soon, she too might be left behind. At least then I would have someone to talk to.

When they are all gone, I will become little more than a servant to the new master's wives. I will be the distant cousin by marriage, who has grown too big for her own good; someone to put down, who will be forced to acknowledge her true status. I might even be resented for the food I eat. Perhaps this is the sort of seeing that Big Sarah has when she looks into the future. This is not a gift from

God, this is common sense. It is not so very hard to know what will happen to me.

I wonder if I could go with Abigail. Would she even want me to, now that I am not strong, and knowing that I sat beside her husband as he died? It was as if I had to choose between them and like Big Sarah, I couldn't help but show the disapproval that was in my heart.

Miriam might help me think things through. She is growing cleverer and more aware all the time, less blinded by Abigail's perfection. Perhaps, I will seek her out and ask her what she thinks about it all. She has changed these last few months, and not just because she has softened and grown. There is a new look in her eye, one that I'm not sure of.

Instead, I go and sit in my garden, pull a few weeds and watch the shadows stretch long across the wall.

Chapter Thirty-Seven
Told by Little Sarah

Piling her clothes onto the bed, they slip to the floor, a sparkling light pooling across the rug, the colours of summer. I try to concentrate, to gather what she needs, only my hands are trembling. My head is empty, so I press my fingers into my stomach. It's no good; I cannot stop them shaking.

I drag the trunk nearer to the bed. This morning, when the men carried it in, I thought nothing would ever fill it. Now I'm worried we might have to leave some of her favourite things behind. Big Sarah makes me jump when I see her standing in the doorway, watching me. She shakes her head and smiles, and I begin to feel the stones under my feet.

"Start with the things she loves, the things she will notice are missing and then what is left won't matter." She leans close to my ear to whisper, as if what she has said is a secret. It is only common sense. I stand for a moment and then I pick the pale blue tunic of silk. It has cream embroidery and goes with the ivory cloak of soft wool. I hand them to Big Sarah. She folds them carefully and puts them in the trunk. Next, I lift the green silk with the linen undershirt. And so it goes on. We separate the layers using scarves that are old or have fallen from favour. The pile grows smaller. We will have to leave some things behind, but not as much as I feared.

We pull the lid closed and Big Sarah fastens the leather straps. She lays her hand over mine. Mine is swallowed up in hers and for the first time in days, my fingers become still. Her fingers are soft from the goats, although not pretty, for her nails are bitten low and the skin chewed and sore.

Of late, she has been withdrawn, but today there is something about her, a gentle energy, pulsing at her temple. She holds my gaze for a long time, before she loses focus.

"If we are to leave tomorrow, how will we have time to pack the rest of her things?" I ask.

Big Sarah smiles a distant smile. "Don't worry, Little One, there is plenty of time."

I look around at the cluttered space. So many of Abigail's ornaments are fragile, they will need straw and careful handling. I shake my head. Big Sarah is not seeing this clearly and I am worried. Abigail wants us to be gone at first light. There is definitely not enough time.

"Oh dear, Little Sarah, do you not see? Abigail owns nothing. This all belongs to Nabal's cousin. She has agreed with Matthias to take her clothes, some bedding and ten donkeys. And I expect the ten donkeys will be returned when we reach David's camp."

I turn to stare at her. Abigail is to leave it all behind. Everything. I am suddenly overwhelmed by what she is about to do.

"Sit down," Big Sarah commands, but her voice is far away, muffled. "Speak out your fear now, before it becomes too great."

I try to form the words. Instead, I fall to my knees and retch.

"Breathe, child, breathe," she cries.

Jani is here. They kneel either side of me, I am dimly aware of them. It's easy to give in. I feel the sickness rising, the empty heave of my stomach.

I notice that Jani is holding Big Sarah's hand. I try to concentrate on the fingers and the way they are entwined. I can see a deep, pink shadow where they are clasped tightly, the knuckles taut and white.

"Swallow," Big Sarah commands again.

"Suck the air in and think only of that," Jani adds.

I cling to the words and wait, hoping, hoping I will have time to recover before Abigail sees me. What good will I be to her like this?

What good am I to anyone?

"Tell me what brought this on?" Jani asks Big Sarah.

"I asked her to speak out her fear."

Jani laughs, "*You* asked her to do that?"

"I know, I know," says Big Sarah, "but mine is hard to name. Sometimes I can see it clearly, sometimes not. I'm sorry Jani, I shouldn't have asked something of Little Sarah, that even I am not strong enough to do."

I wonder what they are talking about. I don't really care.

"Little Sarah," Jani says, "you will not be left behind."

I feel the floor under my knees, gritty and hard and I try to stand.

"Good girl," says Big Sarah and pushes me to my feet. It's as if I weigh nothing to her, and I almost overbalance.

I sit on the bed and the two women roll back onto their heels; their arms folded across their chests.

"Ask us," Big Sarah says, unsmiling.

I take a deep breath. This is what I vomited up from my stomach.

"If she owns nothing, then what about you, me and Hannah? How can we go with her?"

Jani rises. Big Sarah puts her hand under her elbow so she can come and sit beside me. Big Sarah remains kneeling.

Jani speaks, each word deliberate, as if I will be slow to understand. "Abigail has arranged it all. She takes her clothes and you, Hannah, Miriam and..."

"Me, I hope," adds Big Sarah.

"Matthias will argue for us. He will persuade the cousin that you are hers and that to send her away with less would dishonour the house. She leaves her jewellery, her ornaments, everything. The cousin will not demand the return of four scrawny servants, not from David and his six hundred men. He'd be mad to even think of it."

Jani is speaking sense, yet I am still fearful. She has only said four. I fling myself into her arms.

"But Jani, what about you?" I wail, my heart filling my mouth with such pain. I cannot bear the thought of leaving her behind, left to a strange household, without any of us to care for her.

Big Sarah speaks to Jani over my sobbing. "Make up your mind now Sister, how hard can it be?"

"You are right. There is nothing for me here, yet you must see that my position is unclear. I am neither servant nor a close relative. David will have to feed and clothe me as part of Abigail's retinue. Miriam, at least, goes back to her brother and her sister. I have no one to speak for me."

"If Abigail wants you, surely no one will question it, and who would miss you here?" Big Sarah says, her eyes narrowed with thought.

I feel Jani wince, then she clenches her fists tightly.

"That part is true," she says. "Who will notice or care what I do? They will be too busy expressing their outrage and shame, that Abigail is to become David's wife, only days after her husband has been placed in his tomb."

I hear her anger, I see Big Sarah's sorrow at her own thoughtless words, but I do not care, for I am sure that at last we will leave together and that is all that matters. No one is to be left behind.

Chapter Thirty-Eight
Told by Hannah

Abigail is worried that the cousin will come after her, demand that she stays, and return all that belongs to him. Matthias says he will not. Matthias is surely right. He always is. Still, Abigail is fretful, wanting to be on her way, wandering about the rooms, with little to do, touching things, even picking them up, as if she is checking their worth. We sit and wait.

Since Nabal's death, I have started to see that what is in Matthias's heart, is also in mine. I am surprised by the depth of feeling, the longing that has lain smooth and dark below all that I acknowledged.

For a few days I thought we had the rest of our lives together and there was a glorious joy in all that I did, a marvellous lightness. The only thing in the whole world that was truly my own—until David's men came. Now time has shuddered and faltered to a stop. All has become ashes.

Big Sarah was right about me all along. I was living wrapped in Abigail's world, and only when my heart was challenged, did I glimpse what I might have. It has made me watch my mistress carefully, as she waited for David, exposed in her hope, laid bare for all to see. I glimpsed the rawness, that I think Big Sarah sees and feels all the time. No wonder she lives on the edge of madness.

Has God himself released our Abigail from Nabal? Abigail thinks so, she shines in her sureness. It is harder for us. We are not so convinced. I am not so convinced. What has happened is too human, to have raised her so far above us, for it has happened to me and I am just a servant.

When I can, I stand with Big Sarah, touching her hand so that she knows I understand how she struggles, yet I think we still need her wild strength. We have all come to rely on her, to love her and if we are to set out tomorrow, to leave this place, we must have her with us.

"Abigail, I would ask something of you?"

"What do you need, Hannah? If it's in my power, I will give it to you."

She is generous with what little she has.

"I want to ask whether Big Sarah will be allowed to come with us?"

"Do you think I would leave her behind?"

I will not be cowed by her accusation, and I am less stung by it than I would have been a few weeks ago. We have all seen how Big Sarah has been of late and we can never truly know what thoughts are in Abigail's mind.

"Yes, Big Sarah will come with us," Abigail continues, now a little hesitantly, as if she has only just made up her mind.

"Good, then I will go and tell her."

Abigail frowns at me. I hurry out so she has no time to call me back.

Big Sarah is sitting on her bed, the few things that she owns lying on a shawl. I come and kneel at her feet.

"You are to come; you will not be left behind. We are all to go together."

"She said so definitely? There is no mistake?"

"None," I say. She reaches out her big soft hands and holds my face in hers. I watch the tears roll down her cheeks, gently wiping them away with my fingers.

"What are you doing here? These are your last moments. Don't waste them," she says, hauling me to my feet. "Anyway, I have much to do." She turns to look back at the shawl. We laugh.

I won't waste another moment; I'll go and find him.

For the last time I knock at his door and do not wait for him to call me in, hoping to catch him unawares. He looks grave as he rises to greet me, worried I suppose that I have been seen coming to his room at this late hour. I do not care. He pours wine. He sits without speaking, as if my being here is enough. I want so much more.

"Will you not speak, Matthias?"

The lamp splutters and our shadows fill the walls, as the flame stretches.

"I have to stay, you do see that?" he says, tentatively, as if I might not understand. Of course I know he must stay.

We do not know how to proceed. We have always waited for someone else to direct us.

"Hannah." The sound of my name on his tongue is sweet. "If I am to run things as before, if I am sure that my new master will keep me in place, then may I send for you? Would you come, even if it means leaving Abigail?"

I nod and whisper, "If I can."

I thought that Abigail would fill my horizon until the day I died, but she has shrunk, and I can see past her. She will surely send me back to Matthias, when her own heart is satisfied.

We sit and stare at each other. The lamp is dimming. It is time to leave. He stands by the open door, and I know he watches as I walk slowly across the courtyard. I am disappointed that he doesn't call me back.

There are only a few more hours until sunrise. I lie down but my eyes will not close. I wait patiently for the night to end.

Little Sarah is first to stir. I doubt she has slept either. The next few days will be hard for her. The poor child is sick and pale with anxiety. I fetch warm milk, something to line her stomach. She sips at it although she soon puts it away from her. I am hungry, I did not expect to feel so. The goats' cheese is fine and crumbly. I will miss its sweet, nutty flavour. We'll take some for the journey, but it will grow pungent in the heat.

Abigail calls out. She is already pulling on her clothes. She is eager to be gone and for a second I feel anger.

"Hannah."

"I'll get Little Sarah," I say. "She will come and braid your hair."

"Hannah." Her voice is sharp. She is used to me running to her side. She holds out her hands to me. I take them, because I must. "We'll come through this, you and I," she says, staring into my face, into my heart. I wonder that I still let her.

"Are you sure this is the right thing to do?" I ask.

She looks surprised, then her cheeks grow warm and her eyes glitter.

"Of course, you have not met him. When you behold him, you will understand. When he speaks, all will become clear. Oh Hannah, he listened to me as if I were a man of great wisdom. He said I was the cleverest woman he'd ever met, wise and beautiful."

She drops my hands and turns away, unable to contain herself.

We have always known that she is wise and beautiful. Did we not tell her? Did she truly not know that?

I fetch Little Sarah. The others are eating. Miriam looks so excited she can barely sit still, Jani apprehensive and Big Sarah relieved. I love them so much.

The donkeys wait in the courtyard, shifting from foot to foot. We are veiled and uncomfortably warm. I am glad no one can see my face, the tears running over my chin and down my neck.

I remember when I first came here, when I first turned my eyes up to this huge empty sky. Its beauty astounded me, stretching across us, holding us in place and yet giving us space to dream and fly. I will miss it. The dust is already gathering along the edge of my cloak, and I wonder when I will be able to look up again, without this pain in my chest.

Abigail is speaking to Matthias. She is closing the door on our old lives. His face is still and grave as he listens and I wonder what she is saying to him. How can she be the last of us to speak to him, when I am sitting here longing to fling my arms around his neck? How can she be so cruel as to prolong this moment, when I feel all that I am, is torn in two? There is no hope in my leaving, despite what he asked of me, the parting is too harsh and final.

Chapter Thirty-Nine
Told by Miriam

The donkeys are bony and small. We are all sore. David's men ride up ahead and behind us. They are armed and a little fierce, but still solicitous and respectful, for they do not yet know what we are like. Jani is not managing at all well. We need to stop frequently so she may rest. It is awkward, for Abigail is impatient and Jani does not know how she fits anymore, what she can expect from us. I do not know how to help her.

I am looking forward to seeing Joel again. The last time was too fraught, and we were too full of their meeting to speak of anything that mattered. I wonder that David has not come himself to fetch Abigail, that he only sent some of his men. I hope that Joel will be able to explain it to me. I am afraid that despite her love, she will be of less consequence. Only the second wife or is it the third?

"I hope David will settle somewhere soon," Jani says, through gritted teeth.

We have stopped to walk a little. She is so stiff. Abigail is ahead of us, striding away.

Big Sarah answers, "His followers grow in number, more and more each day. He's sure to settle somewhere soon, somewhere he can find food."

That makes sense, but I still see that when no one is looking, Jani weeps for her garden and the pain in her back. It makes her angry, this weakness, so we pretend not to notice.

"If we live in a tent, will we have to sleep on the floor?" Little Sarah asks, from beneath her hood. She does not like spiders or snakes. Who does?

Big Sarah laughs, she knows what is bothering her, too. "Don't worry, Little One. I'll stand at the door and stop anything that wants to slither in, and anyway, with an army that big, they'll be more scared of us. They'll wriggle away as fast as they can."

Since we've been travelling, Big Sarah has become our centre. She still carries her darkness, her seeing, but I think that now all is settled, she is better. She has straightened her back and is more like her old self. I am glad. I have missed her, and we need her now more than ever, even Little Sarah draws in close, for her shadow is large and reassuring.

When we have travelled half a day to the horizon, once more seated on our donkeys, Big Sarah motions for me to drop back.

"So Miriam, at last you will be free."

I do not understand.

"Surely in your heart, there is now a little hope?" she continues.

She is referring to Heled's servant, Gabriel. I am afraid to speak of him so openly, even to her. So I ask, "How will I be free?"

"We will be living away from convention, away from any settled life. You will have a chance to find your own happiness."

"But David is more devout than any man on earth. Even Joel speaks of God with respect and observes the law like never before."

"Why should that make a difference?"

"It means David will be guided by God and not necessarily by his own heart."

Big Sarah grows impatient with me.

"We'll see just how devout he is," she snorts, tossing her head and pursing her lips. "Just how godly, when we reach his camp, which will, I assure you, be full of very ordinary men."

She does not believe he can be as good as the rumours tell us and her voice is too loud for my own peace of mind.

"Miriam, we have heard that he is a man of justice," Big Sarah continues, "yet he heads up a rebel army. How can both be true at the same time? We don't really know anything about him."

"Except what Joel has chosen to tell us," I remind her.

"Or what we have heard on the wind," she replies.

"Perhaps, if he is in love with Abigail, then he will not stand in the way of others," I say. For a moment I feel a bubble of joy expand within me, like when I was a child and Joel promised to meet me in the stables. I wonder then, if what I feel for Gabriel is love. A man I have seen three times in as many years. I am perhaps mistaking kindness for regard. What do I know of anything? I have grown up a sheltered child when it comes to such things. And Gabriel is only Heled's servant, so his happiness, or mine, would be of little consequence to David. I continue, "And what can David know of love when he has already married for politics? His first wife is proof of that."

Big Sarah frowns and says, "Remember, she is not his first wife.

The King's daughter was that and I have heard it said that her loss broke David's heart. He is already damaged."

"Then surely he would not wantonly cause more such hurt, even if it meant going against convention," I reply, lifting my face to the sky.

"Oh Miriam, be careful what you dare to believe, until we have seen what David is truly like."

That is unfair. Did she not bring up the subject of hope in the first place and now she is cross with me for hoping, although in truth, I believe she is swayed by what I have said. Still, I cannot help but be a little angry with her, for making me talk so openly of what I had kept as a manageable sense of unease. We ride a few more paces before she says, "Miriam, you are wise and clever. You have seen without the aid of God, what I have seen deep in my heart."

"Where does that leave me?" I ask.

She shakes her head and says, "I don't know and I'm sorry that you are now angry with me."

"I'm not really, Big Sarah, but I resolve only to look forward to seeing my brother and brother-in-law. I will not think beyond that." I speak with determination, lifting my head once again to look towards the horizon, as if it were truly so.

She smiles.

"Good, because I would have you happy, Miriam. Of all of us, you have the best chance."

The dust clings to our clothes. It is hot and I am weary. If I am the one most able to find love, then I pity my friends, for that means their hope is barely hope at all.

The sun is at its zenith and David's men have erected a shelter up ahead. We hurry forward. Abigail is waiting for us to put down the rugs, so she can rest.

Chapter Forty
Told by Little Sarah

I concentrate on putting one foot in front of the other. I keep my hood low over my eyes so that I need only look at my feet or if I'm on my donkey, at my hands, which are grubby and dry. As we move further and further from Carmel, I feel as if I grow smaller and smaller, the weight of the sky on my shoulders pressing me down.

David has also moved; he is two or three days further away. At midday on the second day, I crawl to the back of the shelter, where I can sit behind the others. It is stuffy and dim, yet it means the horizon is hidden, that harsh line that holds the earth and sky apart. My heart is always in my throat, and I cannot swallow it back down to where it belongs.

Only another night and a day, yet surely even then there will be no peace, for there will always be more journeys. David is a man who is running and waiting. Now we must run and wait with him.

I whisper, "Oh Lord, that you would settle this David somewhere like Nabal's house, so I may sleep in a room with a window and a door." He does not reply.

Chapter Forty-One
Told by Hannah

One of David's men rode off this morning. We must be getting close to the camp. Abigail watched him leave and is now veiled. She wears a simple tunic and yet there is no mistaking that she is a bride going to meet her betrothed. I watch her and wish that he would come. The nearer we get, the more it worries me that he has not ridden out to greet her. Even she has slowed her pace and scans the horizon with a worried frown.

Jani stumbles and I feel guilty that my thoughts are all about Abigail and my own heart's troubles. This journey, even though of such short duration, is hard for her. She seems always to be in pain, always trying to hide it. We can see that she has lost her place amongst us, being neither one thing nor the other. We do not care about such things, for we love her, but it has made her unsure of herself, as if she is a burden to us. Abigail should do more to reassure her; she could make this path so much easier for our dear Jani, who has to beg to rest again. I am sorry for the look of irritation that passes across our mistress's face.

"Hannah, get me a peach. I am thirsty," Abigail commands.

I go back to the donkey that carries the food. There isn't much fruit left. We are so hot and dry. We have eaten most of it. I pick out a couple that are not too badly bruised. As I turn back, I notice a smudge of grey, far away in the distance.

"Oh Lord, please let it not just be the man returning," I whisper, into the donkey's neck.

We draw together, Abigail in our midst. David rides a black horse. Miriam is nodding, he is unmistakable. The horse is urged on, cantering a trail of dust and stones. It is a good sign that he hurries, despite the heat and I promise God a sacrifice of thanksgiving, when I next get an opportunity. The horse is magnificent, but it is his master that I want to look at, to see.

At last, I begin to understand. How could any woman simply glance and turn away? She would have to be near blind. He is beautiful. Not so tall, but broad and fair and there is a simple eager joy in his coming, that is disarming. We part, so that he may grasp her hand. They do look well together. Abigail is flushed and lovely in her relief; so I see that he does not have it all his own way. His heart is open, worn for us to see. Hers is veiled but she has him, as she had Nabal, at the beginning.

"I'm sorry I could not come earlier. We heard rumours that the King's army was on the move." His voice is mellow, gentle and sure. He does not care that we stand about her, he does not see us.

"My Lord, I am honoured that you have come." And she is so honoured, but I can also detect the shame. "This is all there is," she whispers.

He laughs and I want to laugh too, as he puts an arm around her.

"I need no man's wealth," he says. "It is you who has stolen my heart, not a few gold trinkets. God gives me all that I need."

They stand touching, hand to hand, eye to eye. He is like a boy, and she has shed the years of responsibility in a heartbeat. I am singing and soaring with the eagles. Matthias and I will be together, as soon as we like. There is nothing, absolutely nothing that need come between us.

I look at the others. Even Little Sarah is smiling, for at least this part of the ordeal is nearly over, and Miriam's grin has crinkled her eyes to thin bright lines. Jani, I expect, is relieved, that it is not too far to the camp. I turn to Big Sarah, our dearest friend. She is looking at me in silent desperation, and my own smile tightens in alarm, for she has turned pale and is toppling to the ground, her cloak billowing, her eyes searching for something I cannot see.

We revive Big Sarah with water. She comes to, gripping my hand

and staring up into my face. She seems terrified, her eyes darting this way and that. Then she sets her jaw and grits her teeth, from somewhere she finds a renewed strength, a chilling stillness, so although she is the one who fainted, it is I who feels weak and trembling.

Chapter Forty-Two
Told by Miriam

We make our way into the camp. The noise is incredible, like Carmel on market day or like the feasting at the height of the shearing. Tents are all around us, their ropes criss-crossing our path like spiders' webs. Horses, donkeys, women, children, servants crowd everywhere, the colours and smells like a canopy over and around us. It's a long time before we see the far edge and by then I crave meat—succulent broiled lamb or braised mutton—because the smell of cooking hangs on the air and I breathe it in with every step. Turning this way and that, I see a myriad of pots over fires, and it is almost beyond me to not turn aside and beg for something to eat. There is so much to see, that I almost miss Joel making his way towards us, his dark hair bobbing between the people, as they clear a path for him. Many of the women surreptitiously turn to watch him walk by.

"Sister, dear sister," he calls, I laugh. He picks me up and hugs me, like a little girl and there is a surge of anger within me, that I have so quickly shed my new life, but he feels different too. For a moment, I worry that he has changed. I suppose it's just that this is home for him, here he is at peace, and I have never seen him so.

"We expected you yesterday."

"I know, poor Jani did not take to travelling and we had to come slowly."

He doesn't seem to care about Jani, or perhaps he did not hear me.

"Tonight we will fast and pray. Tomorrow we will feast, and Abigail will be his wife. There is so much I want to show you."

"We will fast?"

"Oh Miriam, how can you think of your stomach at a time like this?" There is a twinkle in his eye and with all my strength I punch his arm. "Mmm," he says, "you are getting stronger, that felt like two butterflies landing together."

I fling myself into his arms again and hold him fiercely. I do not care that he does not always listen and that now I am acting like a child.

He leads us to a tent. As we reach the entrance, I see a woman standing across the way. She watches us, her arms folded over her chest. She does not smile.

"Who's that?" I ask Joel.

"The servant of Ahinoam, David's other wife."

"She does not look pleased to see us," I say.

She does not, this servant. Her eyes are narrowed as she takes note of what Abigail brings. This is obviously not a political marriage and must therefore be important on some other level. The woman is wondering what that might be.

And so it begins. Abigail will be the second wife and although no one can doubt his love for her, she must defer to this princess.

Our tent is large, the floor strewn with rugs. As the others start to unpack, I dart back and forth to the opening, to peer outside. I cannot stay confined. I see Heled coming, followed by a line of servants carrying meat, bread and vine leaves stuffed with fruit. I bow low, only he laughs and catches hold of me. He whirls me round. Why can they not see that I am no longer a child, and should be treated as such? He puts me down, but it is too late, my dignity has fled and my new start is as chaff before the wind.

"Your sister is here and would like to see you."

He frowns, for my face has betrayed me. I had not thought for a moment that she would have left her home to be here.

"King Saul might have come at any time," he says. He does not like explaining himself and I wonder why he does so. "A bit of discomfort now, is nothing to what might have happened to her and little Chloe, when his soldiers came to extract his tithe from us."

Rebekah won't have liked giving up her comfortable house, all her servants and I will not be as free as I'd hoped. She will have eyes and ears everywhere. I stop feeling hungry. Heled watches me closely.

"I would think that you would be pleased to see your new niece, and your family," he says.

"Oh I am, of course I am. Where are they? I should pay my

respects straightaway."

He shakes his head. He is not fooled for a moment, but he manages a thin smile, to cover his disappointment. Perhaps, he thinks I feel too grand for them now, for I will be the companion to a queen, but he never saw how much Rebekah disliked me, how much she enjoyed lording it over us.

"Stay and eat first, the fast starts at sunset and you will be hungry. In a little while, I'll send my servant to fetch you. He will guide you through the camp."

My adventure has hardly begun before it is over. I turn back to the tent, I want to speak to Big Sarah, to tell her of my disappointment. That seeing Gabriel now, will be terrible. She will understand and perhaps she will be well enough recovered to come with me, when I go to visit Rebekah. I feel desperately in need of an ally, and she is the only one who knows the truth of my squashed hope.

Chapter Forty-Three
Told by Big Sarah

The tent is dark and cool. Jani has stopped fussing, and I am sitting back on my bed roll. There is a dimness at the very edge of my vision, so I concentrate on the things before me, the food, the shadows, and the colours of the rug under my feet. I dig my toes in and hold tight to the world. I try to remember the touch of Little Sarah gently washing my hands and face, although her fingers still trembled from the journey, and Jani's grumpy insistence that I eat. She is distressed, because I am not yet ready to embrace such ordinariness. Abigail is not here; I suppose she is with David and that Hannah will have gone with them. She has resumed her rightful place, the only one of us still able to stand beside our mistress on this auspicious day.

I have at least come home, back to where I started. I was born in a tent, with the night sky above me. My childhood was spent running in and out and around such a camp. Part of me acknowledges this homecoming, the gentle release of some of the tensions of the past few months but then it cannot cover that other place within, which is now more tightly bound than ever.

I long for the time before he touched me, before Nabal chose me, before this seeing, that makes everything so clear and bright, and yet which brings a darkness that covers and complicates it all. I want to swear and laugh and look after the others, to be how I was before. They are innocent of what is to come. I alone feel the weight of the future and it falls on me to look out for them, even though I am breathless and weak.

Miriam comes and sits beside me. She is upset but will not talk unless I open the way. So I say, "What ails you, friend?" I lift a lock of her hair and tuck it behind her ear, so that I can see her face.

"Oh, Big Sarah, my sister is here at the camp."

I sigh for her. This is a bitter blow, although we should have realised it would happen, at some point. It means that Miriam's actions will be watched and judged and fettered.

"Have you seen him?" I ask.

"No. I am quite sure it is hopeless. Heled sees me as a child and Rebekah has never wanted me happy." She drops her head into her hands.

I am surrounded by love, and it niggles and grinds with its ferocity. Surely, this is not how it is meant to be. Abigail should help protect us and yet she cannot protect herself, standing out there alone, with just Hannah at her side. There is nothing to be done. I cover Miriam's hand with my own.

"We must eat, becoming weak will not help anyone."

Miriam swallows her food, and her tears. I drink more wine than is good for me. I notice that Jani does, too. The pain is getting worse for her and still she pretends that all is well. She has never needed to keep such things from us before.

We are drawing away from each other. I feel it as a hardness between my ribs. There are too many thoughts locked up in our heads, thoughts that ought to be spilling out between us, as they used to do. We are trying to stand alone, and we are not meant to be like that, we are meant to hold and care for each other.

I must help find a way to unblock the words, to find a way to share them again.

Chapter Forty-Four
Told by Jani

My legs ache and my back is on fire. The floor is uneven, so each step is awkward and jarring. I do not know how to begin to live here. But I will. I must.

Miriam is sad. Something has upset her and without her common sense and good cheer the tent feels cold. Big Sarah and she sit together. They have become close companions. I am glad, it means I do not have to work so hard. I can concentrate on finding some peace and a way of sitting that does not hurt. Little Sarah is flitting about, picking things up and putting them down again. At least I persuaded her to take off her cloak before Abigail came back. She looked so frightened and when Abigail did return, I thought Little Sarah was going to grow roots where she stood, as if her old mistress had been replaced by a stranger. But as far as I can see, her old mistress is just the same. She is sitting near the door with Hannah. I stand and stretch; my bones click and grate. Big Sarah beckons me over.

"How's the pain, Jani?"

"I'm a little tight, that's all. And I miss a solid wall to lean against."

"The pole in the middle will do just as well."

"It looks too narrow and hard for my broad back."

"You'll get used to it," Big Sarah says. "It was my mother's place."

"How old were you, when you were sold to Nabal?" Miriam asks her.

"I don't know for sure. I was small but well able to fend for myself."

"Did you miss your family very much?" she says, tidying the tray of food. It's not like Miriam to notice such a thing, normally it would be Hannah or Little Sarah.

"Of course. It made me fierce and cross with the goats, but I soon learned that if I was gentle they gave more milk, and I wasn't scolded so much." Big Sarah is thoughtful for a moment, and then continues, "It was a difficult few months, but Nabal's people look out for each other. It wasn't long before I began to start my day around the fires with them, learning their names, and how to make them laugh. What choice did I have?"

Miriam seems to be listening with her usual interest, only she spoils it by bursting into tears. I have never seen her cry like this; I don't think any of us have. Even Abigail comes over to see what is wrong. Through her sobs, she wails, "I never asked about my mother. I never thought to ask how she was or if she was even still alive."

I am struggling to rise; I want to put my arms around her. In the end Big Sarah has to help me up. Abigail returns, unsmiling, to her seat.

I say, "Heled would have let you know if anything had happened to her. He takes the care of his family seriously."

"But will she still know me?" Miriam sobs.

I don't think she is crying for her mother. I look at Big Sarah, who is looking down at the floor, her mouth a line, firmly closed, keeping secrets.

Suddenly I am angry; sore and angry. I feel sure that I should not have come. I should have stayed with my garden. Matthias would have seen me right. He is a good man. He was a good man, for I doubt now that we shall ever see him again. I should have stayed and carved out my future there, in a place where I had found some dignity.

This pain has made me selfish, and unreliable. I don't know what is going on with Miriam. I should know! I should be the one she confided in. Perhaps, I'm getting too old, after all, at the last count, I was beyond forty. How stupid I was to think I could start a new life, when I can barely move without gasping.

We have talked about our ages many times. Hannah thinks she is in her middle twenties, although in wisdom she is oldest of us all. Big Sarah isn't exactly sure what age she is, for all her stories but we think she is a little younger than Hannah. One evening they compared wrinkles to try and work it out. We laughed until we ached, particularly when I joined in. My wrinkles were far more impressive. Stupidly, my eyes fill with tears at the memory, even though it wasn't that long ago. Miriam is sixteen and Little Sarah fifteen, and at their age, I was married, going on two years. I had lived a whole life before I ever came to Nabal, one that they have not shared or could understand.

I shouldn't be chasing across the desert to God knows where, a burden and a worry to those I love, with no one between God and me.

I want to rest, but these thoughts have made me decide to speak to Big Sarah and Hannah, of the pain in my back, how it burns, and that it is worrying. Perhaps Hannah can mix something that will take the edge off it.

I feel better, thinking they will soon share again what is in my heart. It's silly to keep such a thing from them and it means I can stop battling a little. My eyes are heavy. They will wake me if I am wanted, and Little Sarah is buzzing around the tent doing all that needs to be done. When I shut my eyes I no longer feel the ache around my middle.

Chapter Forty-Five
Told by Big Sarah

Miriam's sister is pregnant, large with child. I look at our flat stomachs and cool faces. No wonder she isn't pleased to see us. Miriam has also introduced us as her friends. Rebekah doesn't know what to make of that, she thought we were servants. I don't think she is as clever as Miriam, nor as beautiful. I think Miriam should be glad that Heled still treats her as a child.

Jani has just told Rebekah that she is a relative of Abigail's. Rebekah is a little more impressed. I'm glad. I do not think Miriam's sister's welcome should have been quite so cool.

Rebekah sent an old servant to fetch Miriam, and she cried again when she saw him, but it was not the man she was looking for. When we crossed the camp behind him, Miriam tripped and stumbled as if she were old and blind, until Jani and I took her between us.

"So are you well, Miriam?" Rebekah asks.

"Yes Sister. May I see little Chloe?"

"She is sleeping. There will be plenty of time for that later."

I wonder if Rebekah thinks Miriam will come back into her household.

"Are you comfortable?" Miriam asks.

Rebekah stares at her, she is searching for insolence. I do not like this woman.

"Jani," I say, "do you remember the goat?"

Jani smiles, Miriam grows pink and stares at the floor. She is not sure that this is the right moment for such a memory.

"Your mother had a goat called Jani," I say to Rebekah, "it was quite a joke for our own dear Jani, when Miriam first came to us."

Rebekah is confused but something stirs in the dimness behind her. A tiny figure emerges, wringing her hands, her eyes bright and blinking. Miriam stands and my heart aches for her.

"Mother, how are you?"

"She will not know you," Rebekah says. She rubs her stomach and sighs. She is long suffering and no one understands.

"I had a goat called Jani," the little woman says, staring around her. She looks at the tent, her eyes blank, as if where she stands is nothing to do with her.

"I remember Jani," Miriam says, her eyes clouded with tears. "She was such a dear little goat."

"She was." The little woman nods her head, bobbing up and down like a bird.

Rebekah claps her hands. Two women appear.

"Take Mother to rest."

Rebekah is ashamed of her own mother. It is very hard to like this sister of Miriam's. She seems a woman tight with worry about what other people think of her. I suppose, there are many coming and going through this important tent. Heled is close to David. The light from the door darkens and Miriam, who was uncomfortable before, now stiffens. Gabriel has come. When did she go from a carefree girl to this young woman, with a heart so bound?

"My Lady, Lord Heled would like you to know that he will stay with his men tonight. Do you want anything?"

The man is trembling at the sight of Miriam.

"Gabriel, tell him that I have everything I need. Tell him to come as soon as he can."

Rebekah tries to sound gracious, instead she sounds petulant, a child forced to give up her favourite toy. Gabriel bows. Miriam is staring at the floor. She must know every lump and bump of it by now.

When I think of Abigail, there is darkness, and I'm afraid. When I think of Miriam, there is a sliver of silver, like the moon, a shaft of hope, tenuous and yet splendid. I want to reassure her, except that it is only what I feel. Big Sarah, the goatherd and her dark premonitions.

Jani rises.

"We too, must go. Abigail will need us. Perhaps you could guide us back to our tent on the way to your master," she says to Gabriel. Clever, clever Jani. "We are so new to the camp, I'm sure we won't find our way back," she continues, smiling at Rebekah.

Miriam kisses her sister, and we wait for her to go ahead of us. I cannot read Gabriel's expression. He is a good servant, if he can remain so impassive, under such provocation.

"You look well, Mistress," I hear him say, as we emerge into the noise of the cramped life around us. They walk together. He asks her gentle questions. Her wits seem to have left her, and I think all she can do is nod or shake her head.

"Except, Big Sarah, he is still only a servant," Jani whispers.

"I am hoping that when they are discovered, no one will remember that," I reply.

She purses her lips.

"If Abigail were not so preoccupied, I would speak to her of this matter."

"Please don't," I say, as darkness floods my sight. "Not yet, Jani, I beg of you."

"Goodness Big Sarah, you're not going to faint again, are you?"

I shake my head, as I cling to her arm. The tent is not far. When we get to the entrance, we slip past them. Miriam has found her voice at last and is questioning him relentlessly, as only Miriam can, afraid that he will leave if she draws breath. I do not think there is any danger of that.

Inside, it is dark, and I am reluctant to enter. I want to stay out in the light, near Miriam and Gabriel, but I am weak, and my head is beginning to pound above my eyes.

I sit with my back against the pole allowing my heart to slow, trying to still my thoughts. I am a woman who looked after goats. I am a woman who sees into the future, whose heart is darkened with fear. I am a woman who fears God and what he asks of her.

Chapter Forty-Six
Told by Little Sarah

Miriam's brother, Joel, has come to see her. They are standing outside, their voices light against the usual riot of noise around us. Sometimes, I hear them laugh.

It is easier when I have my back to the light, and I don't know why I am the only one who sees how much there is to do. When Abigail returns from David's tent, we must be ready. I fold a scarf. Big Sarah is watching me, the shadows running across her face, like clouds across the desert.

It's only been a couple of days since we arrived. I think I am growing used to it, although I haven't ventured out except for the necessities.

For now, Abigail is with David, across the way. Hannah slips between the two tents, fetching the things she needs and bringing us her clothes to wash.

We have heard that the camp will be moving on quite soon.

There is even a rumour that the King is getting close. He can only mean harm to David, and I try not to think how it would feel to run before an army, coming fast to kill us, trying to lay waste to all that David holds dear. At this moment, there is nothing dearer than his beautiful Abigail.

I notice Joel's voice. He speaks quickly, as if he is constantly catching his breath. He speaks of needing to be ready at a moment's notice.

How can we be ready at a moment's notice? I do not know what needs to be done and that causes my stomach to burn.

Now they are talking about their mother. She has lost all memory. Joel does not feel it as deeply as Miriam, for he left home a long time ago. Then I hear my name. I do not want to listen to what they say.

"Big Sarah," I call, as loudly as I dare. "The sand is getting into everything. Would you help me repack the trunk?"

She shakes her head but still lumbers to her feet. Then a shadow fills the entrance and for a moment I cannot see.

"Hannah, is that you?" Big Sarah calls past me.

"It is."

Hannah looks tired and worried. I suppose none of us know what to expect and she is the one who stands between Abigail and the camp. She is the one who takes responsibility for our mistress.

"What does she need?" I whisper.

"The red cloak and the gold tunic."

"Ah, she will be so lovely," I say to myself.

"And will you come and dress her hair?"

"Of course. When?"

"Now," she says, picking a fig from the bowl. "It's growing dark, you won't need your cloak."

She is staring at me.

"I may need it later," I say, pulling it around my shoulders and over my head.

"At least try walking without the hood," she says, quietly, so that only I can hear, "it's not far."

Big Sarah has come to stand just behind me. I feel her.

"I'll come if you like," she says.

She sounds like her old cheerful self, only Hannah looks up and says, "No, Big Sarah, you know what Abigail said."

Big Sarah turns away and sits back down. She chews her bottom lip and closes her eyes,

"Come on you," Hannah says, shrugging. She cannot be worrying about Big Sarah's hurt feelings. She tugs my sleeve, so that I must follow her into the light. I must try to manage without my hood, perhaps if I walk looking down it will be alright. Joel and Miriam have moved away, at least I think they have, for I dare not look up to see.

"Is she happy?" I ask Hannah.

"The most I have ever seen her. She will come back to us tomorrow, as we are to move camp, very soon."

"Oh," I say, trying to stay calm out here under the sky, which is sure to be large and deep blue, hanging above me, pressing me down, worse than ever before. It's hard not to sink to the ground with the weight of it.

"Tomorrow, he is going off with his men, there is talk of the King being near."

I clutch her arm. She shakes me off.

"You mustn't be alarmed, Little One. You are so fearful. I wish you'd raise your head, just a little."

What she asks is too hard and I start to cry, because I am letting her down.

Chapter Forty-Seven
Told by Jani

I'm going back to see Rebekah. I have been to visit her two or three times since we arrived. It's near her time and she's scared. She's only managed to bring one child to full term, perhaps I can be of help. There is nothing I can do for Abigail. The others won't let me. They want me to sit and rest. They don't seem to understand, that working takes my mind off the pain.

"How are you?" I ask.

"Jani, is that you? How kind of you to come back. Is Miriam with you?"

I hear the rebuke in her voice, because Miriam has not come. I make some excuse.

"I am so hot today, I cannot get comfortable," she says. She is indeed hot and irritable. She is shifting her weight, first onto her elbow, then onto her hip.

"I've bought juniper berries. I thought I could soak them and bathe your head. It will make you feel less heavy."

"Nothing will make me feel less heavy. Oh, when is this baby going to come?"

Her women stand around the edge, on duty, anxious.

"Has Abigail come back yet?" she asks.

"No. What a good time they must be having."

Rebekah does not know how to react, she doesn't know me well enough, but one of her women giggles. I have spoken like Big Sarah. No, like my old self. I have nothing to prove to this woman.

"He is a fine man," Rebekah whispers. "She is very lucky, very blessed." Rebekah, too, is under the spell of David of Bethlehem. "Their children will be beautiful," she continues.

"They will be," I reply.

She catches the caution in my voice.

"Of course she's never had any children before, has she?"

"No," I say, feeling disloyal, but it is only the truth.

Rebekah lays her hand on her stomach.

"What about you?" she asks.

That regret is long since over and done with, for me.

"I never had any and now I am well past that part of my life. It has been a great sadness to me."

Her face clouds.

"They are more than a great deal of trouble, and I'm sure you have enough to do already." She groans and her belly grows taut. She frowns, but then says bitterly, "Don't worry Jani, this has been going on for days. The midwife says it will be at least another week. I hope the woman is right and that we will have moved and settled again, before it is my time."

There is a commotion outside. Heled is here, so I take my leave. She sees little enough of him, and I don't want to spoil their time together.

"Who was that?" I hear him ask.

"Oh, just that Jani woman. You know, Abigail's poor relative."

It was not said with malice.

I do not want to go back so soon to our tent, so I walk a little; besides it eases the muscles that always seem so tight. The men are watering the animals around the spring. I stay to watch, only they begin to talk of Abigail and David. Their language is coarse, their imagery vivid. Most of David's followers are, as Big Sarah predicted, just ordinary men.

The camp is pulling up its roots, loosening the things that bind it to the earth. I can feel it all around us and I long once again for my garden, for my trees and the sun spotted shade beneath them.

"Oh Lord, I am too old for all this," I groan. "I should never have come. There is nothing for me here, I am a burden, I'm back to being that poor relative, that Jani woman."

I hurry back to find Miriam and Little Sarah walking around the tent, working out what can be put away and what should be left out until the last minute. Little Sarah is pretending to listen, but she is really trying to stay away from the entrance, as if the sun will burn her. I want to sit down so I move my bed roll to the centre pole. If I sit just right, it is not too painful, although I shall never be able to doze for fear of slipping. I hear Big Sarah chuckling behind me, and I wave her away. She can be so annoying.

I wake much later to the murmuring of a camp after dark.

Abigail and Hannah are back. We are all together again. I hope they have saved me some food.

Chapter Forty-Eight
Told by Hannah

We ride at the centre of the women. It is his wish. Abigail is clearly favoured over Queen Ahinoam. I am sure that is trouble stored up for later. Ahinoam, the first wife, is dark, striking and defiant. It may have been a political marriage, but he visits her just the same. Abigail chooses not to see.

Big Sarah listens to the gossip about this princess, but we have decided that we will keep such things to ourselves, that we will not share it with our mistress. I am worried about what we've heard, about Ahinoam's strange beauty and her fierce temper. Her ways are not our ways, although all that is said about her, cannot be true. We know how gossip runs and twists and becomes an animal of its own making, based on the tiniest of glimpses. What is certain, is that she is no friend of ours.

I hope Jani is alright. We are moving fast and there is little time for resting or stretching. She rides mute, tight lipped and pale beside her mistress. Big Sarah fusses around her until Jani begs her to leave her be. It is grim watching her suffer, none of my herbs are strong enough.

We have seen nothing of David since we broke camp. The women and children are heading south; if we go much further we will leave Judea behind. Despite my worries, I smile. Miriam has always wanted to travel but even she couldn't have imagined this. She is riding up ahead, she wants to see everything. I only hope that she skirted around Ahinoam's entourage, as she is already well known among the women. They are sure to notice her roaming free and if it is commented on, Abigail might feel the need to clip her wings.

The dust hangs like a cloud above us and although we are honoured, here in the middle of all that he commands, I am sure it is the hardest place to breathe.

As if Abigail has read my mind, she twists around and says, "Hannah, fetch Miriam." Then she swallows and runs her tongue around dry lips.

"She has ridden on ahead," I reply.

"She won't have gone far. I want to talk to her."

I kick my little donkey forward into a trot. David never returned them to Nabal's cousin, so we each have one to ride. I move through the households. I cannot see Miriam anywhere.

I look back at the company as it stretches into the distance. David's six hundred are with him. There are at least that number walking here and surely a great deal more spread out across the plain. We would be an easy target for the King, but I have heard he has gone back to his palace. If that is so, why are we still fleeing with such haste from our homeland?

At last, I see her. She is riding alongside Heled's servant, Gabriel, mounted on a small horse of all things, a present from Joel. She was beside herself with joy at such a gift and is even trying to think up a name for the beast. As I approach her, spurring my donkey on very much against its will, I can see that she is speaking animatedly, her hands flashing about her. I must caution less enthusiasm, though it would be like telling a cock not to crow. Heled may be preoccupied with David's business and his baby's imminent arrival but anyone can see that Miriam is well beyond her childhood and should be back with the women. Gabriel sees me and he touches Miriam's sleeve. The movement is both intimate and discreet.

As we ride back, I say as gently as I can, "Take care, my love."

"What of?" she asks.

"He is just a servant."

"Oh no, Hannah, he is much more than that." Her face is glowing. "He has ridden into battle alongside Heled. He even stands next to him when he speaks with David." She turns her head away from my gaze and whispers, "No, Hannah, he is so much more than just a servant."

I must get Big Sarah to speak to her; Miriam listens to her and Big Sarah will put her on her guard. Perhaps she is disappointed that I cannot perceive what she sees in this man, but I will not reassure her with false hope. I know too well where that road leads.

Abigail is waiting impatiently for us to return to our place in the dust.

"Miriam, what is happening up ahead? Is there any news about where we are going?" she asks.

"David is seeking the protection of Achish, King of Gath."

Miriam has heard this from Joel or perhaps Gabriel. I watch Abigail carefully. She is thoughtful, her face full of questions.

"Will he welcome so large a family and for how long I wonder?" she says to no one in particular.

"I don't think David would lead us into danger and Joel says"—here Miriam lowers her voice—"that David does not trust King Saul. He is sure he will come after us again and that is why we must flee so far from home."

Abigail pales.

"How can King Saul hate David? He must be a very stupid man not to want David as an ally."

Miriam and I look around us. Even Abigail should be careful what she says about King Saul. David will have nothing said against our anointed King, even though we run from him and our dust is the dust of injustice.

"David is too honourable," Abigail continues. "In truth, I think he should be king."

"Abigail, my lady," I say, frightened at her boldness, "please do not speak of such things."

"Don't worry Hannah, love has not scattered my wits entirely. It is only to you I speak."

Miriam and I exchange glances.

When I look back, I wonder how far we have come today. We are further than ever from Carmel. I wonder if he thinks of me and I wonder what changes the new master has wrought on our old home.

I hear Jani groan. She is sitting hunched over her animal, taking the weight of her aching back on her arms. She is in agony, my herbs are no good, I must find some other way of helping her.

A bubble of bile rises from my empty stomach, as I understand that I will never be able to leave them. I look across at Miriam, and then at Jani. I think of Big Sarah and Little Sarah, hazy in the dust and I wonder that I can love out of such disappointment, such resentment, and yet I do. The sum of these women perhaps outweighs the weight of his fingertips on mine.

In the end I take a skin of wine to Jani. It is old and musty but strong. It might be enough to get her through the next few hours. It surely can't be that long now, before we stop for the night.

Chapter Forty-Nine
Told by Miriam

I sit by the fire prodding the dust with a stick. The sky is dark purple with clouds stretched like lace, the moon thin. Rebekah is birthing the child and Joel, and I are waiting. Heled has been sent for, but he has not yet come. He is a sensible man. I would be anywhere else in the world but here. My nerves are tight, my temper short. We can hear her groaning and crying and I am afraid for her. It has been going on too long, I think, for a happy outcome. There have been many children born at the camp and it is always noisy. The men and women standing around me smile, only their eyes are full of flames, and I want to run away.

She screams again. I stand quickly and walk off into the dimness, searching for somewhere to hide. It is childish and I am ashamed, but then Rebekah did not ask me to go and be with her. I don't know why that should cut me so deeply. It seems I still want her regard, without any sisterly affection on my part. Her cries are getting weaker, and yet they still make me squeeze my eyes shut. At my age, most women should be well used to such things but for some reason my life has skirted around the birthing tent. I move as far as I can from the light of the fire.

I find some bushes. David has sentries posted, but I cannot see them. I stamp my feet to scare off the snakes and then squat down in the darkness. When I am done, I straighten my clothing. She screams again and I turn my back to it. A breeze blows gently into my face. I try to relax in this dark beauty, try to feel God's peace as her cries tear the night.

"Miriam."

"I am here."

"I was afraid for you, out here in the dark."

He should not have come, and yet I am glad. He is not so tall as Heled and stockier than Joel. If we are caught, he will be whipped, and I will be disgraced.

"Miriam," he says, and he catches my hand and holds it to his cheek.

My throat closes and I swallow hard. I am so weak when I need to be strong. I lean towards him just a little and he wraps his arms around me. I feel his lips on my hair.

"I must speak to Abigail," I whisper.

"It will not do any good, except to bring our separation. Please don't say anything."

I lift my face to his. He steps back. He is miserable, his hands are shaking.

"Go back, please go back," he growls.

His agony is clear, and I know that I could ease it, if he would only let me. I turn away, but I'm not sure in which direction I should go. The night is so dark now, I wonder that I did not notice the moon dipping below the clouds. I peer about until I see a smudge of red that must be the fire. I have walked further than was wise and as I begin to make my way back I realise I have not heard Rebekah's cries for some time.

Chapter Fifty
Told by Jani

I want to die. Every muscle aches, every step is agony. Big Sarah rides alongside me, chattering away like some deranged crone.

"Shut up, Big Sarah. Leave me to my misery," I say, unkindly, "I can't bear your pity."

She stops talking but refuses to go.

Rebekah has had a little boy, another Heled to stride about the world. She is well, but weak and is carried in a litter. She lost a lot of blood and for a while they worried she would not come through. I cannot imagine how she feels now, stretched and sore. Miriam says she is triumphant, for it is a precious son.

My bones pull against my muscles as if trying to burst through my skin. At least her discomfort is tempered with joy. I do not know when my misery will end.

Heled comes to ride beside us. I try to listen to him, but I am finding it hard to concentrate.

Big Sarah says, "Don't worry, Jani. I'm sure tomorrow will be easier for you."

I cling to her words, even though they are worthless. There are three or four more days to go, at least that is the rumour. I do not think I will get any relief until we stop. I pray that King Achish will not send us away or invite us to go much further into his kingdom. I want to get off this donkey and its nasty, bony back. As the Lord lives, I will not moan and wail ever again, if he will just end our journey.

"Jani," Heled calls to me, as he nudges his beast over to me. His horse is tall, and I must stretch to look up at him. "Are you not delighted at our news?"

At least he has remembered my name.

"I am, my Lord."

"Will you not go back and see him? He screams for milk, as if he were months old already."

"I'm not sure I would be such good company."

He frowns and I am forced to continue.

"I am not comfortable on a donkey. And if you hadn't noticed, I am not as young as I used to be."

I have snapped at him like some old harridan. He simply laughs and my thoughts turn dark.

"Talk to Miriam," he says. "She cried all day when we first travelled to Abigail." He claps his hands and Gabriel rides up beside us. "Gabriel, can you not find this dear lady something to help her soreness, as you did for Miriam."

Gabriel grimaces, as if it is a bad memory. When he returns, Big Sarah and I stop. He asks me to sit up a little and tucks a cushion under my back. It tips me forward.

"Relax, if you can," he says.

"It's impossible," I cry, but I try anyway.

He looks at me, remembering someone else and says, "It's the best I can do."

It does feel more comfortable.

"You will ache again soon, only it will be a different set of muscles."

Big Sarah leans over to speak to him; it is too good an opportunity to waste.

"Be careful, friend," she says, her voice soft, "your misery is plain to see."

He stares at the ground, then mutters, "I am careful that Heled does not notice."

"Yes, but Rebekah is surrounded by women with little to do except gossip."

"I will heed your warning," he says. "I have thought much about it since the master's baby was born. Would your mistress speak on our behalf? Heled would listen to her."

"She might," Big Sarah replies, "but not at the moment. David fills her thoughts from horizon to horizon, and she has no space left for the likes of us."

"But if you leave it much longer, you may not have a choice," I say. They both turn to look at me. "Surely the men around Heled and Joel cannot have missed the fact that Miriam is more than ready for marriage and is turning into a very beautiful girl."

Big Sarah sucks in a lungful of air.

"Gabriel, have you heard anything?" she asks.

"Heled has a friend, one of the thirty, Ira son of Ikkesh. He is a good man and recently widowed. He and Heled spoke of her."

"Is anything set?" I ask.

"No, it was just an opening, but she is so lovely, he will not be the only one to enquire."

His heart is breaking, with the knowledge of what he speaks. He turns away abruptly. I stretch, the pain is a little better, at least for me.

"Come," says Big Sarah, "let's get back to the others. I am worried about Miriam."

"Yes, she will have crept ahead again on that silly horse of hers," I reply, "And will stand out like a sore thumb. Joel is a stupid boy to have given her a present like that, not even Abigail has such an animal. We must fetch her back. Dear Big Sarah, tell her I need someone to talk to, someone to distract me. We must keep that lovely face of hers out of the light."

Big Sarah nods and rides forward to find her. I'm not quite sure where the others are. I peer up and down the column for a long time, until I recognise our people. I ride through the clouds of dust to them. Hannah and Little Sarah are plodding behind Abigail. There is a ring of David's servants around them. He is taking no chances. Miriam and Big Sarah soon join us. I can see that Big Sarah has told Miriam all that passed between us, for she has pulled down her veil and is riding with her head bowed low.

"Jani," Miriam asks, "do you really want distracting from your aches?"

"No child."

"Do you want me to talk at all?"

"No child."

"Do you think anything I do will make a difference to my love?"

"I hope so," I say, but a truer answer would be, "No child."

Chapter Fifty-One
Told by Little Sarah

We are come at last to rest. The King of Gath has given us the town of Ziklag. It is not beautiful or large but there are a number of good wells and streets filled with buildings that have solid floors and doors, although ours will need scrubbing out. We are near David at the top of the hill. We have a bedchamber for Abigail and another room for the rest of us, which has a fire that bleeds smoke into our eyes. It is bigger than Ahinoam's residence and closer to our master. From the roof we can see the plain spreading away to the North. I don't go up onto the roof, unless I have to. The sky is still too big and heavy.

Abigail's clothes are in a dreadful state. They are full of grit and some of the embroidery is curling. It all needs pressing. Big Sarah and Jani are supposed to be helping me, but Big Sarah keeps losing concentration and Jani takes every opportunity to go and see Rebekah. I don't really understand why, she does not particularly like Miriam's sister, although she does seem to have grown fond of the children. She brings Chloe to see us whenever she can, she thinks that now the precious boy has been born, she is less loved and cherished. Miriam stays inside almost as much as I do but loves to see her little niece. They often go up on the roof to play.

I do all the work.

There is a small alcove to sleep in. They have fixed me a curtain that only stirs if the wind is from the south, although I may sew some weights along the bottom to keep it secure. Jani says it is little more than a cupboard, but I do not mind, it suits me well. Miriam thinks she would not be able to breathe in it, for there is no window. What she does not understand, is that it's the only place I can breathe.

I am worried about Abigail. She has begun to show but she is sick most days and I do not think she is gaining weight as she should.

There are little spots of dirt, wood and sand from around the fire even though I swept the floor this morning. I reach for the broom and begin again. I won't mention my fears about Abigail; it will only be more worry for everyone to carry.

Chapter Fifty-Two
Told by Hannah

David lies with his head in her lap. She is sitting hunched over him, her leg bent awkwardly underneath her. It is clearly uncomfortable, but Abigail will not move unless he wishes it. He talks of leading his men out from Ziklag, to ride away some of their frustrations at being here for so long. He does not know what else to do, for his beloved brothers are used to roaming free and there is muttered unrest amongst them at this prolonged confinement. He hopes that such an expedition, a raid on the Amalekites will bring some wealth and food into the town, that it will lift their spirits.

He speaks all this into Abigail's heart, all his thoughts, around and around. I do not think he is being kind. She listens intently to every word and when he is gone, she broods on what he has talked of, worrying for him, worrying about him, worrying that what she has replied in turn, did not help him.

She strokes his cheek. He brushes her hand away. She tries to speak. He places a finger on her lips. He kisses her gently and gets up. Big Sarah is in the outer room, she was not expecting him to leave so soon and must step aside for him, remembering at the last moment to bow low. She watches him cross to the house of Ahinoam. He does not stay there long either, but it is long enough. Tonight, Abigail was not what he needed, and our mistress feels it as an open wound.

"Sarah!"

"Yes, Mistress."

"I have told you to stay out of sight when he is here." Her voice is raised, fraught with anger and frustration.

I'm not sure where she expects Big Sarah to go.

"I'm sorry, I did not think he would leave so soon."

Abigail clenches her fists. She thinks Big Sarah is criticising her. Through gritted teeth she says, "If you cannot obey my orders, then you had better leave."

I never thought I would pity Abigail, but she is suffused with insecurity and jealousy. They constantly war within her. Today Big Sarah is standing in the way. Yesterday, it was me. Big Sarah sinks to the floor, dropping into a squat, to rest against the far wall, her head tipped back. Abigail returns to her bed. I sit near the door, waiting until I am needed.

Little Sarah creeps from her alcove. She scurried away at the first sound of David and would not venture out while Abigail was shouting her displeasure. Miriam beckons her over. Little Sarah tiptoes across, to avoid waking Jani, who is snoring in her corner. Tonight we are all together, but Abigail's unhappiness sits in the middle of us like an angry swarm of bees. We are cast down, each of us weighted with her sorrow.

I get up and move to the fire. There is wine and I warm it. Big Sarah comes and stirs the pot as I drop in cinnamon and just a little shaved cedar. The smell fills the room, fills the dark spaces between the lamps. Jani ripples and snorts in her sleep and we laugh. It is a small thing, and although quiet, it wakes her too.

Big Sarah makes her as comfortable as she can, with extra cushions, and a blanket. She is not such an old woman that there should be these lines and shadows about her eyes. Her movements should not be accompanied by such pain and stiffness. She sleeps when she can, and I try to dull the aches with barley and castor oil compresses. They don't seem to do any good. We must get a doctor to see her, for what ails her is beyond me.

I have been staring at Jani, and she has read my thoughts. She shakes her head, even though the movement hurts her. I look towards Big Sarah as she stirs and sniffs, until her hooded eyes meet mine. From her I gather strength. We all do.

Little Sarah is still sitting by Miriam. She scarcely ventures out at all, and her limbs have become weak and thin. She needs sunlight, yet she shuns it and works hard all day on things that do not need doing. I worry for her, too. When David comes, she scampers to her bed and will not come out. Abigail sees it and chooses to remain silent, about what she cannot change. Little Sarah will not, cannot listen to reason, it is beyond her. It is beyond us all.

We have begun to settle in our sun grazed town and I had hoped that with peace and four solid walls Little Sarah would begin to come back to us. But I fear she has travelled too far. Indeed, it seems she is hiding away more than ever.

None of us can escape. We are here because David is here. A troubled man who is waiting, lost between two worlds. There are too many of us beholden to his fate; the town is beginning to feel small, and too far away from our homeland. I pray that God will speak to David soon, that there will be some relief.

Little Sarah gets up and starts to brush the floor. Miriam rises and takes the broom from her hand.

"It's late, Little One," she says. "You should rest, and you don't want to disturb Abigail."

She looks as if she might argue with Miriam, then drops down beside Jani. Jani strokes her hair and eventually Little Sarah's fingers stop drumming the floor.

"I think you should speak to Joel," Big Sarah says, turning to Miriam. That makes us jump. She has obviously been brooding on this thought for a while. Her voice is too loud. Miriam looks scared, she does not want Abigail to hear us. Big Sarah continues, "Your brother loves you. After all, he gave you that silly horse. It is a gift of great value."

"It will make things too difficult for him," Miriam replies, looking over her shoulder at Abigail's door.

"Why?" I ask.

"Because," Big Sarah replies, smiling, "she thinks her brother would have difficulty lying for her or understanding that his little sister has fallen in love. And I suppose the horse may have been the perfect gift, to get her noticed in the first place."

We hadn't thought of that before. Now it seems obvious.

"Miriam, dear," Jani says, "Joel is not stupid, and he might be able to give us warning or even put off the day when some man enquires after you."

Joel will not collaborate with us in this. He is looking for a good match for his sister.

"I don't think I can talk to him of such things. It's not my place and anyway, you know he is hoping to marry Talmai's daughter. His head is far too full of her to think of me. He's hardly been to see us in days."

It is a good match for him and it's true that we have seen very little of him of late. Little Sarah, who might have cared a long time ago, does not seem to have heard her.

"Ask him to come and visit. As long as Abigail is busy we can talk to him for you," Big Sarah suggests.

She's right, in that Miriam is not good at reading Joel, whereas to us he is open, transparent as water. But we do not have a hope of persuading him to argue Gabriel's case. There are too many young men who follow David, who are brave and strong and in need of a dowry.

I think of Matthias. I allow myself a few moments. The others are watching me. What does it matter? They understand it is but a dream. I've lost him, I know that, for I cannot leave Abigail, and I was a fool to think I ever could.

Chapter Fifty-Three
Told by Big Sarah

Abigail calls me, and when I have scraped the sleep from my eyes I realise it is not long after the second watch of the night. It is the first time I have heard my name on her lips for many days. I irritate her, I know I do. Always in the way; I must always be stepped over or around. I wish I were more like Hannah, who seems able to disappear into the walls.

As I cross the room, I see the glint of Hannah's eyes watching me, for she too will have been woken by her mistress's call. I think the others are asleep, although Jani is restless, as usual.

Abigail's stomach is round and her breasts plump. She is unused to the weight of them and lies awkwardly, her brow damp, her hair curling darkly around her face and even though the shutters are open, the room is stuffy and hot. There is no breeze, even here at the top of the town, in this airless, desert summer.

"Sarah, I cannot sleep."

I stand crookedly as if that might make me smaller and then I squat down with my back against the door. She does not react; her thoughts are already far away. David came to see her tonight for he is riding out again tomorrow. It is the third raid. Each time the men come back laden with riches; animals, food, and wine. Abigail herself wears a bracelet of fine gilt, with polished opals, and our rooms are full of golden beauty. Yet I think she would exchange it all in a second, to know that he was safe, that he would remain here peacefully with his people, with her and her unborn child.

The time they spend together is never quite enough. Abigail is jealous of every moment, and we keep from her any talk of his visits to Ahinoam. If she finds out David has been there, she vents her anger on us. As if there was anything we could have done to stop him. Or, worse still, that she could have done something more; that she is not enough.

He loves our Abigail and wants her baby born, a son of course, but there is talk in the taverns that it might not be his, that she was Nabal's wife not that long ago. The rumours anger him, and I know that Abigail's neck is stiff from walking with deaf ears and a tight jaw. I am sure that it is the Princess who is behind such talk. She is his first wife here and I do not think she is given enough precedence. She lashes out with whatever is to hand and although such rumours about the child are just malicious gossip, it rubs us raw all the same.

David is sure that God wants to bless him through this child. Abigail wants to give him a boy, one born out of their remarkable love. I would have it over and done with. I would have it born a girl. Why not?

"Oh, Sarah, my head aches."

I get up and trim the lamp, even though the light is already shaded. She watches me and I feel her impatience. She is desperate to release the words that tumble about in her head. I need do nothing but wait.

"Last time he went away, he raided the Philistines, before that the Amalekites."

"Yes, Mistress."

"But he has told King Achish that he is going into Judea and is attacking our own people."

I had wondered how David explained to our patron what he was doing. David is playing a dangerous game, as both the Amalekites and the Philistines are at peace with King Achish.

"How is he covering his tracks?" I ask.

Abigail shudders and presses her fists to her eyes.

"Sarah, he kills everyone. No one is spared."

So that no one is left to tell who has raided them. She is bewildered by the blood. I am not.

"Abigail, he is a warrior, how else can he feed us? Would you have him steal from his own people, from our own kin?"

"No, but why must he kill everyone? It seems too high a price to pay for secrecy."

She is weak. That's what I think. She reads my face and turns away from my sullen looks. I cannot help myself. I should wear a veil, to keep such thoughts hidden.

"It is my little one," she says. "He makes me want all those I love, to live safely."

When has that ever been our lot? She will not catch my eye. I wait, watching the lamp sputter as the oil starts to run dry. After a while, she whispers what is deep down, under her heart, where all our deepest fears lie.

"Surely, when King Achish finds out what David is doing, he will come and kill us."

"David is clever. You must trust him."

She lies back, her hands resting on her stomach.

"To put a sword across a woman's throat is a terrible thing."

"He is keeping safe those he loves."

She does not hear me.

"What will happen to us," she cries. She drops her head into her hands so that I barely hear what she says next. "David is so restless, so unhappy. He talks constantly of the time when he lived at the palace, with the King's son. He misses him so much. I cannot be enough to fill that kind of emptiness, that longing. And despite all that King Saul has done to hurt him, David still loves the King, although I do not understand how."

She is not speaking the complete truth. It is too painful for her. She is thinking of Michal, David's very first wife, the King's own daughter. She was given to David and then taken away from him; a petty gesture of revenge, which seems to have ravaged David's heart.

"I would have killed myself," she says, striking the floor with her fist, "before I let them separate us."

"I wonder," I whisper to myself.

We sit in silence. The lamp dies. The room is dim, not dark. Dawn must be near.

"I am loved. It is all I have ever longed for," she says, her voice trembling with the weight of the words, "and yet his love is so fierce, so passionate. I'm a little frightened. I need this baby; I need a son."

"He will be of fair countenance like his father." It pains me to say it, as I am not charmed by him, as the others are. "Or she will be beautiful like her mother,"

"I do not want a daughter."

"Please don't say that."

"What will she have to look forward to?" Abigail spits. "She will be like Ahinoam, married for an alliance, no matter how lovely she is. Miriam is the same. She is beautiful and clever but let's hope she never falls in love, unless it is with her husband to be."

I stare at the floor.

"No, Sarah, what has Miriam done? Didn't you or Hannah warn her?"

"It wasn't our place to destroy such hope."

"Then whose was it, if not yours, you who see everything so clearly? You should have seen it coming and stopped it."

I remain silent. I am hurt by her disappointment in me, and I am wondering if she is right. Perhaps, I could have done more to prevent Miriam from falling in love. Indeed, did I not light the spark myself all those months ago?

"You think I should have noticed, don't you?" Abigail says, almost choking over the words. "Why do you always have to condemn me?"

I am startled.

"Sarah," she says, "are you angry because I had the courage to pursue love?"

"I am not," I say. Of course, I am lying, and I am sure that she knows it. I hate their love and where it leads us. The darkness comes and I cannot escape. It catches me and pinions my arms to the wall, my legs to the floor. There is a roaring in my ears, dragging me down. Every breath is terrifying, because when I am held in this place, I can't see her anymore.

I'm not sure how long I am away and when I am aware of the

room once again, Abigail is standing awkwardly over me. Behind her, the rising sun is washing the wall with a blood red glow. We stare at each other.

"Are you alright?" she asks.

I nod and then I speak rashly, for I know that she is about to dismiss me, and I may not get called again, for days.

"Please Mistress, about Miriam. Isn't there anything we can do to help her?"

"Who has she given her heart to?"

I know it's hopeless before I have finished saying the words.

Abigail begins to laugh. She laughs until she cries. I do not think she is being cruel, she is simply seeing more clearly than any of us. When she stops to wipe away the tears she says, "You must talk to her today. She is destined to marry one of the thirty. David himself has decreed it."

I am just a woman who looked after goats. What do I know of anything?

Chapter Fifty-Four
Told by Hannah

At last Abigail can feel the baby kicking, it has given her a new heart. After I help her dress, she comes out of her room and stands looking at each of us in turn. Miriam is sitting by the fire, her face pink, her eyes red and sore. Abigail walks over to her and takes her face in her hands.

"Bathe your eyes, you are going to walk with me. You too, Hannah." She looks for Jani, but she has already gone to Rebekah's, slipping out when we were busy, shaking and brushing the morning to rights. Little Sarah has our cloaks ready. Her hand trembles as she passes them to us, for she is worried that Abigail will insist that she comes too. Miriam's eyes are swollen but she is not a girl used to weeping and I do not think she will let her sorrow overwhelm her.

Abigail does not command Big Sarah. Theirs is a strange relationship, which I cannot fathom. Big Sarah will come or not of her own choosing, although today she also seems to be a little different. Perhaps Abigail's mood is affecting us more than we can resist.

Big Sarah was praying when I woke this morning, her face wreathed in smiles and yet she has refused to speak one syllable since. She is unsettled and has not finished any of her chores. It cannot be her usual darkness; there is too much of a spring in her step and a glint in her eye.

I would so miss her if she left us. Since Nabal, she has stood beside me, helping me run our small household and now that Miriam's heart is broken, she is the only one of my sisters who can make me smile.

We step into the sunshine and walk down through the town to the outer walls. We cannot venture beyond them, it isn't safe. Many of the women watch us pass. All are looking at Abigail, trying to gauge the size of the child. Abigail is well covered and gives nothing away. We head for the lowest level where the street is paved and there are olive trees growing through the stones. They make dappled shade that is a little cooler. It is a good place to pass the time, still better in the evening when a breeze blows in through the gate.

Big Sarah has decided to come with us. We walk together behind our mistress, she is still annoyingly silent. I wonder at my friend and steal sidelong glances at her strong profile.

Abigail is pleased to be out, pleased to be moving. She will be glad when this baby is in her arms and not clinging to her spine, when it is no longer stretching and pulling her, this way and that. I wonder what it must be like to have something so precious so close but that is a thought which must be chained and silenced. I will not allow it to fly free, not on such a lovely day. Big Sarah catches hold of my hand, raises it to her lips and kisses it. I turn and frown at her. She drops my hand and smiles at something just off to my right and then makes a most peculiar hopping step, as if she wants to run and jump like a child. I stare at her quite bewildered. She is exasperating. I sigh, what more can I do?

The town is not large and before long we have passed the main gate twice. There are two watchtowers and a guard room. David is making them bigger, reinforcing the walls either side. It makes me sad, he must think we are here to stay. We pick our way past scaffolding and the clatter of masons. The gates themselves lie amongst a nest of carpenters who are patching them with precious wood from the north. The noise beats against our ears and I cannot believe the men are safe, balanced precariously above us, chipping and levering such huge stones. I stare up as we walk through the chaos around our feet and I do not notice, until we are well past, that the guards are gathered around a stranger. Gossip spreads rapidly in Ziklag. Jani, up at Rebekah's house, will know who he is almost as quickly as we do in this closed, crowded place.

"We had better go back," Abigail says. She is worried it may be news of David.

A woman from the house of Heled hurries over to us. She is puffing with self-importance and barely dips her head to Abigail.

"There is a man. He has come a long way. He is looking for you, Mistress."

"Then bring him here at once. He may have news of my husband."

"No, he does not have news of David. He comes from Carmel," the woman says, barely concealing a smirk.

I do not wait for Abigail to let me go. I don't even think to ask as I run into the gathering crowd. He might bring news of Matthias, or he may simply have come to get the donkeys back. I don't care. Perhaps, I will know him, and I want to hear the news first, without having to keep my face calm and empty, in front of the others.

The sentries surround him, the crowd also leans in. It is precious news from home; everyone wants to hear it. They know me as Abigail's handmaiden and part to let me through. I am breathing hard. I am not as dignified as I ought to be.

He carries a bag over his shoulder, a skin of water and a cloak wrapped around his waist. His face is dark with dust and his beard long. I cannot believe that it is him and for a moment I can only stare at him, then I am in his arms. We cling together until I remember that we stand in a circle of strangers. I feel like a girl of twelve again and remember a similar feeling from a long time ago, when I stepped into the light on the edge of a different courtyard.

"Matthias, you must come to Abigail," I say, drawing him away from the smiles and nudges.

He held me. It was the first time, and I know only a soaring hope. Surely, he has come for me. It is of course beyond foolishness, yet I am unable to stop my heart from running ahead, with such joy.

Chapter Fifty-Five
Told by Jani

Rebekah is still a little plump from her last child and hardly does more than raise a hand to me, but she has her questions ready, only waiting a brief moment for me to find my favourite chair.

"Jani, how is Abigail? She must be getting close now?"

It's what all the women want to know. The rumour, that it is Nabal's child, is dying as Abigail's pregnancy continues. Those with a practised eye, count back an impossible number of weeks.

"She is ready, only she worries about David," I say, settling myself. This seat is low and is surprisingly comfortable so I am able to relax a little.

"I used to worry about Heled, too, when I was about due. It's a difficult time. How long do you think it will be?"

"Two, three weeks. No more. And how are your little ones, Chloe and Heled? I heard there was fever in the town, are they alright?"

"They are both well, Jani. You are so kind to ask after them. But you are looking pale. How are your bones?"

Today I feel stiff and bruised and I ache, which is better than yesterday, when I longed to die.

"I am well," I say. "Much better than of late."

She looks relieved and my heart softens a little towards her.

"Is Heled with David?" I ask.

"Of course," she says, although there is something in her expression that makes me sit up a little.

"Bring us the last of the wine from Jerusalem, I am thirsty," she calls.

We sit and wait for the servant, who brings two gold goblets. They are Egyptian and very heavy.

"Leave us now," Rebekah commands and I wonder where the girl will go. This house is much smaller than Abigail's and is crowded with children and servants.

"These are very beautiful."

"Yes," says Rebekah. "Anyone can see that these did not come from a Judean village. It's obvious David is raiding the people of Amalek."

I'm disappointed, I had thought I was going to be able to take back something more interesting than this old news.

"The thing is," she continues, "I don't think that is where they've gone this time. Heled was worried. He's not sure what David is up to."

"What did he say, Rebekah?"

"He said that they were going into battle alongside King Achish and that can only mean one thing. David intends to fight King Saul."

I am impressed that she has worked that out, but she must see by my face that I don't believe it. David would never fight against his own king, against his own people. I pretend to be in pain. I often get spasms that leave me breathless. It will cover my look. She bends forward in concern.

"Rebekah," I say, gasping a little, "this is grave news indeed."

"I suppose it means that we will never be able to go home again."

"Unless they triumph," I say, but I will need to talk to Miriam or Big Sarah to know whether such a thing is possible. "Surely, if David rides with the Philistines then..." but I'm not sure how to finish that sentence either.

Rebekah says, "Would they trust him to fight? If I were Achish, I'd be worried that David might turn on me halfway through the battle."

"I think that's only because we know that he has not been raiding Judean villages these past months, that he has been raiding Achish's allies. I think King Achish still thinks that David is going to stay in Ziklag for good, that he's loyal to him now."

"Oh Jani, I want to go home," and to my surprise she begins to cry. "Mother grows frailer, and I want to bury her by my father or at least in our own soil. Here we are strangers and will be forever."

She's right. And I realise that every day we live with this great sadness. It sits so close to us, that we no longer see it or acknowledge it, but it is in all of us, colouring our days and nights.

I do not feel like gossiping anymore and my bones have begun to burn. I rise to go, carefully weighting each leg before I take the first steps, hoping the stiffness will wear off and that my back will ease.

"Call for me, if you want anything," I say.

"You too," she replies, and I think she means it.

As I climb back up to our house, there is a strange buzz about the streets that I can't help but notice, even though my pain is beginning to surge and roar. I hurry, as best I can, in case the others need me.

Chapter Fifty-Six
Told by Hannah

Big Sarah danced around us the day he came, she said that she had known that something good was going to happen but had dared not speak of it, had dared not speak at all, in case God changed his mind. Matthias was surprised to see her swaying and stamping to music no one else could hear but we only laughed. We are all so changed, he is not sure how to be. I suppose, I am changed the most, although he says not.

"I didn't know it was Matthias," Big Sarah sang, as she swooped and swirled, jumping in to pinch his arm. "All I could see was a great happiness following you around, like a cloud of finches." She twirled around and around, her skirts flying and her arms outstretched. She only stopped when she became dizzy and knocked over a basket of figs. Abigail welcomed him gravely and walked us home as quickly as she was able, wanting our celebrations to be held behind closed doors.

Big Sarah still hugs me when I pass too close, as if in my happiness she has found some peace of her own.

Matthias left his new master because he was cruel and mean, a different sort of cruel and mean from Nabal. It takes him a long time to tell me all that happened, so many quiet hours sitting together in front of the fire and sometimes I am so happy, I do not follow what he is saying, so he has to start again.

Nabal's house became careful, the food and drink dull and ordinary. The shepherds, on whom the wealth was built, were less respectful, for the man was small and afraid of them. He used his own stewards to do business, and Matthias knew they were less than honest. The shepherds took advantage of that. Profits began to dip.

"Nabal always commanded respect, despite being feared. It is a fine line between the two," Matthias said. "The new master lost both, quite early on."

Jani's beautiful garden had become a place of vegetables and when Matthias walked through the yard, he missed the early morning fragrance of the flowers. It reminded him constantly of those who had left him and made him long to follow.

He waited for news. He questioned every merchant caravan that came near and was frustrated for many months. It was a sign of the times that it took him so long to find out where David had gone, many of the travellers hiding the truth. When at last there was a rumour that we had settled in Ziklag, he packed a pouch with oatcakes and a skin of wine and set out to find us.

"It felt more like a travelling to, than a leaving of my old life," he said, curling his fingers over mine. "That I was going away to find what I had lost, when Nabal died. I had nothing to stay for, nothing at all. I was not owned by the new master, and he didn't trust me. I was useful in the first few weeks but after that he couldn't find enough for me to do."

He lifts my hand to his lips, and I shiver with delight. We sit our arms touching but I don't care. Big Sarah calls me wanton, only she spoils it by laughing. I do not know what Abigail thinks. She always trusted Matthias, respected him, although she was very angry with me when I ran to the gate. All those people watching, wondering what her strange household would do next. They were not disappointed when I flung myself into his arms. Still, she is glad to add a man to our numbers and such a man. She cannot regret his coming, only the welcome, that I gave him.

Abigail was also surprised by our love; she did not know. I thought she knew everything. When I explained how long it had been, she looked dismayed, a shadow passing behind her eyes. Perhaps, she remembered when we left Nabal's house, how her heart had soared, not aware of how mine was breaking. I'd like to think there was a pang of remorse, perhaps a little shame, but I'm not sure she would see it as such.

"I am happy for you both," she had said, smiling and nodding. "But you will have to wait until David returns." Abigail will do nothing without his permission. It is not such a hardship, for we are together. Sitting or standing, working or sleeping, I can see him and touch him whenever I choose.

Matthias is sure that Jani is very sick. And because of what he has said Abigail is trying to find someone to help her. None of my remedies have worked and I am afraid that I will hurt her if I try anything stronger. Matthias thinks it is some form of wasting disease, but I think it might simply be pain, bending her limbs this way and that. I have examined her and there is nothing to be seen on her skin, except a deep red weal where she has kneaded her back to try and get to the source of the hurt.

Little Sarah will not come out of her alcove when my beloved is here, even when Jani calls to her. It is as if she has forgotten him, but he is a patient, kind man and he perseveres. He talks to her as if she were in the room with us, always greeting her by name and saying goodbye to her when he leaves on his errands. One day even she will learn to trust him again. He takes such trouble over us, and whereas, before, we were unbalanced and stumbling, now we begin to stand firm and straight. Big Sarah says that is nonsense, that it is just that I am standing firmer and straighter. She is probably right.

This morning, he has gone down to the lower town to find goats' cheese, simply because Miriam said that she would like some.

"You look ten years younger," Big Sarah says to me, shaking out a blanket. She is looking for holes. It's a job I would normally do but one that she is more than capable of, if she is feeling patient enough.

"Do I?" I put my hands to my cheeks.

"You know you do," she says, poking a finger through a large tear. "How did I miss this one I wonder?"

"We all miss things that are in front of our eyes, dear Big Sarah," I say.

Big Sarah laughs, her head on one side. Her strong face is etched with lines, her dark eyes crinkled with seeing. I step close to her and put a hand to her cheek.

"Sister, it is so good to see you laugh."

"I'm sorry, Hannah. The last months have been hard for you but at least now you do not have to choose."

I look at her narrowly. She turns away, towards the light, she is pretending to thread her needle.

"Big Sarah, what you hadn't realised, what I never told you, was that I chose a long time ago."

"Really," she says, looking up.

I would love to tease her, as she teases me, but I cannot resist that open heart and I do so love to talk of the moment I saw him clearly.

"You have forgiven me, haven't you?" Big Sarah asks. We remember the time she slapped my face. I touch my cheek.

"Of course, almost as soon as it happened," I reply. "I was blind, you were only offering me happiness. I am grateful you risked our friendship so that I might see for myself, even if for a little while I didn't understand. It is you, who has helped Matthias and I get to this moment. No doubt about it."

She sits down on her stool, close to the door.

"I was not responsible for bringing him here, I didn't do anything," she says, frowning at the blanket on her knee.

"But if I hadn't let him know of my regard, would he have risked such a journey? That was entirely your doing. You must see how much we owe you, him and I?"

I am sure she is glad to hear such things, but she does not receive them well. She is happiest when she is teasing us, when she is making us laugh. She doesn't like it when we tell her how much we love and rely on her. She is difficult to please.

Jani is dozing and begins to stir. Big Sarah goes to her side to help her wake.

"Come on old woman," she says, "I have a list of jobs as long as my arm and you can help me."

Jani smiles wanly. She still likes to think that she can be of use. I go to the door, and pretend I am just taking the air. Of course, I am looking down the street for his return.

Chapter Fifty-Seven
Told by Little Sarah

I cannot breathe. Jani's weight is pinning me to the floor; her hand is across my mouth. Since the trumpet stopped blaring there were screams and shouts, screams that made me want to melt with fear. I ran to my bed, squeezing shut my eyes and pushing my fingers into my ears so hard I thought I might scrape those terrifying thoughts out of my head. I want night to come, for darkness to cover us, because even from beneath her I can see around the edge of the curtain. My eyes cannot shut out the light. I count heart beats. I count breaths. Jani stiffens. Someone has come into the room. They speak a language I do not understand. They are dragging things, smashing things. Sometimes they laugh, but it is a nervous-looking-back-over-your-shoulder sort of laugh. They are frightened.

The curtain is pulled back. A figure blocks the light and Jani becomes still.

"An old woman," he says, in our tongue.

"Kill her," says the voice from behind him.

Jani goes limp. She is ready to die for me. Under the cloak she clasps my hand and holds it tightly. The man stands a long time, so long that I wonder if he is still there. Perhaps the blood lust has drained away, perhaps Jani reminds him of his mother, perhaps she is not worth the effort of killing. He turns back to the room to help his companion drag the gold and jewels into the street. They do not come back. We lie together Jani and me. Eventually she rolls off, but we still sit tightly wrapped around one another, not daring to move. There are tendrils of smoke upon the breeze.

Night comes. I want to stretch only Jani will not let me, she clutches my arm tightly and places a finger on her lips. We wait through the night, until the stench of fire, damp with dew, clogs our nostrils. I think I may have slept a little. I am comfortable, curled up here in my little bed, leaning against Jani. I know she will not let anything happen to me, although I would like something to drink, something to fill my stomach.

At last, she whispers, "We should go and look for them." Her face is all scrunched up and she seems to sip the air through gritted teeth. "Or perhaps, we should stay here. Only what if they are hurt and need us," she continues, tears rolling down her cheeks.

I wonder who she is talking about. If anyone were hurt, Hannah and Big Sarah would deal with it, they do not need us. I pat Jani's hand, only she doesn't seem to notice.

Many breaths later, she says, "Little Sarah, I know they are gone or dead. There is no inbetween, for Big Sarah would have fought them and Hannah would die before she let anyone touch Abigail or..." she begins to choke, "our dear Miriam, our own beautiful girl."

Miriam is beautiful when she laughs. She sparkles and shines and does not mind the sunshine.

Jani sobs, over and over again, calling for Miriam, but so quietly,

I am sure that Miriam will not hear her. I sleep and wake to her crying.

Light crawls into the room. I crawl into the room. The others have not come back and there is so much mess. I am worried that I will not get it cleared up before Abigail returns. My knees are cut by the broken pottery. I stare at the blood. Even the sun has given up on us and the day is grey and heavy. We are cold in our shattered house. In the corner, a pitcher lies tipped but not broken, with a beaker of water unspoilt. I take it to Jani. Her lips are cracked, and she swallows a little. She does not open her eyes. I go to the door; there is no one about and I wonder if I dare go and see where the others are. I take a step, just one and then I cannot move. The sun begins to set, which is strange because it has only just risen. I turn to go back into the house and my head swims, the room tips and the ground moves.

***

I am lying on the floor, there are pins and needles in my arms and legs and the pain of it makes me cry, then I hear shouts and horses and wails, like a funeral. I want to get back to my alcove, back behind my curtain. I begin to rise but I am too late. My heart hammers in my chest, in my ears. They are here. I keep my eyes tightly shut. David is calling from outside, "Search everywhere!" His voice is hoarse, as if he has ridden a long way without water. I must crawl away and hide.

"Little Sarah!"

It is Joel. I cannot open my eyes or move but I hear Jani. She groans from behind my curtain and through clenched eyelids I see her stretching out a hand. Joel has heard her, too, he puts his dagger back in his belt and I see his eyes are bright with tears. He shouts for David to come. Jani cannot stand, so David drops to his knees and leans in close to her.

"Who were they?" he asks. Her lips move, only there is no sound. Our voices have been taken away.

"Water, now," he cries.

He can't be talking to me, so I wait curled up in the shadows, except that Joel grabs my hand and before I realise what is happening he is pulling me up. The light is harsh, the sky heavy, I cannot lift my head, and my neck aches with the weight of it. I do not know where Joel has got to. I do not know where I am, where the door to our house is. I drop down onto the stones and cover my head with my skirt. I am trembling. I begin to wretch, my stomach heaving and then I remember Big Sarah's voice telling me to speak out my fear. I do not know what to speak out, except that I long for the dim tightness of my bed, then I am lifted and carried by someone who is strong. It is not Big Sarah. I am set down near the door. I know it is our house, the air feels right. I begin to crawl towards my curtain; I need to open my eyes a little to avoid the shards on the floor. I see that David has put a pillow under Jani's head and with tenderness is dripping water onto her lips.

"Amalekites," she whispers, "I recognised their speech, although they tried to disguise it."

He looks at me and I am frozen here in the hard light of his gaze.

"Stay with her. Take care of her."

And they are gone.

I find bread, only Jani will not eat so I take up the broom, mercifully unbroken. What a terrible state the room is in and there is no one here but me to do anything. Abigail will want it tidy, swept clean before she comes back.

Chapter Fifty-Eight
Told by Jani

I can see light and dark. I cannot move. The pain is down in my depths now. I wonder that Hannah has not given me something to numb it, if only a little. Perhaps she has, and I have forgotten.

Sometimes I hear Little Sarah chatting to someone, while she sweeps dust into my eyes. My throat is parched, and I cannot swallow. My heart is hard in my chest, and it does not feel like there is enough space for anything else, beside its frantic beating. It is pushing everything else up against my skin and I wonder if I will split in half and spill across the floor.

Chapter Fifty-Nine
Told by Big Sarah

My arm throbs and I cannot bend my fingers. When I look at my hand it does not feel like it belongs to me. The bandage is grubby and tight, Hannah checks and cleans the wound, but she has none of her herbs to help with infection or pain. I must bear it.

Ahead of us are two days of misery, as we pick our way back to Ziklag, back to the place which causes us to shudder with fear and fills us with harsh memories. Images that make us jump and spin at every shout, even though we are safe now. The men look sheepish and then impatient in turn, as we try to slow our panicking hearts. We feel our mortality, like a shadow just out the corner of our eyes and I wonder if this is what David's six hundred feel all the time.

He and his men came to save us, screaming their rage and anger, vindicating themselves for having left us so poorly guarded. We were rich pickings, too tempting, when they went away to war. David trusted the patronage of his friend, King Achish. He trusted his own reputation. He has learned another hard lesson in the craft of war and sovereignty. Or rather, we have learned it for him.

Abigail never doubted. She believed that he would come for her. I doubted him and when we first heard the sounds of battle it did not occur to me that it was because he was fighting his way through to us. I listened and thought that there was an argument that had spilled over into a squabble. I imagined our captors grabbing some tunic and wrenching it apart. I wanted it to be a small inconsequential thing; I wanted our captors diminished and human. Only when the men around us began to turn back the way we had come, when they began to unsheathe their swords, began to clench their jaws white, I realised they had not travelled far enough. They had taken David's precious jewel, and he had come to retrieve it. They would have needed the wings of angels to escape his wrath.

They withstand the first onslaught out of sheer desperation, but strength and fury overwhelm them. They run, scattering before the six hundred, as we crowd together to protect our mistress.

Hannah holds me up, for the loss of blood makes me weak. Abigail kneels behind us, silent and tight.

We do not know where Miriam is, we haven't seen her since the marketplace. I hope she is dead.

David strides through the women, blood dripping from his sword, his face spattered and running with sweat. When he sees Abigail, he weeps. Ahinoam turns away in disgust. He is a man who is not afraid to show his heart, it does not seem to shame him as it would other men. We step back as he gathers Abigail tenderly into his cloak. He holds her for a long time, mouthing words of thanks to God, before carrying her to his horse. She rides with him, a place of singular honour, except for the blood she trails and the spasms of pain. Her precious son is draining out of her. I hear her saying, again and again, "It's not time."

That night it is time, but our baby prince comes too late, or too soon, one tiny breath. Abigail is weak and does not cry out, the loss has left her speechless and bewildered. Ahinoam does not smile but watches with satisfaction. I bury him under a little cairn of stones, and I worry that Abigail will soon join him. Hannah and Matthias stay close, as David leaves us and does not come back until dawn.

I wonder what bargain he made with God because she lives. He is made unclean by her but still holds his arm out to take her up onto his saddle. I lift her up to him and for once he does not turn away, for once he looks deep into my heart. He is a man walking a path of which he is sure, but it is a stony, precipitous path and those who follow are not so sure of their steps. The world spins with the effort of lifting her but I still catch his look of pity, for our beautiful mistress. She leans back against him. He wraps his arms around her and murmurs in her ear. Her silent tears begin to soak her hair and cloak.

We follow them, eating the dust of the horses, it feels fitting to mourn so. The other women behind us begin to chatter and laugh, they are saved, they are relieved, but we do not join in. How can we, for Abigail's heart is broken and our household is splintered beyond repair.

When I hear that Miriam is found, that she rides with Joel and her sister Rebekah, I want to go and find her, to see for myself, only Hannah shakes her head. Matthias is sent, so that she and I can stay in our place, behind Abigail. Hannah does not like to be so far from Matthias and constantly looks over her shoulder until he returns. They walk close together, sometimes holding hands, as if they are already married. Hannah does not care about the stares of Ahinoam's women. I am proud of her; she has changed much over the last few months. She is stronger and despite her weariness, stands tall for all of us.

Matthias says that Miriam is safe, but she is cloaked and silent.

She would not talk to him or raise her eyes from the ground, so she is not the same, not undamaged, as we had half hoped. And she is for now out of our reach.

We stop often to rest.

David's men are torn. They want to rejoice, only David's sorrow at the loss of his son is too heavy for them and they remain silent and sad.

I think a lot about Jani and Little Sarah. They were not with us when the Amalekites came. We were down in the marketplace, they stayed as usual in the house, Little Sarah, because she seems unable to leave it and Jani because the pain was bad and she wanted to rest. We joked of it being Abigail's very last walk before the baby. We were so happy. I did not kiss them or take my farewell with anything more than some nonsense about Jani cooking lamb while we were gone. Now I fear them dead and wish my last words had been of greater worth. A part of me is desperate to see Ziklag, to get there, to discover the worst, to start grieving for my sisters, but there is also a part of me that wants to stay out here in the desert, where nothing is certain, so each stride seems too long, and we make too much progress.

At last, we begin to climb up to our home, stepping over the debris of our lives, scattered because it was valueless. When we get to our street I cannot contain my impatience, and I manage to slip past the horses. I know that Hannah will help Abigail and I *need* to see. I peer into the gloom, there is no fire, no lamp but gradually I begin to make out Little Sarah. She is sweeping and singing and for a moment I think all is well. Then I see Jani lying by the empty grate, her eyes staring, and I think that she is dead. I call her name; she doesn't blink or turn her head. I kneel beside her and take her hand. It is cool and light, her fingernails dirty, she smells soiled, and her clothes are damp and stained. I call out to her and put my cheek close to her mouth. There is a tiny breath.

Suddenly overwhelmed with the pain of it all I lift her onto my lap. I hold her tight like a child and marvel at how thin she is.

"Don't go, Jani, don't leave us," I cry.

My tears drop onto her face and I brush them away. In that moment, I feel the life that is Jani, melt away. She has gone. She has left me.

Little Sarah sweeps an endless circle. When I take the broom out of her hand she just stands where she is. It's as if she is deaf and blind. When I lead her to a chair she sits, if I place food in her hand she eats, and if I tip water into her mouth she swallows, otherwise she does nothing for herself. She brushes the dust to no great purpose. Any other task seems beyond her. I suppose, she thought we were never coming back so she has taken herself off to some other place. We cry for her, and call out to her, but she is completely lost to us, as if she too were dead.

David has gone away again. He is mourning alone in his room, with his God. We manage the best we can. Hannah weeps while she and Matthias clear away the debris. When they sleep, they lie touching, fingertip to fingertip, shoulder to shoulder. Hannah cannot even bear him to go down to the market for food. She must be with him. So it is up to me to stay in Abigail's room, I sleep across the door. The wound on my hand opened again when I wept for Jani. Hannah has bound and cleaned it, but it throbs and tightens, and I often cannot sleep for the pain, but it does not seem to be infected. I miss only a couple of fingers, it is not such a loss, I shall have to learn to sew with my other hand.

When I dream, I see the dagger flashing and the spray of blood. I hear Abigail scream as they pull me away from her. I feel again the surprise I felt when I realised that the blood pooling at our feet, was mine. Hannah saved me. She tore strips from her skirt and bound it tight around the wound. She knew what to do, when I was blinded by pain. I had tried to save them all, but what could I do against men with knives? When Hannah had staunched the blood, it was she who went to try and find Miriam. It was no good, none of us could reach her. We had to watch as she was dragged into the guard room. They did not take long, for they wanted to be as far away as possible when David came back. They should have killed her but instead they trailed her behind us, where I could not get to her. She remains in Heled's household now, secluded, until they can work out what to do with her.

I saw Gabriel yesterday. He looked gaunt, his eyes dark. I almost caught his arm as he passed me. His misery is plain, and I drew back from it. It was too raw even for me to touch. It makes me shudder even now and I try not to think about their love and where it is gone.

"Sarah, are you there?" Abigail calls.

I am always here. I roll onto my knees so that she can see me.

"Has he come today?" she asks.

"No, Mistress, not today." She turns away to stare at the wall.

David still cries for his son. He also cries for King Saul and his men, for they too, are dead.

We are consumed by the dead.

We should be rejoicing because now we can go home, only David cannot raise his head. He mourns his child and his king. Can there be such blindness in a man so close to God? I remember my own blindness, that it did feel as if I was too close, that I could never stand back far enough to see properly. Miriam understands that now, now that it is too late.

Heled came to tell us that she was safe. He couldn't bring himself to speak her name. He told us what happened. That the Philistines had gone out to fight the Israelites and that David had wanted to go with them, to stand alongside our enemies, to kill our own people just as Rebekah had said. Of course, the other kings that rode with King Achish didn't trust David and it was they who sent him back. Sensible men, I would not have trusted him either. I do not believe that David would have fought against King Saul. He loved and bowed his knee to him, even after we'd been chased into exile.

So despite everything, David never did raise a hand against God's anointed. I wonder at that and realise that David is wider and deeper than I will ever understand.

Still, we were saved by our enemies' mistrust, for if David had not come back to Ziklag when he did, we would have been lost – David might have hunted for Abigail, I doubt he would have bothered with the rest of us.

And while we were being rescued by David, the Philistines were riding through our kin, slashing them down, cutting them to pieces. King Saul himself fled and died, running. It is fitting that he was fleeing and yet, David still fell to his knees at the news. He wailed and cried out as if it were too much to bear. Perhaps he thinks he could have done something to prevent it. Perhaps he thinks that he and his men might have made a difference, perhaps might even have saved the ungrateful King Saul.

I think it is a mighty blessing, this death of our king, conveniently at the hands of our enemies. David should not mourn but dance, for at last we will be left alone. He is wrong in this crying for his past life, for a king who wished him nothing but harm and I wonder that there is no one to tell him so.

Chapter Sixty
Told by Miriam

I don't sleep. If I close my eyes I feel the weight of them on me. I smell them, I breathe in the stench of them until I wretch, so I sit in the shadows, my eyes dry, my heart like stone. It is all I can do.

Heled and Joel will not look at me. I am a thing of pity, of shame. When they come near, I stay quiet and still, it's the best way. These men killed for me, killed without mercy, but nothing was changed by the blood. It would be better if I were dead. Like Jani.

Rebekah is kind. She finally sees me, and she wept for Jani, which made me look at her less harshly. Like all who returned, she feels great relief for her own safety and that of her children, but her grief is ruined with guilt. All their grief is ruined with guilt as I am here, and many others, to remind them of what might have been.

They do not know what to do with me. They wait to see if I am with child, whether a small bastard Amalekite grows in my stomach.

We will move to Hebron as soon as the weather warms a little.

Jani is buried in Ziklag with my mother. I should have been buried there too.

Chapter Sixty-One
Told by Hannah

The brazier is topped with cedar chippings; it breathes a warm haze that hangs above our heads. I love the smell, the glow, the change in light from the smouldering wood. If I have nothing better to do, I bring my sewing in here and work by the fire. The furniture is solid and comfortable, and everyone knows where to find me.

I look at what we have laid out for her; a gold tunic and a shawl of white wool that has a fine silver thread sewn around the edge. It catches the light when she moves and will match her colouring, at least I hope it will. This is when I miss Little Sarah the most. When she chose Abigail's clothes, she was invariably right, and I think Abigail only disagreed with her when she woke in a contrary mood. Since I have had to start doing this, Abigail often changes her mind. It is understandable. Now she is a queen and there is more at stake.

When we first came to Hebron it was difficult knowing what was expected of us and I often caught our mistress watching and wondering. We all felt the strangeness of it and for a long time, we did not know how to be. I am still wary of how we live, for Abigail feels a little less than she was before, less able to protect us, to provide for us, but perhaps only I have noticed. David still comes every day if he can. She waits for him, dresses for him, stays away from the other women just in case he needs her. That is not wise, as she is creating a gulf that cannot be crossed. Her love for David seems to leave no room for common sense and our lives are distorted by it, distilled down to the simple task of having to hand what she needs to look her best. I feel the thinness of our existence and I do not think it bodes well.

We have many rooms here in Hebron, perched high above the citadel. The town is spread below us like a mat of pulled wool. Jani would have loved it, being able to watch the soldiers marching under our windows and she could have grown fat on the rich food we eat every day. We even have a small courtyard with a fountain, that fills the house with its splashing and brings a mottled light that soothes and lifts. It is fed from a huge cistern under the hill. I do not think Ahinoam has a fountain in her quarters.

David is King and rules half the kingdom and Abigail has a fountain.

We were fortunate, that after Ziklag she regained her strength, and he soon began to visit again. Despite that, she is not pregnant and Ahinoam has started to swell with her own child, which she never tires of showing us. Love is not enough. Abigail needs to bear him a son.

Matthias comes into the room. I know it is him by the way he stirs the air. He stands behind me and stretches his arms around my stomach, his lips brush my neck. I lean into him so that for a few seconds he takes the weight of all of us.

"How are my two best beloveds?" he whispers.

"We are well," I say, placing my hands over his hands. We stand quietly, until I feel a kick, deep inside my belly. He moves in front of me, his face a picture of wonder as he feels our child.

"I think he knows your voice," I say, laughing. Matthias drops to his knees to put his ear to my stomach. "What can you hear?" I whisper.

"Lots of gurgling. What did you have for breakfast?"

I laugh.

For a while I did not think we would ever laugh again and even now it is still a guilty pleasure. Abigail reserves such things for David, the rest of the time her spirits hang heavy. Lately, she will only allow Big Sarah and I to come near her. She knows that we will not gossip of her listlessness to the other servants.

But I cannot hold in my own joy, not all the time, for we are going to have this child here, where we are safe. Big Sarah teases me that I am too old. I am only just thirty, but sometimes I do wonder if it is too much to dare hope for, this blessing. I pray that God will help balance some of the terrible things that have happened, with this baby, our baby, who reminds us that there is some love that does not drain and imprison.

Little Sarah appears at the door. She has slipped past Mary, who is supposed to keep an eye on her. She sees the dresses laid out on the bed and runs to them. Matthias and I come quickly to her side. This has happened many times before. She picks up the silk and lets it run through her fingers. When it has slipped to the floor, she snatches the shawl, pulling and stretching it in her hands. Matthias tries to prise it away, but her fingers are tightly clenched, and he does not want to hurt her. She counts as she twists and pulls. Abigail will be angry if she knows we have let this occur. Matthias has no choice. He carefully puts his foot behind her and then pushes sharply. Her hands fly up as she tumbles backwards. I catch the shawl as it sails into the air.

She lies there winded, just as Mary runs in, out of breath. Mary is careful not to catch my eye, she knows I will be angry. Later, I will have to have words with her, reminding her once more of her duties. Matthias gently helps Little Sarah to her feet and guides her from the room, Mary following behind them. Big Sarah appears; she is also out of breath. They have all been looking for her.

"Give it to me," she says, reaching for the shawl.

"It might be ruined and it's one of Abigail's favourites."

"Fetch the purple one instead. If Abigail asks, tell her I caught this one on a nail and I am darning it. I will steam it and see if I can't get it back into shape."

She is already turning to go, but there is something I want to ask her, now that we are alone.

"Dear Big Sarah," I say, reaching out and touching her arm, "did you see Miriam this morning?"

She nods and her eyes fill with tears. There is never a good moment to ask about Miriam.

"She is like her old self around the children but with anyone else, even with me, she was…"

"Can't she come back to us?" I ask.

We have talked of this, many times. We miss her terribly, Big Sarah and I. Jani can't come home, and neither does it seem that Little Sarah will ever be herself again, but Miriam could return, and we are sure that she needs to be where we can take care of her.

"They just don't know what to do with her," Big Sarah replies. "At least there is no child. But I will ask Abigail again, surely Heled would not refuse her twice."

"We could help her," I say, "I'm sure of it."

Big Sarah looks at me and stares beyond my eyes.

"You and I, together, here. Yes, it would be the best thing."

She comes and puts her hand on my stomach and mouths a blessing.

"Are you ready for this, Hannah?" she asks.

"How can anyone be ready for such a thing," I say, laughing and the little one kicks, as if to agree with me.

We hear Abigail and David. They have been walking on the ramparts. Big Sarah moves quickly, to stand in front of me. Too late, we are caught, and Big Sarah and I feel his displeasure. Abigail's joy is tainted by my swelling belly, although she pretends that she is happy for us. But I know that I am a source of disquiet, a reminder, for I am bearing a child out of love, and they are not.

Chapter Sixty-Two
Told by Big Sarah

After David has gone, Abigail sends for me. He has been called back to the throne room; there is more trouble with Saul's followers, or his relatives. They nibble at the borders and cause strife where they can, hating that Saul's son was so weak he lost half the kingdom. David, it seems, is not to be left in peace by them. They buzz about like annoying flies.

Abigail lies where he left her, staring up at the ceiling and I must wait. I wonder if she has even remembered that I am here. My impatience grows for there are many things I could be getting on with. I believe she should be grateful that David comes when he can and yet when I see the sorrow, amidst the desire, I do try to understand. He has less and less time for her as matters of state grow more complex. She is squeezed and stretched and although he undoubtedly loves her, he loves his God and Judah more.

He is currently negotiating a treaty with the King of Geshur. This king has a daughter. David speaks of it quite openly. He does not see that although Abigail strives to be rational, her heart is thick with jealousy. He will sleep with this new woman, as he did Ahinoam. He professes to love Abigail, yet it seems he will not rely on her alone. It is wisdom, it is statecraft, but I wonder that he does not trust his God enough for a son, with the woman he loves so well.

"Sarah," she says, at last, "now that we are settled, do you think the darkness is behind us? That the future, you were so afraid of, was the loss of my little one? And Jani," she adds quickly. "There has been so much sadness. How can there be more to come?"

I was not expecting this. We have not spoken of such things since we left Ziklag. I sit down and stare deep into my heart. I can see nothing more than the dull ache, left by our beloved Jani and the deep wound that still festers for Miriam and Little Sarah. I shake my head.

"Even though the kingdom is split, David grows stronger every day," she continues, desperately searching for some small reassurance.

But I'm not sure that she is right. Every day, David has to battle, to guard his back, and his borders. It feels as if he is having to fight too hard to keep what God has given him, and why isn't his beloved Abigail pregnant again? Ahinoam is ripe with child, glowing amidst the women, more beautiful than ever. Her son will be the first born now. She is daily assuming her rightful position. Abigail has his heart, his confidence, his love but to retain her position she needs to carry his seed.

"I can't see," I reply, and I sound irritable, even though I do not mean to.

I am still too much for her, I still take up too much space. I have not told her what she wants to hear. She waves me away, only when I reach the door she speaks again and I realise the disappointment she feels in me, is only a reflection of what she feels about herself.

"I would like Miriam back, too. I miss her but I'm not sure I can cope with another damaged woman in my household. I am laughed at by Ahinoam. Did you know that? We are a laughingstock."

I know that and I wonder if she is stating it simply to needle me, or to justify her inaction. We are all aware of what is said, not so quietly, behind our backs.

"They talk of my household as a mad house." She continues, "You frighten them, Little Sarah is ridiculed and if we brought dear Miriam home then… it would be too much."

I stride away from her. I am angry because I want her to be stronger than this. It is so unfair. She is seemingly weakened by love. Why should she care what the other women think? David is the King, and he loves her. She is not a political appendage; she is his heart. Can she not see that bringing Miriam back to us would show great strength not weakness?

I pace along the battlements, calling out to God for Miriam and for Abigail. Not out loud, I am mindful of our reputation and that the sentries posted up here would be happy to have something more to gossip about than the colour of the sky. I try to look as if I am simply taking the air, but I am aware my stride is long and my turning sharp. At last Hannah comes to find me, to soothe me. She knows that I cannot be upset when I see her belly, tight and full.

"Give Abigail time," she says.

"But poor Miriam. That she is stained and damaged she must already endure. That we do not care enough to bring her home must be agony for her."

"She will know that we still love her, that we do not care about such things."

"How can she know when she does not dare lift her head for shame?"

"It was not her fault, no one with an ounce of kindness would ever think that she brought it on herself."

But I am sure that there are many who remember Miriam riding through us on that stupid horse. That she had been linked with one of David's men, one of those who stood closest to him in battle, that her beauty had been talked of, her enthusiasm, her laugh. That she had been allowed to roam freely, and unfettered. Hiding under her veil had come too late for some blame to stick, for that blame to take root and grow and twist and maim our beautiful girl.

Chapter Sixty-Three
Told by Miriam

It has been half a year since we came to Hebron. I have only seen Big Sarah and Hannah a few times and then only when Abigail released them from their duties. Most other people avoid me. I think it will always be so. I live in a strange dim place. I hoped I wouldn't care what others thought of me, that I would one day straighten my back and walk with my face once more turned up to the sun, but I find that I care very deeply and if it weren't for the regard of Rebekah and the children, I do not know what I would do. I do lift my face to the light, when we are together, because Chloe and young Heled do not care what was done to me, and for my sake Rebekah tries hard not to remember.

Chloe is sitting on my lap while I braid her hair. It is pale and wispy, and I do not like to pull it tight. She leans comfortably against me as she sorts through the sewing box. Rebekah is embroidering a tunic for Heled. I don't think he will ever wear the garment, but he might keep it near him, for it has been lavished with love and much time.

"Oh, dear, I must unpick this last bit. What do you think, Miriam?" Rebekah asks.

She holds it out for me to see.

"It's not so bad. It's a little tight, that's all. I think when it is done, if we flatten it under a hot iron, it will look splendid."

"Are you sure?"

I am sure that it would look terrible if she unpicked it and tried to sew over it again.

A servant enters and I instinctively pull my veil over my eyes. Chloe sits upright as if to protect me or perhaps she is simply trying to hide me.

"You may go," Rebekah says, after the girl has leant over to speak quietly, so only her mistress can hear her. I smile at the formality, but Rebekah loves all such things, and the servants are well versed in what she and Heled expect of them. Once the girl has left, Rebekah turns to me excitedly.

"It's a message from the Palace, from Abigail."

She is grinning, something she will only do when we are alone, and it reminds me that she is but a few years older than me.

"Abigail would like you to go and see her."

I had wondered if she would ever send for me and I wonder what has happened that has made her do so now. Her place is too fragile within the Palace to have such a tainted woman near her, but perhaps a short visit wouldn't do much harm. Abigail needs another child, she needs a boy, even I can see that. Despite myself, I would love to know what is going on and I do long to hear Hannah and Big Sarah's voices.

I haven't left Heled's house before and as I step into the street I pull my cloak over my face so that I must breathe through its heaviness. It is a joy to feel the breeze and the heat of the sun, even through the dark wool. I have been closeted too long, sitting in shame. I cross to the other side of the road where it is shady and the walkway less sodden. Hebron is a town bursting with people and the streets are full of dung and rubbish. I hope I will not lose my way. The Palace is not far and towers above us, more like a fortress, so it is always within sight. I think it would be a good place to hide, high above everything and everyone, but I know that that will not be my future, not now.

Someone walks behind me. I hear the scrape of a sandal. I slow down so that they can pass me, for I am walking quite slowly, enjoying the light and air. But they don't seem to be in a hurry either. We are nearly at the street where the silk merchants have their stalls. I am trying to remember all that Rebekah has told me of

Hebron, where I should turn, so as not to get lost. I take a deep breath before I move into the crowd and am almost overwhelmed by the noise and colour. Excitement begins to bubble in my stomach and it makes me reluctant to walk into the dimness of the alley beyond, even though it is the path to the Palace gate. Then I hear a shout. It is a boy, no more than ten years old, surrounded by his friends. They run towards me, shouting words they should not know the meaning of. The injustice of their taunts, the untruth of them tears at my heart. I hurry forward. I am afraid and angry, as the bubble of excitement turns to acid. Why can't they forget? I ask nothing of anyone, I expect nothing and yet I am dogged by other people's memories.

Rebekah did offer me protection for my short walk and many instructions about the way, she was most insistent. I refused. I thought it would be alright after so many months. I should have listened to her. I am damaged. It doesn't matter that I was not to blame.

A stone skitters along the cobbles. They are only children, but I am still worried. I do not want to run for fear that it will force their hand, that others might join in or worse that they might start throwing more than stones. How can I arrive at the gate of our queen smelling of faeces and rotting food? I would have to turn back to Rebekah's; I would have to hope that Abigail would understand and send for me again. I am undone by such a thought and my breath gets shallow and harsh with panic.

Suddenly the children are scattering, yelping in surprise. I turn to see what has happened and my heart stops. This is almost more than I can bear. Gabriel stands where the children had been. Rebekah must have sent him after all. She wouldn't have realised how painful it would be for him, how difficult. For a moment our eyes meet but he is too far away for me to judge his thoughts and then my own eyes leak tears. Now I cannot see very far at all. I continue on my way. At each turn I glimpse over my shoulder. He walks behind me, a good way back, staying with me, protecting me. I suppose he must be too ashamed to come any closer. It should make me angry, instead I feel only gratitude. It is these tiny moments of humanity that bring meaning to my life.

The Palace guards let me through with barely a glance, for Big

Sarah waits within. She is not ashamed of me, engulfing me in her arms; a sudden darkening and holding that somehow fills me with light. I know now, that if the men had dared mutter of my state or even looked at me askance, she would have turned on them. Their eyes remain level and grave. How I have missed her, how I have missed them all. Just before I turn to follow her broad tall back, I look around one last time. He is turning away and does not see my glance. Big Sarah has stopped and pulls the cloak from my head.

"No need of that here," she says. "Still lovely, although a little thin and far too pale."

I look down. I cannot bear her kindness. She takes me by the shoulders and gently shakes me.

"No Miriam, do not be like that. Head up."

She pulls her arm through mine so that we must walk together. Hannah is also waiting and weeps as I enter, dripping tears onto my neck.

"Don't worry about her, it's the baby," Big Sarah says. "It's due any second and she cries all the time." It's as if I have only been out for a walk.

Hannah sniffs and nods and wipes her nose on her skirt. She looks me up and down and then begins to cry again.

Big Sarah snorts and starts to tidy my hair, to straighten my dress. Hannah's tears turn to smiles as she elbows her out of the way. She deftly winds my hair around her fingers and re-pins it.

"That's much better," she says. "Much more like your old self."

But my old self has gone, and I ache for the time before Ziklag. Now my eyes fill with tears, which I don't want them to see. I would not spoil this comfortable love that we have for one another, which I have pulled on like an old shawl. Back at Rebekah's I am wreathed in pity and invisibility. Here, I can almost feel my spine unbending, the muscles itching as they stretch far beyond what they are used to.

"Do you think she is ready?" Hannah says to Big Sarah, as if I am not here.

"I don't know," she replies. "Why don't we ask her?"

Hannah covers her mouth with her hand, as Big Sarah turns to me.

"Are you ready, our Miriam? Are you ready to meet the Queen?"

"I think so," I whisper.

I wonder how she is changed, the woman who when I first met her, seemed able to stare into my soul.

Abigail rises to greet me. I kneel before her.

"I've missed you Miriam," she says, reaching her hand out to cup my chin. Her dark eyes peer at me, as of old, seeing through my skin, her lips pursed in thought. I see that she has aged, no not aged, faded, just a little. I am not the only one touched by that raid, I see that now. I should have realised that the loss of her child would mark her deeply.

"Yes, indeed," she continues. "We have suffered your absence for too long but now that you are here... I am the wife of the King, surely I can have what I want?" There is a smile playing around her lips.

Big Sarah folds her arms and stares at her. She is frowning. Abigail returns her stare, only her face is smooth and untroubled. She is so beautiful. I had forgotten.

"Sarah," she says, "today I feel a little stronger. Today is different."

Big Sarah's eyes narrow as she looks her mistress up and down. This is a conversation that has spilt over from another time.

"You're pregnant, aren't you?" Big Sarah whispers.

"Perhaps, but it must be kept between ourselves, until we can be sure."

Hannah is counting on her fingers. How long since our mistress last bled? She nods, though Abigail is only a little late.

We sit as we used to, except that now there are only four of us. Hannah calls for dates and wine, as if she is the mistress. Much has changed since they came here, much that I have not been a part of. Abigail is distracted but that smile is still playing around her mouth. She looks at each of us and then says, "Miriam, I know what a terrible gossip you are." Hannah and Sarah nod in agreement, I am mystified. "So we must keep you here, until it is safe. I don't want you to tell anyone my good news before I have told the King."

The others laugh. I realise she is teasing me. No one would dare tease me at Heled's house.

"And you'll be a real help, for we'll have our hands full, God willing, over the next few days," Big Sarah says, smiling at Hannah, who blushes pink, as her eyes fill with tears again.

Matthias enters and bows solemnly to Abigail. Abigail points to the food. He offers it to Hannah and when she shakes her head, he pushes the plate closer, right under her nose. She takes a small fig.

"She must keep up her strength," Abigail says, although she is looking down at her own smooth stomach.

When the servants come to clear the plates they stare at me and wrinkle their noses, as if I am unclean. Big Sarah tenses, until Hannah catches her eye. She shakes her head, a tiny movement that I am not meant to see. Abigail notices and claps her hands in irritation.

"What is wrong with you today?" she says, to the now trembling girls. "Why do you lift your eyes in my presence? I will not be served by such insolence." The women quickly back away. I look with wonder at our mistress. She always had some strength within her, now it is like forged iron and easily seen. I almost feel sorry for the servants, who I suppose were only curious.

They leave and another comes, cloaked in black. She is led by a young girl who bows to Abigail. There is nothing to see of Little Sarah but her hands. She is taken to a corner, and the servant Mary gives her a basket of clothes. She pulls them out, one by one, until they are all laid across her knees in a shining pile and then she puts them back, one by one, carefully folding them again. She does this, silently, continually.

"Hello, Little Sarah," I try. She does not stop sorting her clothes, nor does she look up. I look over at Big Sarah who shrugs. There are no words.

"Does she not speak at all?" I ask later, when Mary has led her away.

"No, but she will cry out if you surprise her or when she hurts herself," Big Sarah replies.

"Her voice isn't gone, just her wits," Abigail adds.

Hannah says, "None of us know what happened to them while we were captive."

Hannah has reminded us of my true state. All know what happened to me; I was dragged low in the strong light of a midday sun, where there was nowhere to hide. She is sorry and blushes and pulls my hand up to her cheek. I do not mind so very much. It is bound to be like this for a while. They will tread on eggshells around me and growl at the servants, when they whisper behind my back. It is all they can do. Even with my beloved sisters, it must be so.

"How is Rebekah?" Abigail asks, turning the subject to something easier.

"She loves Hebron," I say, smiling. "She has a much bigger house and Heled has bought many servants for her to order around. More than you even, Mistress."

"I thought she was looking a bit fuller the last time I saw her," Hannah says. "She's not pregnant again, is she?"

"Not all women have to be pregnant to be happy," Big Sarah says, laughing at her.

"I don't think she is with child. Heled's hardly been home at all, in the last few months," I reply.

Abigail's face clouds. It is also true of David. Absent so much of the time, only able to snatch a moment here and there.

"Will there ever be peace?" Hannah asks.

"I don't think so," I reply. "Peace means that someone must relinquish power, and I don't think any man would do that easily."

There is silence.

"Miriam, I have truly missed you," Abigail says. "You always understand what is going on. You will be a fine addition to our household."

It sounds so ordinary, but it means that I am going to stay. I try not to cry again. It is hopeless but I manage to weep silently.

"I have missed you too," says Big Sarah, taking my hand in hers.

Hannah tenses and we all turn to look at her.

"It's alright," she says, sucking in her cheeks. "It was only a little pain and it's gone now."

Big Sarah kneels in front of her.

"Where was the pain?"

"Around here," she says, groping under her stomach.

"Does your back ache, too?" Big Sarah asks.

"On and off for a couple of days."

Abigail stands. "I will leave you now. Call me when it's time."

Hannah tenses again and Big Sarah rocks back onto her heels.

"Are you ready for this?" she asks.

"I think so," Hannah whispers, although she is gripping Matthias's hand, so I can see white around her knuckles.

"Matthias, go and fetch the midwife. Miriam, will you stay?" Big Sarah asks.

I nod, unsure that I will be of any use. The last time a baby was born, I escaped to the desert.

Chapter Sixty-Four
Told by Big Sarah

The midwife has come. She is short, round and fierce, and we are careful to do what she tells us. She brushes aside our anxiety with a snort, for she has walked this journey with a thousand women. There is no mystery here.

The pain is rising and falling but there seems no space to rest. Hannah has stopped talking, her eyes stare at nothing, concentrating on putting one foot in front of the other, pausing only to sweat and tremble. She is exhausted and afraid. She grips our hands as if she were drowning.

"Walk her round again, keep her moving," the midwife commands.

I want it to stop, to be done with. I have helped with many birthings, and not just goats, but none so dear as this one. God, I cry out silently, why do you make it so hard for us, why do we have to pay so high a price for our happiness?

Miriam leads Hannah around the room once more. She keeps staring up into Hannah's face, smiling, encouraging her, but when she looks down, her own face is squeezed with fear. This might have been her a few months back, she will not have forgotten that and that she would have had to face it alone.

We are both praying for God's mercy. There is so much blood, so much sweat. I had not thought it would be all so consuming. I look to the midwife to take courage. She simply nods as Hannah stops pacing and almost straightens. The look of fear is gone, and she squats. The midwife drops in front of her. Hannah reaches out for us, Miriam on her left and I on her right, as she begins to strain.

"Again," calls the woman.

"Again," I say. "Again, Hannah."

She uses us to pull against. Miriam looks at me with a desperate determination.

"You certainly picked your moment to come home," I say, through gritted teeth.

She braces herself against Hannah's grip.

"I wouldn't have missed it, for all the world."

She is crying, crying from a well deep inside, tears soaking her dress.

Chapter Sixty-Five
Told by Miriam

She is the sweetest little girl I have ever seen, with smooth, perfect skin and large black eyes. Her hair is dark and plastered to her scalp, where it frames long lashes and rose-pink lips. Hannah and Matthias are stunned. They stare in wonder at their daughter. Matthias can't stop shaking his head and I am sure that he is wiping away tears. Big Sarah is leaning over the crib. When the baby slips into sleep she is gripping her finger and Big Sarah will not leave her.

Even Little Sarah comes and peeps down at our new sister, but we don't let her stay, for fear of what she might do.

"Jani would have loved this," Big Sarah whispers and I think of her standing with her hands on her broad hips. She would be laughing at the fuss we are making over a baby girl.

They call her Esther.

***

Abigail gives birth to a son, David's beautiful boy. He is healthy and golden, and Abigail is also struck dumb with joy. All her longings rest in that crib and for the first few days she barely sleeps for the wonder of him. We are all changed by his arrival, by a sense of completeness and when she holds him, she whispers, "Shlemut, my perfect boy." He brings hope and light, our Lemi. I had forgotten what that felt like. I laugh at the silliest things and believe that we are blessed. Of course, not everyone is pleased. Ahinoam is furious. She told David how very happy she is for him and Abigail, but when he left the women's quarters, even I could see the danger our little prince was in. Ahinoam screamed at her women and tore her hair out in chunks. She had been so sure that Abigail would miscarry, like last time. She had thought that Abigail was weak and would never bring a healthy boy to full term. The breadth of her tantrum is spoken of all over the Palace.

Why is David so blind to these things? His succession is not something that only concerns him and God, it is also what makes the rest of his household turn, and turn again. Those around him do not share his joy, his faith is not mirrored by those who sit at his table or share his bed. I wish that he could see. He is filled to the brim with the birth of his son and seemingly blind to everything else. At last, his love has borne fruit, and it does seem fitting to us, who watch from close by. He often comes to stand by his little son, his lips moving silently, as he prays blessings over him. I have heard that he has sacrificed so many animals as thanksgiving offerings, that the altars run with blood. There will also be a feast in the boy's honour, so the people can rejoice with him. Abigail and Lemi will attend.

David calls him Chileab, son of my own heart, I am perfected in my son. To us, he will always be Lemi.

Hannah will go with Abigail to the banquet. I will stay back to mind little Esther, as Matthias has more than enough to do.

***

The evening of the celebration comes too soon; we are not prepared. There is a sense that something is going on, something that we should be aware of and yet can't quite put our fingers on. I wonder at my capacity to pretend that everything is as it should be, as I decide to take Esther up onto the battlements, to see the moon but it is cold, and we don't stay long. When I get back, Big Sarah is pacing up and down. I try to settle Esther in her crib, but Big Sarah's shadow keeps brushing past the child and her sandals slap the floor with irritating irregularity. Esther won't sleep, and she begins to whimper. At last, I turn and stand in Big Sarah's way.

"What is the matter? You are like a camel in heat."

That stops her.

"I'm fine and when did you get to be so gracious?"

Esther begins to wail, a frightened cry, so I pick her up.

"You're upsetting Esther."

"What does she know of anything?" Big Sarah says, with wonder, and then peers closely at the child. Too closely, Esther's big black eyes widen as she gasps down enough air to scream again.

"Perhaps she understands more than you think," I say, pushing her away. The jobs will never get done now. I will have to spend my time soothing her.

"I'm sorry, Miriam, I am just tired and out of sorts. Look, I'll go and get some milk and perhaps a little honey, all that howling will have made her hungry."

I have known Big Sarah for far too long to know that it isn't tiredness that is worrying away at her. Something is wrong. It begins to feel as if some wave is about to break over us, as if a dam is breached and the water is coming like a wall. Perhaps, I too have a little foresight.

Matthias looks in at us. He reaches for his daughter.

"What are you two fretting about?" he asks.

Big Sarah almost looks as if she might speak, but no. She turns on her heel.

"I'll fetch Esther that drink," she says.

Esther is beginning to settle in the arms of her father.

"Hannah is worried too. That something is going on," he says.

"There is always something going on, in this place," I say. Neither of us are reassured.

Chapter Sixty-Six
Told by Hannah

Abigail herself holds Lemi while we wait for David to call us. He is wrapped in purple silk as befitting a prince. It is garish and doesn't suit his colouring, but it is a gift from one of the local kings and David said it must be worn. The antechamber is crowded and hot. We are surrounded by guards and servants, and we wait so long that I wonder if David has forgotten us. I am wrong. He comes himself and takes his son in his arms, kissing his forehead with tenderness. He holds out a hand to Abigail. She is so lovely in her motherhood, there is more colour in her cheeks and lips than I have seen in a long time, and she has not lost the roundness that came with the birth of her son. None doubt the rightness of her place beside him, as his queen, none but Ahinoam.

They enter the banqueting room to silence, the men around the tables holding their breath, wondering what David will do. He is not a man who can be second-guessed; he is a man who asks God first and God's ways are not always obvious. Those that know him best, know that it is wise to wait.

At last, he and Abigail reach the end of the hall. At a nod from David the men rise to their feet, forcing me to flatten myself against the wall, and begin to roar their approval. David holds his son aloft and cries again and again, "The son of my heart."

The men love David, and this is what they know how to do. They know how to shout their love, they know how to bellow, so that your ears are hammered with the noise of it, they know how to stamp their feet and thump their fists. Miriam's brother-in-law Heled is seated close to the King and not far away is her brother Joel, newly married and flushed with wine. They are welcoming David's heir; they are acknowledging that the succession is assured. The uproar makes the Palace tremble and all who live within its walls can clearly hear it. There is talk later, that Ahinoam went to her bedchamber and closed the door.

Lemi starts to cry. Abigail tries to take him. David laughs and lifts him higher out of her reach. She beseeches him to let her soothe their son, but David cannot hear her, or perhaps he chooses not to. This is his child, his strength, and the boy will need to be as strong and wise as David is himself. Abigail lowers her arms and stands beside her King, trying to smile but I can see that something has changed within her, as she watches Lemi gulping and choking. At last, he is handed back to me. Abigail longs to come to him but instead she can only watch as I wrap him in my shawl and hurry from the hall. She must remain seated in the high place of honour, beside her David, until he dismisses her. She is as trapped now as she was back in Nabal's house.

I think, amidst the roar of his men, when he held her son aloft, away from her, the scales fell from her eyes. I hurry to our quarters afraid and desperate to share what I have seen with Miriam and Sarah.

Chapter Sixty-Seven
Told by Miriam

I hear his screams from a long way off. Big Sarah and I stare at each other, and we wonder what has happened. When Hannah hurries into the room she looks worn and worried. She holds Lemi very close. Perhaps he is too hot. I reach out to him. It does no good. In the end we take it in turns to soothe him and Esther, too, who quickly joins in the wailing. Rocking and singing we stay with them, but nothing we do seems to help, and we do not notice Little Sarah creeping into Abigail's bedchamber. What delight she has in taking down every hanging, cushion and sheet and folding them into a great pile in the middle of the bed. When Abigail returns trembling with tiredness, she stumbles into her room and stares in disbelief. This upheaval, I think, mirrors her own heart and the silence before her scream of rage is deep and profound.

That night she almost sends Little Sarah away, for good. Why not? She is making us all a laughingstock. And it seems the rest of us are helpless in the face of so much anguish. It is Big Sarah who pleads with Abigail to let Little Sarah stay. It is Big Sarah who braves her wrath, and it is Big Sarah who persuades Abigail to change her mind.

In the morning I am exhausted, and it reminds me of the night that Abigail first went out to meet David, when we rode through the darkness to find him, when she returned to us changed. Something here has shifted too, the ground no longer feels solid beneath us, and our mistress does not know what to do. We sit around her, the children sleeping late. She breathes deeply, frets about the light, and a draught. She wants watered wine and then does not touch it. When finally she begins to speak we all lean in close to hear her.

"My eyes are opened, and I don't think I shall ever be able to close them again," she whispers. "I do not doubt that he loves me. I am treated ahead of all his wives, only he is God's servant first, king second, father to his sons and then my husband. When I reached for my beautiful boy, he simply lifted him higher, beyond me."

We breathe and wait.

"Little Sarah may stay, only you must increase the guard over her. She will have no other chances. Do you understand?" she says, looking at each of us in turn. "I cannot afford to be worrying about a mad woman, when my own son's future has to be my main concern."

It is the best we could have hoped for.

Beyond this, I pray that things might settle. They do not, for Abigail has seen her son's life mapped out for him, the path clear, narrow and dangerous. He will be the first of the princes because it is what his father wills; he will be the heir to all that his father is. He will become king – but only if he lives that long.

Before the banquet, Abigail saw no further than her love for David, for his longing for a son. She hadn't really thought of what might be required of that son, particularly now that David rules half a kingdom. It greatly disturbs her, and we do not know how to help. Abigail paces the room while we try to put the rest of it to rights. She does not know where to sit but does not want to leave us and when she finally falls into a fitful, exhausted doze, we stay near.

Chapter Sixty-Eight
Told by Big Sarah

Abigail begins to see what has been gnawing away at me from the beginning, that in giving birth to her precious Lemi, she will lose everything. It does not matter how much she loves him, that love is nothing compared to the regard of his father. I gnaw at my thumb nail, worry at it with my teeth, until I pull away the soft white skin beneath. If only the child had been a girl, then Abigail could have let Ahinoam and David get on with it. Our mistress does not care for power, just for love. For a woman so clever, she is remarkably blind, which is why, maybe, God sent me to walk beside her.

Hannah brings food. Abigail won't touch it, which is foolish, and she snaps at us for pressing her. We are tired, stretched thin and are scratching away at each other, even though we don't mean to. In the middle of this, when we are out of sorts and struggling, Ahinoam comes. She stands at the door with all her women, waiting politely to be admitted, although by rights she does not have to. She is reminding us that she is the first wife, despite all that has happened. We are not calm and ordered, how can we be? Queen Ahinoam has chosen her moment very carefully.

She comes as a sister, all smiles and gentle concern, for she has heard there has been disquiet in our household. She is a snake. She comes to offer help. She is a scorpion with her tail raised to strike. We three women stand behind our mistress, although we wish we could stand in front, to protect her. Abigail must be strong, but she trembles in Ahinoam's presence, and we cannot be sure if it is fear or anger.

"Dear Abigail, are you well?"

"I am quite well. David's son and I are greatly blessed. I am grateful."

Ahinoam's face clouds and I tense. Our mistress, in her tiredness, has not used her words well. Already she has antagonised this woman. It is foolish.

"We are blessed, too," Ahinoam replies, sweetly. "My son, who looks more like his father every day, is a joy to our hearts. We should let our little princes play together."

Abigail smiles in return, she seems to have regained some of her composure, however we know she will not let that monster child anywhere near her Lemi. He is large for his age, spoiled and mean.

"Of course he is still such a little babe," Ahinoam says, seeing that Abigail's face is like stone. "But as they grow older it will be good for them to know they have a brother to look out for them." Her voice is firm, almost warm, only her eyes glitter with malice and I am reminded once more of a viper, waiting to strike. I move a little closer to Abigail, I long to place my hand on her shoulder, except I know it would just give Ahinoam more fuel to burn us with.

Ahinoam's son was presented at a feast at his birth but not from his mother's arms; she waited in her rooms for her maid to return him to her. David, who is so clever about so much, is foolish not to see how dangerous it is to show his preference so soon. Abigail suddenly looks frail in the shadow of this woman and we, who know her best, can see that she doubts herself. How can she keep Lemi safe until he is grown? How can she?

We wait for Ahinoam to speak again.

"Come and share food with me," she says. "Our husband will be off soon enough, protecting our borders, protecting all that is ours. While he is away, let us be friends."

Abigail manages to dip her head graciously, only I can see her fists are clenched at her sides. They bow to each other and Ahinoam sweeps away. We remain as statues where the first queen has left us, unable to move, our minds spinning into the future.

"I am not mistaken, am I?" Abigail speaks, into the silence, her voice unnaturally loud. "She will stop at nothing for her son."

I nod and say, "Would you not die for Lemi, because you are his mother?"

Hannah clutches my hand. She is imagining what she would do

for her own dear Esther.

All is set. What happens next cannot be changed, except if David had kept but one wife.

"We must protect Lemi, at all costs," Abigail says, staring at us, gathering us in.

"Can't you speak of your fears to David," Miriam asks.

Abigail shakes her head.

"Remember where I stand. I am getting older and there is already talk of another wife."

"He brings trouble on his head," I mutter.

"On all of us," Abigail replies.

I don't think I have ever heard our mistress, ever allude to David except as a perfect being, one so blessed as to stand beyond us and our simple lives.

Hannah hurries away to find Matthias, without waiting for Abigail to release her. She will run to find her Esther, pick her up to hold her close and will weep sad tears upon her head.

Chapter Sixty-Nine
Told by Hannah

I cannot believe how quickly Abigail's regard for David has broken into pieces, how quickly her all-consuming passion has turned to pain. Perhaps, because I love my own dear Matthias so well, I see more clearly than the others.

On the night of the banquet, Abigail's concern for Lemi ran through her love for David like ice, and like ice it hardened and split her in half like a stone. I am frightened and hope that I will never have to choose between Esther and Matthias. It is almost impossible to watch Abigail stand over her son and weep for him. I try to hold them both.

"Will God not protect him?" Miriam cries out.

"Did God protect you?" Big Sarah retorts, from a dim corner, where she sits back on her haunches, her face dark and shadowed. Miriam pales but does not weep. Big Sarah jumps to her feet and flings her arms around her, pleading forgiveness.

"I'm so sorry, so terribly sorry. You cannot think that I meant to hurt you? I am stupid, I speak before I think."

I hope Miriam will not be too upset by what Big Sarah has said and although I cannot hear what passes between them, she eventually does persuade Big Sarah to let her go. We are all disconcerted and do not know how to be.

After Ahinoam's visit, there are many rumours flying about the Palace, and that night I watch Big Sarah taste Abigail's food for the first time. It soon becomes part of our life. We take it in turns, surreptitiously. Abigail pretends not to notice, she is still too frightened to admit that what we are doing is really necessary. We also take it in turns to watch Lemi. He is never left alone. Even Matthias takes a turn, if we are too busy. Our prince grows to love us, not realising that we are his keepers, his jailers. He is a beautiful boy, kind and gentle, however there are the odd flashes of temper which take us by surprise. Each of us believes we are his favourite, for when he looks at us, it is with such warmth, that it makes you feel as if you are the only other person in his world. I suppose, in that way, he is like his father and will be able to command loyalty with a glance. He is even able to sit on Little Sarah's knee, although she sometimes squeezes him too tightly.

I think that his true favourite is Matthias, who always speaks gently. He treats him as a little man and yet makes him feel protected and loved, although when I said as much to Big Sarah, she laughed at me.

Chapter Seventy
Told by Miriam

I miss playing with my niece and nephew, Chloe and Little Heled. I try to walk down to see them as often as I can, as it enables me to forget, for a few hours, the daily tension under which we live. The only problem is that Abigail says that we must be accompanied by Matthias and perhaps a maidservant of our own, for she has become more conscious than ever of her standing. Whenever we venture out, we must be attended by as many servants as she can spare. Even Little Sarah is treated with respect and guarded like royalty. The unspoken message is that if Abigail favours you, she will be loyal unto madness and shame. It is a good message, for I think the household cares and serves her accordingly.

There is no question of our devotion to her. It has been tempered over the years, but is deeply rooted in our knowledge of her, and I do not think it would occur to her to doubt us now.

I hardly ever think of Gabriel. I suppose there is too much else to worry about and sometimes, I think love survives because it is pragmatic. There is no hope, so I have put him to one side and since my walk to the Palace that first day, I have seen him twice. In fact, both times it was only his voice I heard, which I inadvertently picked out from the household noises. There is no reason for our paths to cross and I think that like all men, except Matthias, he does not know how to look at me. Heled continues to treat me with sad pity and is uneasy in my presence. I do not doubt that Gabriel would be the same.

Rebekah understands where I fit, that there is nothing more to be jealous of. What happened to me, makes a shadow cross her face, she still shudders if it is alluded to and that warms my heart towards her. It has enabled us to become as sisters should be. I am always assured of a welcome whenever I visit. Perhaps, it is because of what I might do for her children, as they grow, because of my influence with the favoured Queen, but that doesn't matter to me, for I would help each of them gladly. I am still known as the whore of Ziklag, yet she holds me when I arrive and will not let the servants gossip in my hearing.

As I have regained my sister, so I have lost my brother. Joel and I have not spoken alone since he pulled me onto his horse and carried me away from my captors. Gradually, I came to realise he only did that because that's how David had treated Abigail. When he got married I did not attend his wedding. He did not ask me, and I have never met his new wife, nor have I ever been invited to their home. That hurts, although I try to understand, but it is hard to forgive him for not loving me enough, when I loved him so well.

Today, when I woke, the sun was spattered across my room like gold. I could hear Lemi laughing and decided that I would very much like to see my sister; well, her children really. It has been many weeks since I last managed to get away. So at breakfast I ask Abigail if I might have leave, but she shakes her head. There is a banquet and although I will not be needed, there is no one spare to walk with me.

"Do you think I might go alone?" I ask, unwilling to give up my idea so easily. "The town is safe and there are lots of patrols."

Abigail shakes her head, again.

"No, you must travel adequately protected. And it is not the townsfolk I fear."

The others nod and I swallow my disappointment. I will have to visit another day.

"Wait," Big Sarah says, shrugging. "Why don't we ask Rebekah? She has servants galore and would, I am sure, love to send some of them to collect you from the Palace."

Abigail thinks for a moment and then nods. Rebekah's household is richly robed and numerous. I would certainly have a large escort, just for the sheer joy of showing the world how many servants Rebekah has at her beck and call. I love my sister. All I need to do is send the message.

Later, Big Sarah comes to tell me that my escort has arrived.

"Your entourage is here," she calls. Her voice is light and sunny, yet her face is grave. She catches me by my arm and says, "Be prepared, for he has come."

I feel a little sick, but I have a strong heart, and I want Big Sarah to be proud of me, so I shrug and say, "What is that to me?"

"Nothing," she replies. "It is nothing to you. Only I would have you walk tall and with great dignity, when your heart starts to race and your eyes cannot tear themselves away." Her stare is deep, but I manage to turn away, laughing.

So I walk straight and tall, with dignity, to show him I am no longer ashamed, that I am a maidservant to the Queen now. My effort is wasted. He cannot look me in the eye, he does not lift his poor face beyond my knees and despite what Big Sarah said, I pull my cloak over my hair to spare him the sight of me, for I find that I would save him pain, if it's in my power to do so.

Of course, he walks behind me, so it is only when we reach my sister's house that I need to move close to him. I undo my cloak and lay it across his arms and wonder that he trembles.

All day, as I play with the children, he comes backwards and forwards. It is too cruel, that he is sent to tend us. He comes with food, he comes to make sure that there is nothing else we would rather have, which makes the children laugh and they begin to demand all sorts of impossible things. He comes when the clouds briefly shut away the sun to make sure that I am not cold, which makes Chloe demand a cloak that she is far too warm to wear. He comes with the children's servant when it is time for them to come in and when I go to follow he says, quickly, "Mistress, you look well."

I do not answer, for I am staring at his hand resting on my sleeve. He steps back, dropping his arm as if I am a burning coal. I peer up into his face and frown. I cannot read what is there.

"Please, before someone comes, speak just one word to me so that I may hear your voice," he asks.

I am stuck in a place without words.

At last, I say, "How can you speak to me like that? Are you not ashamed to stand so close?" My voice is edged with the hurt and pain, that I thought was gone, or at least tempered.

He steps back, his face a mask of agony as if someone has just thrust a sword into his side. I find that I am drawn to close the gap.

"I have never been ashamed. How could I be? You know how I love you. More than any man. But your pain was my pain, and I could not bear to see it.

"But Gabriel, you must look to love elsewhere. No one will ever touch me again. How can they?"

"But that is not your fault. It cannot be what you want. I know I am only a servant, I know I am unworthy, but I love as any man loves, and I will never love anyone else."

I do not know how long we stand together, two arm lengths between us—a gap that is no longer empty—until Rebekah's servant comes to find me, as I am taking so long to come in.

***

I begin to hope. In my dreams Gabriel and I become like Hannah and Matthias. He leaves Heled and comes to the Palace, where we serve Abigail together. In the quiet of my bed chamber, it makes perfect sense. It is only when I try to voice my longing to Big Sarah or Hannah that it becomes as it was before, too difficult, and my tongue becomes swollen, with frustration.

In the meantime, Ahinoam is encouraging David to take more wives. She obviously hopes that the more women there are, the less influence Abigail will have. There are few arguments that Abigail can use to counter such thinking. David's position was undoubtedly bolstered by his taking of Maacah, daughter of the King of Geshur.

And so when Lemi is a year old he also takes Haggith, another princess to bear him sons.

Abigail is beginning to feel her age. She is older than Ahinoam and worries that David will not count her wisdom beyond her fading allure. How far he has fallen from the pedestal that she had perched him on. Now, when he comes to see her, our task is to make everything perfect. She will demand nothing from him, she must always be at her most beautiful, so that in her quarters he leaves behind his kingdom. He has stopped speaking to her of all that he is doing, preferring to play with his son. And so her power is lessened. Yet still he comes to her.

Ahinoam does not, cannot understand what there is between them. David does not visit her son Amnon; he does not come to visit her, only to sleep with her and that is not as often as before. There are more wives and less time, but Abigail and her son remain his first and last thought.

I am sewing beside the brazier. Truth be told, I am sitting trying not to think of Gabriel. It is hard not to get lost in a wood smoke of dreams, that are as unrealistic as they are pleasurable. Hannah is here too, intent upon mending a tear in one of Lemi's robes. We have not spoken of anything of great consequence but that doesn't matter, there is plenty of time for words. When Abigail calls out from her room I jump at the sound of her voice. Hannah looks up but does not move, it is Big Sarah and I who are wanted. Hannah smiles, but only I see it, and peers back down at her work.

David has spent a precious morning with Abigail but has had to leave to hold audience with some visitors from Egypt. Abigail hates it when their time is cut short and it will have left her irritable, so Big Sarah and I enter a little reluctantly to see what our mistress wants of us. Abigail is sitting on the edge of her bed, staring at the floor, her hair loose around her shoulders.

Eventually, Big Sarah says, "Mistress," if only to remind her that we are here.

"Sarah, loyal Sarah," Abigail whispers and takes her hand. Big Sarah's hands are large, the gap where her fingers were sliced away, smooth but still red. Abigail traces them with her own small fingers. I am unused to such a show of intimacy, perhaps a little jealous.

"We are yours," Big Sarah says.

Abigail looks at me. I am under her protection, no doubt of that, but she still seems reluctant to treat me as a servant. After Ziklag, it all changed. I feel I am no more than Big Sarah, Little Sarah or Hannah, perhaps even a little less.

"I will do whatever you ask of me," I say shrugging, "I have no status except what you choose to bestow on me, although I would ask one small thing of you."

Seeing Abigail so pensive, almost vulnerable, I have remembered Gabriel, and it makes me bold. Big Sarah is puzzled. She thinks she knows all that is in my head, yet even she does not know what I am about to ask.

"What do you want of me, Miriam?" Abigail replies, understandably a little curious.

"Get another servant."

"Why? Do we need one?"

Abigail's confusion is plain. Big Sarah begins to understand.

"Yes, Mistress," she says, smiling. "Another manservant to work with Matthias. Lemi's protection is paramount and two such men, men that we trust implicitly, can only mean that he would be safer."

"A man who understands battle and strategy," I say, "because we are at war, even though there is no roaring and splashing of blood."

"Where is such a man?" Abigail asks, almost laughing, "and what are you up to?"

I begin to falter, but not Big Sarah. She does not give in, not for a moment. For my sake, I think.

"Gabriel, of the household of Heled," she says, as if she has just thought of him.

"No," Abigail replies. "I will not ask Heled to give up so precious a servant. He has ridden into battle at Heled's shoulder."

I did not know that Abigail knew so much about him. It makes me proud and a little giddy.

"But Heled's household is large now and Gabriel is one of many. He is mostly used by Rebekah to run errands," Big Sarah continues, although it is my hands that are clasped together in supplication. Big Sarah fills me with such hope, that I dread the fall. But the nature of hope is that it does not look too far ahead.

"Heled will refuse you nothing," I plead. "He knows you are the King's favourite and that your son is next in line."

"Please Abigail, just ask him," Big Sarah begs. Abigail's brow furrows in thought.

"But why would I want him? It is too specific. Heled would suspect and if he thought I was doing more than procuring a servant, I would lose his regard forever and so would you Miriam." She shakes her head. "No, I cannot do this."

She is right, of course. I thought *husband* in my muddled longing, but I would still have had to ask Joel for permission, and it would surely be too much for him, after all I have put him through. It would also be ammunition for Ahinoam. Abigail's house is already filled to the brim with mad women and shame, how could I add to it by marrying so far beneath me, or even have the gall to think of marrying at all?

"I'm sorry, Abigail, I should never have asked you," I say, tears filling my eyes, tears that I simply cannot swallow away.

"I'm sorry that you still yearn for him. And him for you?"

I nod miserably, but Big Sarah is not done.

"My Lady, if we can arrange for him to come to your attention, then it would be natural to ask Heled, if he would consider selling him."

"Sarah, do what you can for love's sake but tell me nothing so I can act in truth. I would not anger God by sinning on purpose, nor anger Heled after all his kindness to me." Abigail is adamant on this.

Big Sarah is satisfied and so am I. I understand Abigail's need for caution, it is often all that protects us from the twists and turns of palace life, but she has not refused outright and that is a golden sliver of hope, that I will cling to.

"Now Mistress, what do you need?" Big Sarah asks.

Abigail frowns as she remembers why she has summoned us. Then we hear Lemi waking and tears fill her eyes.

"I cannot keep him safe. Lemi is not strong like Amnon, Ahinoam's child, and I fear for him. Too many people would gain too much by his death." As she speaks the words catch in her throat, so that they become difficult to say. "I am always worried that we have not checked his food properly and my stomach hurts with the anxiety of what they might do to him. And now David speaks of teaching him to ride; he will be gone from me for hours at a time.

How can I protect him then?"

We do not know what to say.

"As he gets older I will have to leave him to the care of others, more and more, and I know he will be in danger. How could I live if anything happened to him? David does not lie with me like he used to and so I do not think Lemi will have a brother or a sister. What can I do?" She sucks in air and breathes it out so hard that she seems to shrink. "He is my all. I would give up David for him, even though it would mean that both our hearts are broken."

Big Sarah and I exchange a glance. This is wild talk; it is almost hysterical.

"You cannot give up David. It would be impossible," Big Sarah says.

"What if he thought we were dead?"

"How could that be?" I ask. "For he wouldn't just leave your body lying where it fell."

"There are potions that make it look as though all life has left you and then a few days later your breath returns."

Big Sarah shakes her head.

"Mistress, that is ridiculous. There are other ways of keeping Lemi safe. The dose for such things needs to be exact, it is far too difficult. You love Lemi, yet a future danger to him cannot outweigh this desperate course."

Lemi comes in on Matthias's shoulders and his mother reaches up to him and weeps again. Lemi wants to play horses, like he does when his father is with them, so it is easy to distract him from her tears.

Big Sarah and I are unnerved. We cannot think what to do to help Abigail or how to stop her.

***

The next royal bride is prepared, Abital. David's political ambitions grow with each of his new allies. Abigail welcomes her and tries to make her into a friend, an ally. It is already too late. Our closed, tight little household does not compare well to the vibrant openness of the other women's quarters; free as long as they accept the rule and ascendancy of Ahinoam. So, when Abital comes to see Abigail, she asks in wide eyed innocence about the madwoman and the whore of Ziklag.

"Can I see them?" she asks.

Abigail is so angry she can barely speak. The visit ends not long after. I'm not sure Abital knows what she has done to make Abigail turn away, but it confirms that what Ahinoam has said of us, is true.

From then on, Big Sarah and I are called on to listen endlessly as to how Abigail is going to smuggle Lemi away, far away from the fear and intrigue, away to a place of safety. We don't believe she will do anything, but something has become tightly wound within her, something that makes her believe she can give her son certainty and a future away from the Palace.

Chapter Seventy-One
Told by Big Sarah

Mary, who often looks after Little Sarah, is tasting Lemi's food, just a spoonful as usual. As I take the plate from her she staggers, her face turning grey green. She slips to her knees and vomits like a dog. Her chest heaves and her forehead becomes slick with sweat. She remains sick and weak for two days after. Abigail becomes like stone. She takes to sleeping with Lemi, and two of us taste their food, no longer making any pretence of it. We stand like a ring around them. Abigail even speaks to David of her fears, and he agrees that she should increase her household.

I know that this is the moment, and I go with Miriam to see Heled. We go dressed in our best clothes and we go surrounded by as many servants as we can find.

Heled has grown older, his hair is grey, his face jowly, although he has not yet turned to fat. If I were a different woman he might turn my head. I have always admired his strength, but I doubt that even he would be strong enough for me. He is clearly surprised at Miriam's request to see him, until we hear Rebekah stress that it must be the Queen's business. His regard for Abigail has always been high and perhaps, like most men who have known her a while, he is a little in love with her. I am glad, for it can only work in our favour.

"Sister, how goes it with you?" he asks, managing not to look at Miriam at all. That stirs my anger, although I knew it would be so and now I think that he is rather an ugly man.

"I am well, Heled, but have you heard of our trouble?" Miriam replies, smiling at him, as if all were as before. Dear, brave girl.

"Yes, that some meat was bad. The boy had a narrow escape," he says.

Like everyone else, he is careful how he speaks of what happened. I raise an eyebrow. There are lots of rumours flying about Hebron.

"The servant was very sick. We were surprised at how ill she became. How quickly. She did not feel herself for a few days."

For a man who has fought in battle he is surprisingly squeamish. He does not want to hear the details or perhaps he is just being cautious.

"How is Abigail?" he asks.

"She is worried. Lemi, I mean Chileab, is a delicate child and such a dish could have proved too much for him, perhaps even killed him."

"What do you want from me?" he asks, his eyes narrowing and I wonder that I ever thought him handsome.

Miriam continues, "David would like Abigail to extend her household, and she only wants the new servants to come from someone she knows and trusts." He nods. He does not need it spelling out. "You and Rebekah have one of the largest establishments in Hebron and all your people are loyal to you, for you are a fair master. You are also my kin and one of Abigail's closest friends, where else would she go except to you?"

He nods again.

"What do you need?"

"We need more men, those that understand the running of a house of rank."

I list two or three that we know of from Miriam's visits. We do not mention Gabriel until the very end.

"I would miss Gabriel. You cannot have him. The others I hardly know, and you are welcome to them."

Rebekah, who has sat silently until that moment, lays her hand on his arm. I wonder at that and look for some sign of his irritation. It seems much has changed in this house since last I observed them. Instead, he turns to her, his face softening, a smile beginning to play around his mouth.

"What is it, my love?"

"We have many servants and Abigail is our queen. If she asks this of us surely we should give generously, even if it hurts us a little. If you don't know much about the men that—" Rebekah cannot remember my name, which is of no matter "—that she spoke of, how can you know their true merit, whereas Gabriel, we know would serve her well? After all, Chileab will be king one day and his mother will not forget such a favour."

She continues sewing while she speaks, peering at her work, as if it is not quite right, and that what she has said is of no consequence. Heled stares at her and so do I. I do not dare look at Miriam. I wonder if Rebekah understands what she is giving to her sister. She resolutely examines the embroidery, she even holds it up to the light, as if she has forgotten we are here. Heled tips his head to one side. I think Rebekah rarely interferes with anything he ever says or does. I watch his strong features soften again. He is swayed and will indulge her, for her gentle cleverness.

"Why not have the Queen in our debt and Gabriel is a good servant. He will be my gift to her."

Rebekah allows herself a tiny smile.

As we return to Abigail's quarters, Miriam cannot speak. I think she is being discreet but even when we are alone, she still cannot seem to form any words. Hannah brings her a glass of wine.

At last, Miriam whispers to Hannah, "My heart is in my mouth, it is dry, as if filled with dust." She gulps the wine, and it helps her find her voice. "Rebekah," she says in awe, "does she know of our regard and yet still intervened for us?" She looks around in wonder. "And Heled listened to her, so Gabriel is to come. Heled's gift to Abigail."

"Then you must go and speak to Abigail immediately," Hannah says. "Let her know that Heled has come to her aid, so that she can thank him."

Miriam nods. It is all she can do.

Abigail sits up and narrows her eyes.

"You two are full of surprises," she says, but there is also a little wonder in her voice. "Heled gave him to me, just like that? As a gift! I am glad you are my servants. But Miriam, you must be patient. You must learn to be guarded about what is going on in your heart.

We want no scandal attached to this gift.

"My household must be perfect. I want no whispered rumours that there is anything amiss. And I must say again to you dear Sarah, hide away when David comes. You disconcert him, I know you do."

We bow low and leave. Once we are out of sight we dance inelegantly around each other. Miriam is so happy, I think her heart will burst. Hannah hears us and brings little Esther to see what her silly Aunts are up to. It is a moment I will treasure to my grave.

Chapter Seventy-Two
Told by Miriam

Hannah, Matthias and Esther are the first to leave. They disappear into the north, Matthias knowing several villages that he thinks might be suitable for us. It is madness. I cannot believe they have gone. Abigail must have been planning it with them all along.

They could not refuse her and are to send a message when they are sure that they have found somewhere safe. I wonder what that village might look like and how we could possibly blend in. I look down at my hands, soft and manicured, and then to the fine dyed cotton that I wear, the silk scarf around my hair and the bracelet on my wrist. I remember beating carpets with Little Sarah back at Nabal's house, how my shoulders ached and my eyes itched. I haven't done a proper day's work for years. How would we keep ourselves in some quiet village? What would we do except draw attention to ourselves?

We wait, and Big Sarah and I begin to despair. How we miss them. It is as if part of our hearts are missing. Lemi speaks constantly of his sister Esther and keeps asking why they can't play together. When he talks of her we feel grubby and deceitful, as we retell the story Abigail has decided on; that Hannah and Matthias have gone back to Carmel because a relative was sick and needed looking after. But it is not a good story, just the best they could come up with. It will seem strange to everyone that Abigail would allow loyal, familiar servants to leave her at a time when her household is increasing in importance and numbers. I think Ahinoam will realise this too. She probably had them followed; we can never be sure.

Matthias is to run a small flock of sheep bought with the money Abigail gave him, something she knows he will excel at. They are to keep a house ready for when his sister comes to live with them. Her husband is dying and when he goes to be with God, she is going to join them with her son and her servants. Although why such a fine lady and her family would want to move to an obscure village, for it will have to be obscure, would be anyone's guess?

Mad Sarah, dear, silent Little Sarah is next to go, packed into a closed carriage. She takes some of Abigail's most precious things stored under the floor. We spread the rumour that she has a fever and that Abigail is afraid for Lemi. That she will be allowed to come back when she is well. Matthias is to meet her on the plains and take her north so that no one will know her true destination. We hope that people will soon forget about her, she was seen so little except by us. I am pleased that Abigail thinks her worth the trouble but in the end I suppose she is simply ensuring our silence.

I miss Little Sarah's quiet presence. It is like losing our dear Jani all over again. Now there are only the two of us left, Big Sarah and I. Gabriel thinks we are mad, he thinks we will all die at David's hand and yet he walks beside me regardless and every moment is precious.

David comes to Abigail more often than ever, however their time is increasingly brief and hurried. Our king is troubled, preoccupied. The dual kingdom, instead of birthing peace, is bringing only bitterness. David's own men grind and rage quietly to themselves, for they miss the desert and the freedom. They are constantly fighting when there is nothing to fight about, squabbling like children. There is too much bloodshed, an eye for an eye, a tooth for a tooth, revenge and then revenge again. Although David roars his disapproval, he never punishes those who err. The six hundred are special, they are his brothers, and he turns a blind eye, so they in turn become untouchable.

Abigail watches and listens. She is clever and can see what lies ahead. It pulls her this way and that, she is constantly torn, bleeding inwardly, her heart shrivelling as she tries to live. She does not want to leave David, while she is seemingly his only comfort or take from him his beloved child and yet she feels the other women beginning to hem her in, dangerously so.

One day when she and David are walking together out on the battlements, because he is restless and needs the sky above him, Ahinoam sweeps into our rooms. She smiles and laughs and calls Lemi to her. He hides behind Big Sarah. Ahinoam orders Big Sarah to give him to one of her own servants. They have come to take him back to play with Amnon. Big Sarah stands tall and speaks for us, her eyes staring into Ahinoam's soul, only her voice quivers with fear.

"He is not well. He has a fever, my Queen."

"He looks well to me, and my Amnon is strong. We are not afraid of a fever."

I do not know what to do, for if Big Sarah openly defies Ahinoam she will be whipped or worse. I bend down, to pick him up, and pinch him hard on his chubby little thigh. He looks up at me in disbelief and starts to scream. Ahinoam looks startled.

"It is the fever. His tummy hurts and his stools are loose," I say. I dare not look at her because I am still the whore.

Big Sarah moves in front of us, and I twist his little fingers until he is almost apoplectic with pain, pulling away from me as I hold him tightly. Abigail's household begins to gather. They have never heard him cry out so. Gabriel enters and bows low to Ahinoam.

"The mistress is on her way back; she will be here shortly. Would you like to wait somewhere more comfortable?"

Ahinoam looks at Gabriel, my beautiful Gabriel and she raises an eyebrow, she has taken note of him, and I am frightened. She turns to leave, hesitating at the door, as if she would like to say something more, only with a shake of her head she is gone. We know that she is not fooled by our games.

I hold Lemi, rubbing his leg and hand where the marks are flaming and I kiss his little fingers that are scarlet and purple. Big Sarah brings his favourite sweetmeat, and I weep in fear. He tugs away from me and only allows Big Sarah to hold him. He will not even look at me.

When Abigail returns, I beg her forgiveness for what I have done. Lemi will not come to me, and I feel I have betrayed him. I am ready for my mistress's anger, instead she begins to cry. It builds until she almost howls in relief. I am praised and held, for she is sure that if we had let him go to her rival queen, he would have come to harm. I tell her what Gabriel said, that he had lied for her and that we were sure Ahinoam knew it. Abigail calls him to her and says, "For your quick thinking I will protect you, as you have protected mine. No harm will come to you or Miriam. And when it is safe I will pay her dowry myself."

Then she dismisses us since Lemi will not settle while I am in sight. In the deep shadow of the courtyard, where the night has spilled its covering wings, he holds me and whispers, "Now we are betrothed."

"Did you ever believe it possible?" I whisper back.

"Not until a few months ago, when I heard you come ask for me, you brazen woman."

I blush in the darkness and grow warm.

"Has it been so very hard for you?" I ask.

"From the moment a skinny maid stirred my heart, no beauty then, but so courageous, I have always hoped."

"I wept all that second day, on the ride to Nabal's house. I ached so much. How could you think me brave?"

"Because you wept silently and asked for nothing."

"I was afraid," I say, remembering.

"I hated leaving you there, in a stranger's house, although you did not know I existed."

He cups my face in his hands, and I wrap my arms around him.

"To me you were just some old servant."

"I am only a year older than your brother."

"Joel. What will he do when he finds out?"

Gabriel takes a step back, his arms dropping to his sides. I grasp his hand and hold it to my cheek. He speaks quietly to the stars.

"They will have to accept us for the Queen's sake, but I don't expect I will be asked to dine."

I love my sister, and her children, but I love him more. I make my choice. It is not so very hard.

Chapter Seventy-Three
Told by Miriam

Abigail is living on her nerves. We know that she is not sleeping or eating, and her fine face grows thin and shadowed. We try to make her take food, but she worries more than ever that Ahinoam might bribe one of the servants to poison her or worse Lemi. Big Sarah sleeps across her door again, like she did in Ziklag, and I sleep in a small room off her bedchamber, like poor Little Sarah used to do. We listen to her walk in the dimness of the night, until even she grows too tired to stand. David can't help but notice her weariness and he sends his physician to see her.

The man knows nothing. Hannah would laugh at his remedies. Abigail tries his sleeping draught. It is too strong; she sleeps deeply for nearly a whole day and a night and is groggy for many hours after. It frightens her to have been unconscious for so long and then worse, so slow-witted. Big Sarah has also seen him talking to Ahinoam. After that Abigail will touch nothing that comes from him. She pretends, of course, for David's sake, but with alarming rapidity she begins to fade, to become transparent to us. She tries to rally for Lemi's sake, when even she can see that her clothes hang loose. She eats heartily for a couple of days, only it isn't long before the apathy returns, worse than ever.

We can protect her from the prying eyes of the Palace, we can paint her face and pad her clothes, but it cannot be hidden from David, he clearly sees that something is terribly wrong. He comes when he can and spends whole nights prostrate before God. It does no good, in this matter God is either silent or acquiescent.

When we are alone, Abigail talks of the time she will join Hannah and Matthias in the mountains, a time when she will have her strength back, when we will all melt away to safety, when we will live uncomplicated lives away from Hebron, away from the blood and poison. It is only in the dark reaches of the night that she cries out in fear and Big Sarah comes and holds her, until she sleeps. Gradually, we begin to see that she will never leave David, for the very thought of it, is draining the life from her.

Big Sarah keeps watch, never far from Abigail's side. Sometimes she says she can feel the darkness like never before, so heavy it robs her of any hope at all. But it has also made her plan and prepare. She has asked me to pack a bag and keep it tucked away in my room. I in turn ask Gabriel to do the same.

As winter turns into summer and once again the ranunculus carpets the desert, Abigail begins to drift away from us. Big Sarah and I walk the rooms, holding back tears, as we try and keep our hearts from breaking, and to keep the household running, as if all were as it should be. Ahinoam has not returned to interfere. She has no need. All she has to do is wait.

Then comes an afternoon, when David arrives. His face is naked in its pain, because he knows that her time is done. That God, has heard his pleas for life, but has said no. When he enters her room, his eyes sliding over us, we step back into the shadows.

He weeps for her and so do we. She clutches his face.

"My King, my love." The effort causes her to catch her breath, her chest heaves, so that she can only whisper, "Please let Sarah and Miriam have care of Chileab. I trust no one else, and they love him like their own."

But Big Sarah has always disconcerted him, and he knows me from the sacking of Ziklag. He nods, but without conviction. When he leaves, he asks me to send word of her progress through the night. Even then, he cannot look at Big Sarah, who always seems to stare into his soul. The only woman who does not wilt at his beauty.

When he has gone, Abigail calls us to her side, just the two of us. There is no substance to her face, her skin is pulled taut over bones that are sharp and too close to the surface. She seems to have no strength to even lift her arms.

"He will not let you have the care of Lemi," she gasps. "I know it. You must take him now. He will not last a moment in the household of Ahinoam. Gabriel will ride with you, he loves you, Miriam, and he will protect you. Go south and then east before you head north. At least with Hannah and Matthias, and with you, my dearest women, he will grow up an ordinary little boy. He will not be poisoned or treated badly."

"Are you sure this is what you want? He is David's son, his favourite son," Big Sarah asks. Abigail murmurs but we cannot catch what she says. She turns away from us, her breath shallow and crackly, as if her lungs are brittle and dry. I step back and can only see the turn of her cheek, hollow and pale. The colour is drained from the room, and I am shocked by the pain that pierces my chest.

We tell Mary that her mistress is sleeping, that she is not to be disturbed, that we will stay with her as usual. Mary looks at us and narrows her eyes. We do not play our parts well, but she is not a clever girl and cannot see beyond what we have said. She turns away. I am sorry that we are leaving her on a lie, but Abigail has left us no choice.

In the first watch of the night, we steal away from the Palace, Lemi sleeping in Big Sarah's arms. Gabriel is waiting for us with three donkeys. His face is grim, but he does not hesitate. We cover ourselves in coarse tunics, slipping past the guards on the Southern gate. They are drowsy and sluggish with drink. Big Sarah has done much to clear our way.

I turn back and back, and back again, not only because I fear pursuit, but because Abigail will die alone this night. That when she reaches out for her beloved women, not one of them will be there to take her hand or smooth her brow.

It is something I will never forgive myself for.

Acknowledgements

Thank you, Jutta Mackwell, for your encouragement and wisdom so gently applied from the earliest moments of this book. You underpin much of what I write, and I am always, always grateful.

Thank you to my family who keep me grounded and realistic, particularly to Mike, because you are the place of safety from which I jump. I never take that for granted.

Pip Sanday is an artist of rare and deep-seated spirituality. When I saw her picture *Dawn Illumination 1* for the first time, I knew it was exactly right for the front cover of this book. Like her picture, my gratitude for her permission to use it is infinite. Thank you too to Thomas and Helen Sanday for helping me reproduce it.

Thank you, Bridget Scrannage, for your insightful editing. You always take my manuscript to the next level. And to Ann Peacocke: thank you for your inimitable professionalism — you put the hidden sparkle in. Hidden, because no one will notice your work, they will just read the words with greater ease and clarity.

To my book group of many years: Thank you — you make me read things I would not usually read, and see things that would never occur to me. It is an immense privilege to share a little of our journeys together.

And finally, dear readers, thank you for your valued support and comments — sine qua non.

By the same Author

Watching You Fall
Falling Tide
Missing You